No Rest for the Wiccan

Madelyn Alt

BERKLEY PRIME CRIME, NEW YORK

THE BERKLEY PUBLISHING GROUP
Published by the Penguin Group
Penguin Group (USA) Inc.
375 Hudson Street, New York, New York 10014, USA
Penguin Group (Canada), 90 Eglinton Avenue East, Suite 700, Toronto, Ontario M4P 2Y3, Canada
(a division of Pearson Penguin Canada Inc.)
Penguin Books Ltd., 80 Strand, London WC2R 0RL, England
Penguin Books Ireland, 25 St. Stephen's Green, Dublin 2, Ireland (a division of Penguin Books Ltd.)
Penguin Group (Australia), 250 Camberwell Road, Camberwell, Victoria 3124, Australia
(a division of Pearson Australia Group Pty. Ltd.)
Penguin Books India Pvt. Ltd., 11 Community Centre, Panchsheel Park, New Delhi—110 017, India
Penguin Group (NZ), 67 Apollo Drive, Rosedale, North Shore 0632, New Zealand
(a division of Pearson New Zealand Ltd.)
Penguin Books (South Africa) (Pty.) Ltd., 24 Sturdee Avenue, Rosebank, Johannesburg 2196,
South Africa

Penguin Books Ltd., Registered Offices: 80 Strand, London WC2R 0RL, England

This is a work of fiction. Names, characters, places, and incidents either are the product of the author's imagination or are used fictitiously, and any resemblance to actual persons, living or dead, business establishments, events, or locales is entirely coincidental. The publisher does not have any control over and does not assume any responsibility for author or third-party websites or their content.

NO REST FOR THE WICCAN

A Berkley Prime Crime Book / published by arrangement with the author

PRINTING HISTORY
Berkley Prime Crime mass-market edition / November 2008

ISBN: 978-0-425-22456-4

BERKLEY® PRIME CRIME
Berkley Prime Crime Books are published by The Berkley Publishing Group,
a division of Penguin Group (USA) Inc.,
375 Hudson Street, New York, New York 10014.
BERKLEY PRIME CRIME and the BERKLEY PRIME CRIME design
are trademarks of Penguin Group (USA) Inc.

PRINTED IN THE UNITED STATES OF AMERICA

10   9   8   7   6   5

For those who sleep,
and those who dream,
and those who have awakened . . .

Through the corridors of sleep
Past the shadows dark and deep
My mind dances and leaps in confusion.
I don't know what is real,
I can't touch what I feel
And I hide behind the shield of my illusion.

— SIMON & GARFUNKEL,
"FLOWERS NEVER BEND"

Chapter 1

My name is Margaret Mary-Catherine O'Neill—Maggie, please, only my mother goes the long way 'round the bend—and I am a lifelong resident of Stony Mill, a mostly uninteresting small town in Indiana.

Mostly.

I used to think that living in a small town meant boredom, monotony, and slim pickin's in the way of potential male companionship. On the other hand, I also used to think a belief in magic, ghosts, and witches was a symptom of an overactive imagination, wishful thinking, and possibly even outright insanity.

Kind of funny, when you think about all that has happened here in the last eight months.

And all in this sleepy little town.

Except you won't find me laughing. Would *you*, if you discovered within yourself a previously unacknowledged ability to discern, and even feel, the hidden, secret, most private emotions of others? The ones they don't want

anyone to know about? It's a little unnerving. Unfortunately there are no twelve-step programs for empaths. No
magic pill to make it all go away. Just like all the other intuitive souls out there in the world, we empaths are on our
own, for better or for worse.

And actually, come to think of it, there was also nothing boring or monotonous about the strange disturbances
that had been popping up all over Stony Mill either. Tur-
bulence of a sort in the fabric of energy and matter that
makes up the reality the rest of us see and feel and experience. Ripples that seemed to have opened a door and put
out a great, big welcome mat for all sorts of weird phe-
nomena. In the beginning, only sensitives noticed the
change in the tides, and only those sensitives with a deeper
familiarity with matters esoteric understood the signifi-
cance of what they were feeling.

That chaos energy was on the move.

Dark energy.

That's where the N.I.G.H.T.S. come into the picture.
The Northeast Indiana Ghost Hunting and Tracking Society, that is. Headed up by my witchy boss, Felicity Dow (at
Enchantments, of course—Indiana's finest mystical antique shop), my band of ghost-hunting buddies have been a
big help to me in learning to understand more about myself, and to gain some much-needed confidence while together the lot of us plumbed the depths of the mysteries of
Stony Mill—mysteries both dark and light combined.

For as any good metaphysician will tell you, one cannot exist without the other. I took comfort in that knowledge. That dark could never overpower light. That light
would always exist, no matter what. As long as that was
true, there was always hope.

A girl needed to have hope. Especially when all the signs pointed to the weirdness in town getting worse.

Scoff if you will. I know how strange this all must sound. A year ago I would have scoffed, myself, but all that I've experienced has since opened my mind. I'm still not convinced that's necessarily a good thing, but I am learning to deal with it. My way.

As for the charge of slim pickin's, it seems I might have been too hasty. A girl with two very different men vying for her attention can hardly complain. What to do with the two of them, well, that's another problem entirely.

My name is Maggie O'Neill, and this is my story.

In researching my newly recognized "talent," I'd read that many empaths tend to be unusually susceptible to the weather, reacting to it on more than just a physical level. Perhaps there was something to that theory, because there was something about a hot, sultry night that never failed to set my nerves on edge, and this summer had had no shortage of them. Summer . . . that's the thing. Summer, it wasn't. Not yet. Not quite. The formality of the summer solstice was still a little over a week away, but already we'd seen enough searing heat to brown the grass and drive people indoors to the cool relief of overworked air conditioners. Between the hot sun and a shortage of rain, the green lushness typical of mid-June in Indiana had thus far failed to manifest. Fields of soybeans and corn that should be beginning to flourish struggled valiantly to deepen their root systems in the crumbling soil, while aboveground their growth had faltered, their yellowing leaves coated with the gray dust that was raised from gravel roads with

every vehicle that traveled them. Local farmers eyed the
sky beneath glowering brows, searching for a hint, any
hint, of the much-needed moisture.

How it could be as steamy as it was without rain, I had
no idea, but it was enough to try the patience of a saint.
And Saint Margaret, I was not. Not even close. I was actually beginning to be glad I lived in the basement apartment in the old Victorian on Willow Street rather than on
the upper levels. Home to the occasional shadow creature
my dark little apartment might be, but at least the surroundings were always a temperate (if damp) seventy de-
grees, and without the monstrous electric bills my best
friend, Stephanie Evans, better known as Steff, endured
in her apartment two floors above me.

Still, a girl started to go stir-crazy if she stayed home
too often. Which was one reason why I had allowed
Tom—Fielding, that is, my on-again, off-again, not-quite-
boyfriend—that steamy Saturday evening, to sweet-talk
me into a moonlit drive down to the sunken gardens in the
old limestone quarry. The other reason being that I was
still trying to make up to him, at least in my mind, for my
unplanned lapse in ethical judgment six weeks earlier,
when I'd allowed Marcus Quinn to kiss me. Marcus
Quinn, the delectable male witch I had once mistakenly
written off as being attached to my boss. Marcus Quinn,
who'd let me know in no uncertain terms that he was most
definitely interested in me. Marcus Quinn, who with his
shoulder-length dark hair, blue eyes, and laughing de-
meanor had teased his way into the illustrious position of
Temptation No. 1 in my life.

Marcus, Marcus, Marcus!

Forgive the Jan Brady moment, but I will hereby confess to a general state of man-centered confusion. At least Tom was a known commodity. There were variables when dealing with Marcus. Unknowns. Call me a wuss, but unknowns made me nervous. *He* made me nervous.

Wow, did he ever.

I'd been avoiding him ever since. Or trying to.

Tom, on the other hand, I'd been doing my best to get to stand still. It had been six months since he'd told me he wanted to date me. I'd been trying ever since to figure out what exactly that meant to him. A lot of things had been implied, but never anything definite. There are just some things that a girl needs to get clear in her mind. Like, were we an item, or weren't we? Enter Steff, my very own bona fide Love Guru. She would just shake her head at me and remind me that love was all about the heart, not the head, whenever I voiced my concerns. But then, Steff had an innate confidence I'd always wished for but had never quite managed to acquire.

Back to my Saturday night interlude . . .

Closed to business long ago, the quarry had found new life in years past as one of the top make-out destinations in Stony Mill. Not, perhaps, the usual haunt of a couple of nonteenagers, but desperate times called for desperate measures. We'd been there all of ten minutes, trying to get into the experience, when I remembered why desperation was such a necessary part of the equation for an illicit summertime visit to the local Lovers' Lane: overheated lip-locks, a steamed-up windshield, hip bruised by a badly positioned seatbelt, bloodthirsty mosquitoes, and the constant embarrassment threat of seeing someone you know stroll past did not make for full-blown seduction.

What had I been thinking?

To make matters worse, Tom was "on call," which, as an officer of the law and Special Task Force Investigator, was a nice way of saying he was really on duty but allowed to do things he wanted to do unless his attendance was required elsewhere. Which also meant that the occasional squelch and squawk of the police radio was our romantic accompaniment. Which *also* meant that Tom's attention was—how shall I say?—*diverted*.

When I first realized that he was pausing to lend an ear to the portable police radio he carried as part of the job, I almost thought I must be mistaken. After all, his eyes were still closed; it could just be the heat getting the better of my imagination. With the second lull, though, I frowned and concentrated on putting more effort into keeping his focus on the business at hand . . . so to speak. But by the third breather, when he'd actually lifted his lips from mine and put our proceedings *on hold* while he trained his ears to the numerical call codes and details that followed, I was starting to feel a bit peevish, pent up, and put out. Between the heat, the steam, and the inevitable hurt feelings, any willingness to participate on my part had evaporated in a way that the sweat dampening my frizzing hair would not.

I extricated myself slowly and began to untwist my clothes. Tom shifted to make way for me, but his body was still on high alert, his eyes focused hard on the red power light on the radio as the call detail concluded with a noisy squelch. I don't think he'd even noticed the loss of our romantic evening mojo.

That hurt my feelings even more.

I tried not to let it. His job meant the world to him, and the last thing I wanted was to be one of those needy, self-absorbed women who have to be the primary focus of their man's life. But jeez. Call me high maintenance, but in her more intimate moments, didn't a girl deserve a little priority?

"Maggie." Tom was already buckling himself in on the driver's side as he simultaneously started the engine. I knew what it meant. Without a word I reached for my buckle. "Maggie, we're going to have to go. Both of the guys on duty are in the middle of things right now, and there's been a report of trespass and possible break-in at the feed mill in town." As he threw the truck into gear, he glanced over at me and added as an afterthought, "Sorry."

I sighed. Sorry he might be, but this seemed to be happening more and more often on what little time we managed to find together. Not that it was always Tom's fault; life at Enchantments, Stony Mill's answer to an up-scale gift shoppe and secret witchy emporium, was keeping me busier than I ever would have imagined. Business, as they say, had been booming.

"It's all right," I told him, trying hard for magnanim-ity. "You've gotta do what you've gotta do."

He reached out and squeezed my hand. "That's my girl."

As we left the old quarry, I wondered how many cou-ples had been startled out of their clinches by the bounc-ing headlights that identified our hasty departure. Then again, would I have noticed, had I been suitably enthralled? Hmm, probably not.

I turned my attention to Tom, keeping my expression neutral and my tone light. "Are you dropping me off, then?"

He shook his head. "No time, not if we want a chance

in hell of catching whoever is there. Might be nothing, but better to be safe than sorry. You'll stay in the truck and lock the doors."

It wasn't what I'd wanted to hear, but it was all part and parcel of seeing a cop. Whether I liked it or not, there would be times he would be called in to duty, and whether I wanted it or not, there would be occasions where I would be with him when the calls came in and circumstances would necessitate my being taken along for the ride. Such was life.

I really didn't like it, though. I'd seen enough danger in the previous eight months to last me a lifetime, and none of it had been by choice.

We were traveling indecently fast up the bumpy county roads, slowing only a little before blowing through stop signs at the crossroads. My heart made a scaredy-cat dip every time. I managed to stifle any squeaks of distress, but I feared my fingers would make permanent dents in the soft parts of the doorframe by the time we drew near to the edge of town, where the pseudo-skyline of the feed mill loomed on the horizon, backlit by security lights in the steamy night air.

The Turners had owned the feed mill, the largest collection of grain elevators in the county, as far back as I could remember. A small village worth of silos of varying diameters and heights, the tallest stretching as high as a ten-story building, this hub for the farming community had changed drastically from when I had visited with my Grandpa Gordon as a child. Back then, it had been little more than some old silos, a dusty roundabout, and outlying holding pens for hogs heading for slaughter. Now the new-and-improved array of silos was interconnected by an extraordinary number of ramps and conveyer systems, the hog barns looked pristine—at least on the outside—and the very air itself whirred and buzzed with the noise from drying fans that looked big enough to drive a truck through. I remembered seeing an article in the *Stony Mill Gazette* about major renovations at Turner's and how they were costing a pretty penny, but this was the first time I'd been out this way in quite a while. Technology, it would seem, had arrived at last in the farming sector of Stony Mill.

As fast as we'd traveled through the surrounding countryside, now that we were drawing nearer the feed mill, we were creeping by comparison so as not to broadcast our approach. Next to me, Tom had gone instantly, perhaps even reflexively, into police mode, his entire body on high alert. His eyes grew sharp, moving here and there, taking in all the shadowed coveys, the many pockets of quiet where a person could easily be hiding.

"Jesus," he said under his breath. "Where to start? The guy could be anywhere."

I watched as he unlocked the glove compartment and withdrew his ankle holster, his eyes still on the quiet scene in front of us. Without a word, I reached behind the seat and grabbed the heavy utility belt and bulletproof vest he always kept at the ready like the Boy Scout he was, and handed it to him.

"Thanks." He opened his door and stepped out cautiously, drawing the vest over his head and securing the thick leather belt around his waist with a quick and practiced motion. He slipped his hand into the pocket of his jeans, withdrawing a big pocket knife, which he tossed onto my lap. "Here. Just in case. Stay put. Lock the doors behind me."

He closed the door firmly but quietly and moved away
from the pickup with all the grace and danger of a pan-
ther on the prowl. His plain white T-shirt and blue jeans
stood out all too easily beneath the bright glow of the security lights. A sitting duck, if anyone was out there with
a serious reason for not wanting to be caught. Remembering what he'd told me about taking precautions, I punched
the Lock button, feeling far more secure as the solid *ka-
chunk* of the tumblers crunched into place. The weight of
the folding knife in my hand reassured me even further—
not that I'd need it, but its presence eased my mind anyway.
At least, for myself; for Tom, well, that was another worry
altogether.

This was the hardest part of dating a cop. One never
knew from day to day whether his health and well-being
would continue. I found myself leaning forward on the
truck's bench seat, staring out the windshield at the pockets of darkness as Tom darted in and out of them, hugging
close to the walls. *Why didn't he take a flashlight?* I wondered, fretting. Maybe I should turn on the headlights . . .

I forced the thought from my head and made myself re-
lax back against the seat. There was no way Tom would
see that as anything other than interference, and I'd promised him months ago to keep my nose out of police business. Not that I had ever intentionally intervened. Like my
mom had a fondness for saying, trouble just seemed to
have a knack for finding me.

I fidgeted anxiously. Nine forty-two on the clock,
glowing bright green on the dashboard.

At nine forty-three another car scuffed to a halt beside
the truck, red and blue lights flashing, but no siren. I turned
my head, but the officer who had been driving had already

leapt from its confines and was standing outside my window, face stern, one cautious hand on the butt of his gun as with the other he motioned for me to open the window. Far be it from me to get in the way of the law. I pressed the Down button, posthaste.

Recognition registered suddenly on his face—Jed Something, I remembered just as suddenly, an older, thicker version of Tom, whose gunbelt served only to emphasize the middle-age drift. "Oh, it's you," he said. "Thought I recognized the truck. Tom already here?"

I nodded. "Out there somewhere. I've lost track of him."

"Right. You stay here." He cut the flashers.

"Be careful. I haven't seen anyone yet, but—"

He had already turned away from me. Just then the misty clouds that had been obscuring the moon shifted. I glanced up at the movement. My breath caught in my throat as the glow from the half-moon silhouetted a silo with its system of conveyers and chutes and ladders . . .

"Oh, my God. *What is that?*"

My voice was barely a whisper, but it was enough to make Jed pause. He turned back toward me and caught me looking up, up, up. Almost in slow motion he tilted his head back to follow my gaze to where a silent form hung heavily from one of the uppermost metal conveyer systems, as still as death in the airless night.

"Holy shit."

In an instant he was scrambling for his squad car and the handheld spotlight the vehicle came equipped with. With a flip of a switch the spotlight flared into action, sending the entire area into spasms of light and movement. Officer Jed swung the light beam upward, aiming for the thing we had both seen but wished we had not. The beam swept past it once, twice, as his unsteady hands betrayed his nervousness. Finally he got it just right. The light caught and held on the . . . what was it?

Knowing Tom wouldn't like it, but also knowing I couldn't possibly *not* look, I quietly let myself out of the truck. Just for a minute, I told myself. Just long enough for a quick look-see. I wouldn't get in the way.

In the next instant Tom came wheeling around the corner of the nearest building, gun in hand and held at the ready, his expression uberfierce and ready for business. Seeing it, I will admit—I quailed. Yeah, I know. Cowardly, but true. And in that moment the ten-year-old girl that still lived deep down inside me made the snap decision to try out the Invisibility Enchantment I'd read about and had been working on secretly for just such an emergency. Yes, it was spellwork, and a few months ago I'd have shied away from that—but I'd been working on coming to terms with my special abilities, and an innocuous charm could hurt no one. No, it wouldn't really work like Harry's Invisibility Cloak, but if I did it right, any impact my presence made might be lessened to the point that Tom wouldn't notice or care that I had stuck my nose in things—again. Worth a shot anyway. Was it self-serving? Probably. But a girl has to look out for herself sometimes, and besides, how else was I supposed to satisfy my curiosity about what was going on here?

It took only a split second from decision to execution. Holding my breath deep in my lungs, I drew myself in, making myself as small and inconsequential as possible, holding the *I'm-not-here-don't-mind-me-fading-into-*

the-background thought with as much intensity as I could manage. I was stunned when it actually appeared to have worked: Tom's gaze skated past me without pause. The minute he identified Officer Jed as the reason for the sweeping beam of light, his shoulders relaxed visibly, and he lowered his handgun.

"Glad to see you could make it, Jensen."

"Did you see—"

"Anyone?" Tom finished for him. "Nah. I think whoever was snooping around is gone. I haven't seen or heard a thing since—"

Jensen cut him off by swinging the light up and jerking his head toward the hanging . . . *thing*. For an instant, Tom looked frozen, too, by the sight. Then he revved into action, reholstering his gun and fastening the snaps. "Do you want to take the ladder, or do I?"

Jensen grimaced. "Ho, jeez. God, I hate heights. Why does it always have to be heights?"

"I dunno. You want me to climb it?"

"Nope, I'm on it. You're not even supposed to be on duty, remember?" He girded his loins—well, his utility belt—shifting it around his meaty middle. Jensen did not seem to share Tom's predilection for physical fitness. He cast a mischievous glance at Tom. "You gonna be ready to catch me if I fall?"

"Hm." Tom made a leery face. "You know, you're not really my type. How about if I radio for backup instead, big guy?"

The cop's version of gallows humor. Even in tense situations, nothing much fazed them for long. I, on the other hand, was completely weirded out by the thing hanging above us. I didn't envy Jensen much. That climb looked like a bitch and a half. Since I didn't even manage to pass rope climbing in middle school gym class, I felt his pain.

"What—or who—do you think it is?" Tom mused aloud, rubbing a hand over the jaw I had been nuzzling not so long ago.

Jensen shrugged. "We'll know when we get there, I guess. I don't see why anyone would have climbed up there to off themselves, but stranger things have happened." *Surely the understatement of the year,* I thought wryly as Jensen continued, "What I want to know is, why always on *my* watch?"

Jensen made his way over to the silo and eyeballed his target as Tom called out helpful suggestions. As for me, I edged back on the fringes, as quiet as the proverbial mouse, watching the proceedings from my ringside seat with that heady mix of emotions that comes from rubbernecking at traffic accidents and funerals—half-revulsion, half-fascination, all guilt.

The higher Jed Jensen climbed, the higher the anticipation grew. Behind us in the barns across the way, the hogs were restless. Their strange grunts and squeals rang out over the sounds of the fans and machinery, filling the air with an unease that pressed in on me. I hadn't been expecting that. I took a deep, steadying breath and scuffed my feet against the pavement in an attempt to ground the nervous energy that the animals projected as strongly as any human.

Jensen was at least halfway up when an F350 pickup truck skidded in off the road, spewing gravel in typical testosterone-charged fashion as it shuddered to a halt beside Tom's much smaller version. The driver jumped out, leaving his door open as he pushed back his felt cowboy hat to stare up first at the spotlighted conveyer system high above, then the dark spot of the uniformed officer inching his way up the heights of the round-backed ladder. He stopped a moment with his hands on his hips and mouth open as though stunned by the scene unfolding before his eyes.

The stillness of the moment didn't last long.

"What the hell is going on here?" The man's dark eyes swept from Tom, to me, to the police cruiser, then back to the scene high above. "Can someone please tell me what in the blue blazes is going on?"

Tom was digging in the back pocket of his jeans, withdrawing the flat wallet that contained his badge and identification. He flashed them at the newcomer. "May I ask you to state your business here, sir?"

The man stared at him, his rugged face red beneath a tan that spoke of hours spent in the open air on a regular basis. "My business? Well, that's just the point, Officer . . . Fielding, is it? *This*"—he swept his hand to indicate the widespread grouping of buildings and silos—"is my business. I'm Joel Turner. I own Turner Field and Grain Systems."

Even if I hadn't been gifted with sensitivities from the Powers That Be, I would have known by the set of the shoulders beneath the button-down cotton shirt and the forceful slash of his hand that Mr. Joel Turner was a man of few words and even less patience.

"Mr. Turner," Tom said before the man could get himself even more worked up. "I take it Dispatch didn't get ahold of you. I'm afraid there's been a report of possible trespass here on your property. A driver passing by the place saw flashlight beams and suspicious movement, and called it in."

"No, they got ahold of me, all right. Trespass, huh?" Turner's gaze roved over his widespread property, sharp as a hay fork. "So what are *you* standing around for? Shouldn't you be out there looking? And while you're at it, maybe you wouldn't mind explaining the fool climbing up the side of Big Ben." The silo, I assumed, not the clock tower. "What the hell is that thing up there?"

"That *fool*," Tom replied in a clipped manner that said he did not care much for Turner's choice of words, "is a fellow police officer currently risking life and limb to investigate vandalism of your property. As for what is up there, we don't have an answer to that yet."

As though he had heard the discussion below and sought to put an end to the speculation, Jensen gave a shout. As one, all eyes swiveled upward. Jensen hooked an arm around one of the ladder steps and pressed his back against the safety cage to brace himself. A second later we heard the crackling sputter of his voice coming from Tom's radio.

"False alarm. It's just a dummy that some jackass decided to haul up here to make trouble."

"A dummy?" Tom responded into his own shoulder mike. "You mean, like a store mannequin?"

"More like a scarecrow. Rough. It looks like someone put it together themselves."

"Hm." Tom thought for a minute. "How about it, Jensen? Can you get to it to get it down?"

There was a moment stretched long, rife with hesitation, and I knew Jensen must be surveying the distance between his body and the dummy itself. Twenty-five feet on solid ground was a cakewalk. Twenty-five feet of open air with a freefall of one hundred feet to a hard landing on a concrete slab was not a pretty prospect. The radio sputtered again. "Well . . . yeah, sure I can. I mean, maybe it would be better to wait until morning, since there's no real urgency. I mean—"

Without a word Turner turned on his heel and stalked off toward a low-slung building across the way. A utilitarian sign on the front minced no words to identify it as the OFFICE. Tom whipped his head around to watch him, then spoke into the radio's mouthpiece again. "Hang on, Jensen."

"Copy that. But be quick about it, would ya? Can't say as it's all that fun up here."

Tom stuffed his wallet back into his pocket and jogged after the feed mill owner, who was punching the buttons on a numerical keypad just outside the office door. Turner barely looked back at Tom as he came up behind him; instead, when the system made a high-pitched *blip blip*, he shoved his way inside without further ado. A light switched on, spilling carelessly across the yard. Turner stayed in the doorway, his bulk preventing Tom from following while he worked at something just inside the door. In the next moment, there was a loud clunk from above, a mechanical whirr, and the jingling of metal as the system of pulleys and conveyers lurched into motion, and the dummy right along with them.

High above, Jensen gave a shout. The radio on Tom's hip squawked again. "Well, why didn't you do that sooner, son? That just made things a helluva lot easier."

Tom looked at Turner. Turner turned away beneath the weight of the attention, ducking his head down enough that the brim hid his eyes. He shrugged. "I don't do . . . never mind."

Fifteen minutes of wrangling, adjusting, and reverse-climbing later, and Jensen had hauled the lumpy figure down in a fireman's over-the-shoulder hold, letting himself down one careful step at a time—not an easy feat when you were a good thirty pounds overweight and a little doughy around the middle. Tom and Turner lifted the thing from him as soon as they could reach it, and between the two of them lugged it to the ground. For a scarecrow, this dummy appeared to be surprisingly heavy.

Everyone gathered around. No one seemed to notice or care that I had inserted myself into the circle. The thought made me puff up with pride—my invisibility charm seemed to be working even better than I had hoped. This particular skill could prove useful.

The thing that had been hanging from the conveyer system was not a mannequin, but as Jensen had described, it was distinctly man-shaped, and it was most definitely crafted by someone with a sick sense of humor. Its face was a burlap sack, just like any moldering scarecrow holding court over the crows and blackbirds in the veggie rows, but its eyes were big black X's, its mouth a Frankenstein grimace of stitchery in red yarn. The thing had been suspended from the conveyers by a noose securely knotted—hangman-style, I noted, grimacing at the implied suggestion. It was dressed in an old button-down shirt, clean but worn blue jeans, and atop its "head," a straw cowboy hat.

One after another, three sets of eyes, mine included, lifted from the dummy to Mr. Turner standing at its feet and traveled from his boots up to his low-on-the-brow cowboy hat. He scowled suddenly—the meaning was not lost on him either.

"You wouldn't know who might be leaving this kind of thing for you, do you, Mr. Turner?" Tom asked, his voice neutral. "I mean, it's a weird thing for anyone to do. Kinda eerie, you might say, hanging it up there for you to find."

"Shit." Turner lit up a cigarette, cupping his hand around the tip until it burned Devil-red in the night. He took a long drag, then blew the smoke out, his stare dragon-cold and intense. "What makes you think the thing was meant for me?"

Tom raised a brow and stared him down, just as cool. "What makes you think it wasn't?"

Turner just shrugged. "I didn't say that. I just don't think you can jump to that conclusion without cause."

A tic was making an appearance at Tom's left temple—I knew how much he hated having his authority compromised, and he hated mind games even more—but he kept his cool.

Jensen, as the officer in charge of the scene, rose from where he'd been kneeling beside the dummy and stepped in. "I think this might be enough cause even for you, Mr. Turner." He handed him a piece of paper, wrinkled from handling. "I found this on the, er, the body when I was holding on for dear life a hundred feet up."

Turner accepted the paper, the briefest twitch of his fingers before taking it the only sign of uncertainty. His mouth turned down at the corner in a sneer. "Death threats for unfair business practices." He made a sound of disgust. "I knew this was a load of hog shit. This isn't a case of vandalism, Officers. This is nothing more than a simple case of sour grapes."

"How do you figure?"

Turner shrugged. "We've had a lot of major expenses this last year—purchasing some of the other feed mills and co-ops in the county—"

"All of 'em, I heard," Jensen provided helpfully.

"I guess that'd be about right. In any case, with the economy in the crapper, we've had to make some modifications to our pricing scheme just to stay out of the red and pay our own creditors. You know how it is."

"And this is—"

"Someone who isn't happy about the effect on their own bottom line. It happens all the time. No big deal."

"Well, now." Jensen looked him in the eyes. "That may be, but I'm not so sure that I would write this off so quickly. Death threats are no laughing matter."

I could see that the note was made out of letters cut from a magazine and pasted onto a piece of notebook paper. " 'The mighty will fall'?" Turner read. "Not very original, is it."

"All it takes is one crackpot without an imagination," Tom replied.

Turner shrugged. "I have a security system in place. Unfortunately my brother is often the last one here, and he sometimes forgets to activate it. Family. What can you do." He clamped his lips tightly around his cigarette, a hard man with an even harder attitude. An old-style Hoosier if I'd ever met one. "Look. I know the people I deal with on a daily basis. They may be tight-fisted bastards, but as for a real threat? I think I'll risk it."

I cringed inwardly. Old habits die hard—thanks to my upbringing, my hands downright itched to form the criss-crossed corners of the Holy Cross. There was nothing more arrogant than thumbing one's nose at death, and if I were Joel Turner, I wouldn't have chanced it for all the chocolate kisses in the world. For me, a self-affirmed chocaholic, that was saying something. In fact, the superstitious part of me—the part of me that had just spent the last eight months intimately associated with the darkness that had settled into the cracks and corners of my beloved hometown, and had only barely come out swinging—was a little worried that this new threat was an omen. A sign that things were not yet finished. I had been hoping that the trouble had left us in the way that it had come in: quietly and without fanfare. And maybe it had. Certainly nothing had happened since April, when Luc Metzger had met an untimely demise on a quiet county roadside with a Pennsylvania Dutch hex symbol to mark the spot forevermore. But to flaunt that hope in the face of reality? It was just not a good idea.

Not a good idea at all.

Chapter 2

By the next morning, I had shaken off my fear-tinged mood of the night before. It was Sunday and I woke up early, no longer tense with worry but unable to sleep. I lay there in bed awhile longer, but even the air in my basement apartment was feeling clammy and close, so I thrust my feet out from under the damp sheet and rolled upright in the bed, wiggling my toes against the carpet as I contemplated the day stretching before me.

What to do, what to do . . .

Sundays in this small Hoosier town offered little in the way of entertainment for those poor slobs who woke up without significant others to occupy their time. Tom, I knew, would be putting in a twelve-hour shift today, so any kind of romantic fun was out of the question . . . and I most definitely would *not* allow my eye or thoughts to wander in other directions. Most especially not in the di-rection of a certain dark and dangerous hunk-o'-honey who seemed to be doing his level best to lead me down the garden path to temptation. Avoiding Marcus hadn't been easy. As a key member of the N.I.G.H.T.S. and Liss's partner in magick, he often appeared out of nowhere. I hated to admit it, but lately, just the sight of him set my pulse to racing. It scared me . . . especially since I had the distinct impression that the intrigue was mutual. Why? Gee, it might have been that kiss we'd shared, before either of us had known what hit us—and believe me, it had packed a wallop. And then there was the dancing around the Beltane fires, when I'd discovered the truth about the relationship between Marcus and Liss. As in, they weren't an item. As in, that made my hands-off view of Marcus a moot point. Except for my relationship-or-not situation with Tom, my conscience, and those pesky little things called morals.

Tricky, tricky.

Heading into Enchantments might have been an option, except for the fact that it was Sunday, the store was closed, and I'd been devoting so much time to my duties there of late that Liss had pretty much ordered me to spend more time on myself.

I thought for a moment about calling up Steff . . . except then I remembered that I had seen her boyfriend's vintage Jag parked curbside when Tom dropped me off the night before, and I wasn't about to be the person who pooped that party. Maybe later.

My only other options were grocery shopping (*Wal-Mart on a weekend? Mass hysteria. Fun, fun . . .*), driving around aimlessly by myself (*yawn*), or reading (*and I had just finished my latest library find and hadn't yet found the time to seek out another*). Which left me with either cleaning my apartment or visiting with my family.

Guess which one I chose? I will admit I did check the *Guide de TV* for any reruns of *Magnum P.I.* before deciding, just in case, but even my beloved Thomas had abandoned me. I was on my own.

One thing that families can always be counted on for is to fill up the unwanted nooks and crannies of any spare time that a girl might find on her hands. *Idle hands are the Devil's hands*, my Grandma Cora used to say, and I still find those words echoing through my brain in just that way. My conscience, you know. It comes to me often using the not-so-dulcet tones of my late Grandma C, whispering to me from inside my head, chiding me to behave the way a good Catholic girl should. I don't know why it has to be Grandma C—and I often wish it weren't. There's nothing like your grandmother inserting her judgments into a private moment to make you want to banish her from your thoughts forever. Why couldn't the voice of my conscience be male and intriguing? You know, the Phantom to my Christine?

Then again, in somewhat private moments, I'm not sure that would be an improvement. Could prove a bit of a distraction, that's for sure. Ahem.

Still, now that the decision had been made, I was looking forward to spending some time with my family. I glanced at the clock. Nine thirty-five. My mother would be heading home soon, preferring the quieter early mass to the later one overrun by growing families. If I hurried, I could get there first and have a little time with my dad and Grandpa Gordon without my mom's more . . . *forceful* personality interjecting itself.

The plan decided, I launched myself into action, digging through dresser drawers and the closet for any combination that would be comfortable enough to see me through the steamy heat I knew I wouldn't be able to escape from, and yet leave me covered enough to avoid my mother's always judgmental eye. I settled on a plain old T-shirt, not too close-fitting, and a pair of knee-length shorts—still shorts, but long enough to cover any wobbly bits that might otherwise have been in view on my thighs. One further concession to comfort was a pair of flip-flops, which I knew my mother hated, but sometimes a girl just has to be herself and go with the flow. Especially when the temps were supposed to reach the mid-nineties. *(Help. Me. Now!)* Breakfast was a toasted English muffin and a handful of grapes, both of which were suitable for eating on the run. Which I did, munching my way down sleepy residential streets until I reached the old Indian trail, now residential route, that sheltered the old-fashioned farmhouse that stood out from its more up-to-date neighbors like a plain white hen in a yard full of exotic chickens.

Home.

My dad came out of the garage, wiping his hands on a shop rag, when he heard my old VW Bug puttering into the circular drive that looped around an ancient oak that had once held my playhouse in its bowers. Glenn O'Neill was a quiet man—meek, some might say—who had let kindness guide him throughout his lifetime. It was a quality that made him a wonderful father, but might perhaps have served as a detriment in his accounting career. The stresses of his job at the luxury boat factory were evident in the worry furrows and lines that stretched across his brow, the pinched look at the corners of his mouth. I didn't like it. I didn't like it at all.

I left Christine parked beneath the shade of the oak and went to give him a big hug.

"Hey, sis. I wasn't expecting you today. Good to see you, though."

He gave me one last squeeze and big smacking kiss on the cheek. I laughed and smooched him back. "Hi, Dad. How are things?"

"Oh, same old, same old. You know."

My mouth twisted in distaste. "They're still working you to death, I suppose. How many hours did you put in last week?"

He shrugged and wouldn't meet my eyes. "The work had to be done."

"Dad, it always has to be done, and it's not going to go away. You know that. They know that. I think it's awful what they do to you. Why don't they hire some help, if there's that much to do?"

He mumbled something about the downshift in the luxury markets owing to higher gas prices and worry over the world economy, but I knew the truth of it as well as he did. If there weren't someone there already who was willing to step in to fill the void, more help would have been hired. Still, it wasn't up to me to point that out to him any more than I already had. It was his job. His paycheck. His life.

I sighed, wishing for the impossible for him, then changed the subject. "When do you expect Mom back from mass?"

"She didn't go."

"She didn't . . ." I blinked at him, certain I had heard wrong. In all my years, I could count on one hand the number of Sunday morning masses my mother had missed. Usually it involved one of us kids coming down with something at an inopportune time, but with all of us out of the house, that left only her, Dad, and Grandpa . . . I glanced toward the house, frowning. "She's feeling all right, isn't she? Is Grandpa okay?"

"Fine, fine. It's your sister, that's all. She's been keeping your mother so busy, she doesn't know which end is up and which is down. She's feeling a bit out of sorts and frazzled, that's all. She wanted to go this morning, but I wouldn't let her. Told her the Church could do without her one Sunday out of five hundred." He looked a bit smug about it, too, and I knew why. It wasn't often that Mom let him push her around. Which meant Mom really must not be feeling herself.

"I think I'll go in and check on her," I said, gazing off in that direction. Besides, Dad's attention was already wavering back toward the garage.

"Sure, honey," he said distractedly with a pat on my shoulder. "She'd like that."

My mom and I had enjoyed a somewhat less than perfect mother-daughter relationship for as long as I could remember. Same old story. She didn't think I was trying to make a life for myself. I wanted a life of my own, rather than living out her fantasies of perfection. We were working on that. Not always well, but . . .

I heard raised voices as soon as I approached the screen door. "I don't want to hear about it, Dad, and that's final."

"Don't tell me what to talk about, missy. It's bleedin' hot in here and you know it! My jimmies are hanging so loose, it's a wonder they aren't migrating straight outta my boxers in protest, and at my age, that's not a pretty sight!"

"Oh, for the love of—! If your mouth hasn't been just a-running on and on lately, I just don't know."

"Well, it's true, and I'm too old to be tempering my tongue to keep from insulting a daughter who's as prickly as a porcupine. You have to admit, Patty, you've been a little hard to live with lately."

Everyone else in town had their air-conditioning on full blast today in anticipation of the soaring temperatures. My mom was the only person I knew who had insisted upon having central air but rarely turned it on owing to the wastefulness of it all.

But I've got to hand it to my Grandpa G. There weren't many people who could take on my mom when she was in full-on Control Mode. And I'd lived with her long enough to know that this was all about control. She wanted it, and you were going to give her her due, by golly, or there would be hell to pay. So long as you understood that and stepped aside, you could get along with her fairly well. You just had to be smart and learn how to get around her.

And I had had a lot of practice at that.

Mom and Grandpa both looked up when I walked in. Mom sat at the table with a coffee cup clenched in her grip, scowling.

"Hi, Mom," I said, breezing into the room and setting my purse on the counter. "Dad told me he wouldn't let you go in to church this morning. What's up?"

Still glaring at Grandpa, my mom waved off the question. "Oh, you know how your father is. Always worrying about me."

Grandpa had steered his Hoverchair over to the old, ceiling-high cupboards and was now leaning dangerously sideways on the seat while he aimed the tip of his cane at a lineup of cookie boxes with the skill and strategy of the wiliest pool shark. The tip connected, as expected. The nearest box teetered on the edge of the shelf and fell to the floor, causing my mom to wince and close her eyes.

"I'll get it," I said helpfully, already bending at the waist. "Here you go, Gramps." I handed him the box and wrapped my arms around his shoulders, leaning in close. "It's good to see you."

He kissed my cheek soundly. Scruffy gray whiskers prickled the tender skin over my cheekbone, but he smelled good, like aftershave and licorice. "You too, chickpea."

"Check to be sure that's something healthy and not the Thin Mint cookies," my mom warned wearily, her eyes still closed. "He's always trying to get into the Thin Mint cookies."

Grandpa G surreptitiously slid a tube of the cookies out of the box before handing it back to me with a huffy, "Fine. Fine! Take them. I didn't want 'em anyway." He gave me a broad wink as he steered his wheelchair toward the door to beat a hasty exit. Still, he couldn't seem to resist grumbling under his breath about pushy women and how it was still considered a crime in this country to starve an older person to death, before rolling away down the ramp my dad had built for him with his prize tucked under the flaps of his flannel shirt. Funny, he'd wear flannel three hundred and sixty-five days a year, but he still wanted his air-conditioning. That was Grandpa G for you.

I tried not to smile at his sass as I replaced the box on the shelf. It wasn't easy.

Mom waited until he was gone before pinning me with one of her famous penetrating stares. "He had the Thin Mints with him, didn't he."

It wasn't so much a question as a declaration that she was waiting for me to confirm. I could have lied, but I knew she'd see right through me. "Just one tube, Mom. Not enough to hurt him."

"It's enough to throw his sugars way out of whack, if he eats them in one sitting. Which he has been known to do." She tapped her fingernails against the table, inhaling deeply. "That man will be the death of me yet."

"Sounds like Mel is vying for that distinction lately."

Far be it from me to point out my younger sister's spoiled princess performance to her chief enabler, but . . . oh, I just did that, didn't I? I know, I know. It was a small and petty thing to do. Some things never truly die, and sibling rivalry is one of them. Cain and Abel, anyone? I rest my case.

My mother leaned back with a weary sigh. "I won't deny it. Your sister has been running me ragged." She stopped for a moment to take a sip of her coffee, which I noticed she was drinking black, without her usual heavy dose of cream and sugar. Wow. Hard core. "It's the hormones, of course, and the boredom. Her obstetrician just told her that it's to be bed rest for the next three months solid. Bed rest? *Your* sister? She can't clean her own house. The girls are running amok without constant supervision during the day. Greg hasn't been much help either. At the office at all hours. It's enough to drive any woman around the bend."

Mel was always enough to drive me around the bend. But a pregnant Mel, bored, bedridden, and toxemic? *Yeesh.* "So you've been filling in?"

She shrugged. "During the day, as much as I can. At least the house can be clean, the girls don't have to be with a nanny or a nurse, and Melanie has someone there with her in case of an emergency."

"I don't get it. Why can't Greg just cut his hours short?"

Mom raised her brows and pursed her lips. "Your brother-in-law has a busy schedule. A busy legal practice. You can't expect him to be the primary breadwinner and take care of everything on the home front, too."

Greg Craven and my sister, Melanie, had been married for about six years now, ever since Melanie had graduated from her party-girl-looking-for-a-rich-husband years. Greg won the big prize. Or, perhaps I should say, Melanie did. Greg was as up-and-coming as a young lawyer could be in a small town. His specialty? Divorce and family law, and from what my mom had told me, business was booming, more so than ever before. I guess that would explain his hesitance to scale back his hours to accommodate his bedridden wife . . . or maybe it was just that Mel could be a royal pain in the ass when she couldn't do what she wanted to do.

"You know," my mom said, interrupting my musings, "there's no reason you couldn't help out, too."

Wait . . . what?

"With me there during the day and you in the evenings after work until Greg gets home, the entire day would be covered."

Well, yeah, but . . .

"I mean, you are her big sister. It would be nice if you could be there for her in her time of need."

Warning! Warning, Will Robinson! Guilt trip, straight ahead.

"That is what family does, after all. Looks after each other."

"All right! All right. You win," I said, holding up my hands in submission. I know, I know. I was too easy. But she was right in a way. It would have been awful of me to let my mom suffer alone. "I'll help out for a couple of hours in the evenings. It'll be fun, right? Me and the girls? It'll be like a slumber party. Yeah, lots of fun." Just me, and the girls, and Mel the Prima Madonna.

My mom beamed. "I knew you'd see it my way."

Was there any other?

Oh, my God. What had I gotten myself into?

My mom had decided that, this being Sunday, it was the perfect opportunity for me to head on over to Mel's with her, to let Mel know about my willingness to serve, and to show me the ropes on everything that Mel would need done every day.

Oy.

It wasn't that I didn't want to be helpful. What I didn't want was to see the look of triumph on Mel's pretty face when she realized she was going to be able to order me around.

Everything looked normal when we pulled into the brick driveway that swirled ever-so-tastefully up to Mel's ever-so-tasteful home. Mel lived in the ritzy Buckingham West subdivision, where the houses were all taupe, the men business casual, and the coffee klatch wives in serious need of therapy . . . retail therapy, that is. It was where many of the up-and-comings in old Stony Mill society and the property tax refugees from the city comingled in relative peace and harmony, secure in the knowledge of their continued financial well-being. It was an arrogant view, perhaps, a naïve view, but they had had years of prosperity to bolster their faith and complacency. Welcome to the lives of the rich and fortunate. For all they knew, the world had always been their oyster, always waiting for them to take the pearl. And that was the way they intended it to stay.

The residents liked to think everyone was equal in Buckingham West, and by outward appearances, they were right. There was a sameness here, with the matching color schemes, the garages limited to three cars, the requisite curb appeal. The rules. You see, to be fair to all, the association had put forth many rules with regard to anything that might be viewed by the outside world: frontage size, lot size, style of home, colors of siding, number of windows, those things you could have in your yard, and what you couldn't. Evenly applied rules meant equal footing between the otherwise competitive Buckingham Westers.

Of course, the veneer of equality was nothing more than illusion, and the pretense of fairness was the biggest illusion of all.

Mel was no different from the rest of her lofty-minded neighbors. If anything, she was the queen of the neighborhood watch, if more by attitude than actual status. Mel had always wanted more than what we had grown up with on my dad's salary alone. Landing Greg, a young lawyer, must have seemed a real coup, the first big step in her life plan. She'd lost no time in quitting her job in order to step into the kitten heels of a socialite and starting a family with Greg, and one of the first things they'd done as a married couple was to dig themselves neck deep into debt on this house, to fit in with Mel's concept of the American dream.

Maybe that was why Greg worked all those hours.

A more probable cause became evident the moment we set foot inside the house. It was obvious my mom had not been there yet. Dishes from the morning meal lay where they had been left all over the counter, which was soiled with spilled milk and scattered cereal. The milk jug lay on its side, though at least its lid was in place, thank goodness. Newspaper lay discarded on the counter, the floor, and one of the tall stools at the counter—Greg's doing, no doubt. Coffee was burning in the bottom of the coffeemaker, the scorched smell assaulting the nose almost as much as the smell of soiled nappies coming from the diaper can. A little pink scooter lay discarded on its side in the center of the Mexican tile floor, surrounded by blocks and crayons and a fuzzy purple hippo with a gap-toothed grin. My eyes went wide at the state of things.

"Um," I said to my mother, trying to get the big picture, "you were here just yesterday. Weren't you?"

Mom was surveying the wreckage with the same dazed expression I was wearing. "Yes."

"And this goes on every day?"

"Pretty much."

Together we moved along toward the hall. "Greg?" my mom called out, trying to be heard over the maniacal giggling and yammering cartoon voices coming from the television in the family room. "Greg? Girls? Grandma's here!"

Nothing.

"Maybe they're upstairs with Mel," I suggested, trying to be helpful.

Mom nodded, but instead of walking toward the wide, free-floating steps that led to the upper level, she walked to a box on the wall and pressed a button. "Melanie? It's Mom. I've brought your sister with me."

I didn't need the intercom to hear my sister. Her response echoed off the vaulted ceilings. "Mom! Oh, I'm so glad you're here. I've been so bored up here all by myself, and none of my friends could come over this morning. They're all busy with their churches. I was even starting to think I was hearing things. Why do houses have to make such odd noises? You'd think, with what we paid for this one, that it would be as silent as the grave." She gave a nervous laugh. "I'm going stir crazy, obviously."

"Melanie," Mom interrupted her flow, "where are Greg and the girls?"

"Oh, didn't I tell you yesterday? Greg and his mom took the girls in to morning services. I could have sworn I mentioned it. Well, it's a good thing you didn't get up early to take care of the girls, isn't it? Although it would have been nice to have the companionship." Amazing, how she managed to excuse herself from not keeping Mom up-to-date, while still scolding her for not coming around anyway. Smooth.

"Well? Are you two coming up or not?"

As we made our way toward the stairs, the messes continued. Mom started to pick things up, but I touched her arm and shook my head. "We'll never get upstairs that way."

She shrugged.

"Is it always like this?"

"No. Well, not entirely. They're busy girls, that's all. And without proper supervision, they . . ."

"Wreak mortal havoc? Leave chaos and destruction in

their wake?" I quipped as I double-stepped over an eerily lifelike babydoll and a xylophone on the third riser.

All Mom did was pick up the toys and tucked both under her arm as she trudged wearily up the stairs.

"There you are!" Mel exclaimed as we arrived at her open bedroom door. She was wrapped in a pink bedjacket that wouldn't have looked out of place on a 1950s-era starlet. Razor cut to perfection, her blond hair lay in a soft curl against her cheek, the other side tucked neatly back behind one ear. She even wore a sweep of blush and a light touch of mascara. Sandra Dee, eat your heart out. "I thought you'd gotten lost or something."

"Huh," I grunted before Mom could stop me. "Actually that's not far from the truth. It's like a jungle down there."

"The girls were playing while Greg made them breakfast," Mel said, waving a hand dismissively.

Mom was running on autopilot, straightening bedding, restacking the multitude of fashion magazines that covered the bed, picking up dirty clothes. "I have good news for you," she said as she reached to plump the pillow behind Mel's back. "Your sister has offered to help out with the girls."

Mel's gaze flicked toward me. She raised her brows. "Maggie did? Hm. I suppose that was your idea." Her expression left no doubt as to her skepticism. "Maggie doesn't know anything about keeping a household. The girls need someone who knows what they're doing."

"And on that note of encouragement," I said wryly, "I guess I'll be going. See ya, Mom."

"For heaven's sake, Maggie, don't be going off in a huff just because I hurt your feelings. You're too damned sensitive," Mel said, setting down her nail file and folding her hands primly over her six-month-preggers belly while leveling a pointed stare in my direction. "I mean, if anyone has a reason to be overly sensitive right now, it's me."

"Girls! For heaven's sake. Melanie, I don't want to hear any protests. You need help, and I know I haven't said anything, but it's just too much for me. *I* need help."

Melanie sighed, gazing back and forth between the two of us. "Fine. You're right, Mom. I don't want to stress you out. As long as you think Maggie can handle it."

My pride twisted in my chest, making me long to be twelve again and forgiven for doing the immature thing. Like sticking out my tongue and blowing a big, fat raspberry. Instead, I said, "Don't worry about a thing, Mel. Everything will be fine." Taking the high road was sometimes a lot less soul-satisfying.

"Good!" Mom exclaimed. "That's settled, then. I'll just show Maggie where you keep things and fill her in on the girls' schedules, and she'll stay the afternoon. I could use a day off to get some things done around the house before the week starts over tomorrow. All right, Maggie?"

The moment I had walked into Mel's house, I'd known that the role I'd been conned into would not be easy. But I'd been wrong. It wasn't going to be difficult. It was going to be pure hell.

My sister, in typical Mel fashion, had written out lists of tasks, schedules, warnings, admonishments, and just plain bossiness. "Wow. Is there anything she didn't think to write down?"

Mom shrugged. "It's really made things easier for Greg. This hasn't been easy on him."

Well, with Mom there all day, and Greg not coming

home until after the girls were in bed, I was having a hard time seeing how Greg was being affected much at all . . . unless it was in the bedroom. But maybe I was being too hard on him. A lack of bedroom action was enough to hit any guy where it hurt most.

With a last suggestion to call her if needed, Mom left me alone with Mel.

Chapter 3

Greg and my amazingly beautiful nieces, Jenna and Courtney, arrived home shortly after Mom left. I barely had a
chance to give my handsome-in-a-business-suit-kinda-way
brother-in-law a soapy-handed wave as he walked in with a
cell phone firmly attached to his ear before he headed upstairs.

My nieces immediately wrapped themselves around
my legs and were now bobbing up and down excitedly.

"Auntie Maggie! Auntie Maggie!" Jenna, the elder,
squealed. Courtney just beamed like a curly-haired cherub
and buried her face against my knees.

The two together were a pretty irresistible combination. Looking down into their big, babydoll eyes, I felt a
strong and relentless tug in the vicinity of my ovaries. I've
always known that I wanted kids of my own, someday . . .
but the longer it took to find that perfect man to be their
perfect father, the more I began to worry that love and
somedays were just pretty dreams that had no basis in

reality. Fairytale concepts that single women everywhere liked to believe, because to admit otherwise would be to open the door to depression and despair, and wasn't the world a scary enough place as it was? And it didn't get any easier. Was Tom The One? Was he Mr. Right? Or was he just Mr. Right Now? And how, exactly, was a girl supposed to know for sure?

That was the eternal question. One I intended to get to the bottom of. Soon. Well, eventually.

I dried my hands and knelt down to wrap the girls in my arms for a hug and a big, smoochy kiss. "Hello to you, too, you cuties. My goodness! Look how big you're getting. What has your mommy been feeding you two? Magical beans?"

"Jack and the beanstalk! Jack and the beanstalk!" Four years old and proud of it, Jenna often spoke for both of them. Courtney, at two and a half, hadn't yet mastered the finer elements of speech, and was more than happy to let her sister do the talking. "Gramma read us about the beans."

"She did?" I raised my eyebrows. My mother and magical beans? I didn't think she did magic.

"Uh-huh. I don't like beans. But I'd like magical beans. They wouldn't taste icky like Mommy's. Wanna see what I can do?"

Courtney lifted her arms to me and gazed up expectantly, so I scooped her up, patting her on her padded bottom as I watched her older sister do a somersault in her Sunday best. "Whoa! That was good. Wow. Tell you what, maybe we should go change. I don't think your mommy would like you rolling around like that in your nice clothes."

Right on cue, the intercom buzzed. "Maggie? Helloooooooo?"

Little Courtney's face lit up. She put her hand on my cheek and leaned in, gazing deep into my eyes. "Mommy!"

"I know!" I settled her more securely on my hip as I went to the intercom. "Need something?"

"Could you bring me up a pop or something cold? Please?"

"Um, sure." I wondered why she didn't just ask Greg to do it for her. But maybe he was still on his cell. "Come on, girls, let's get your mommy a pop and go visit her upstairs."

I grabbed a ginger ale from the fridge and, settling Courtney more securely on my hip, headed up the stairs with Jenna trailing behind.

Mel was on the phone, but I heard her telling the person on the other end to hang on. "There's my girls!" she said, opening her arms. I set Courtney down, and she and her sister stampeded forward to leap into Mel's arms. "Oops! Careful now. Watch Mommy's tummy. You wouldn't want to hurt the baby."

"Our baby has to be careful," Jenna told me, her eyes wide and solemn, her arms folded behind her back.

"That's right," I said, equally grave. I handed the can of pop to Mel. She took it, but put the receiver back up to her ear. The girls toddled off hand-in-hand toward their room down the hall.

Mel returned to her phone conversation. "Well, you can't go by what she says, Margo. You know that she just says things to annoy you. She's not really one of us."

I stopped what I was doing. Margo. That could mean one person and one person only. My lips settled together in a grimace. A few months ago, I'd learned that Mel was on occasion having coffee and going shopping with my high school nemesis, Margo Dickerson-Craig. That didn't mean I had to like it.

"Well, what about it? Greg just left, and my mom isn't here to spoil the fun. Why don't we get the girls together here?"

Ack. Wait, what? I frowned at her and waved my hands around to mime, *No, no, no!* And what did she mean, Greg just left?

Mel ignored the hand action. "Oh, good. I have got cabin fever like you would not believe. Can you do the calling around? I have a palm to grease here. Just my sister. She won't say a word. Trust. Yeah. Okay. Talk to you in twenty."

I stood at the end of the bed with my arms crossed, glaring at her as she clicked off the phone. Mel glanced up at me, amusement glinting in her eyes. "What? A girl can't round up some of her girlfriends when her hubby goes off for some fun of his own?"

"That depends on what kind of fun we're talking about here." I said not a word about her friendship with Margo. It wasn't up to me to choose my sister's friends. But oh, in this one case, I wanted to.

"Just a simple afternoon of movies and coffee. A little R and R, girl-style."

"Are you sure you're up for that? You are supposed to be taking things easy."

"If things get any easier, I'm going to be comatose. Come on, Maggie. A girl cannot live on fashion mags alone. I don't even have to get out of bed." When she saw me wavering, she threw in a wheedling, "Please?"

Exasperated that I had totally lost control of my day, I sighed. "What do you want me to do and when will they be here?"

She handed me a(*nother!*) list. "An hour or so. Thanks, Mags."

Mel's estimation was right on the money. I worked like a madwoman for the next hour, vacuuming, stacking things in the dishwasher, tidying, and wiping down the bathrooms. I was in the kitchen, throwing together bowls of snacks, when I heard a car in the driveway. The doorbell rang a moment later.

"Ding-dong! Avon calling!" a muffled voice giggled.

I opened the front door. On the other side stood two women, one stacked high with bags, the other bag-free and witless. The Bag Lady I recognized as Jane Churchill, the hapless friend of the Witless Wonder, Margo Dickerson. Er, hyphen Craig.

Her face froze when she saw me—or maybe that was the result of the Botox she had conned her doctor into injecting into her forehead for her migraines. (*Sometimes Mel's gossip actually was quite entertaining. And useful.*) "Well, well. Look who it is, Jane. My old high school buddy, Maggie O'Neill."

Emphasis on *old*, I noticed. It didn't matter. We both knew she was no buddy of mine. I decided to ignore her instead of rising to the bait. "Come on in. Mel is upstairs in her bedroom. Why don't you go on up while I bring the snacks. Can I get you something to drink? Tea? Pop?"

"Why don't you just bring up a variety, Maggie, hmm?" Margo suggested . . . aka placed her order. She lifted her too-blond hair away from her forehead. "And maybe you could turn up the AC? It's sticky in here."

It was sticky everywhere, but then, in her nubby blazer and trouser-style jeans, she wasn't exactly dressed for the weather. Jane gave me an apologetic glance that almost made me forgive her for her friendship with my least favorite person in the world, but trailed like a puppy at Margo's heels, leaving me to wrestle alone with the trays of snacks and drinks.

No problem.

I followed carefully, feeling out each unseen stair tread with my toes before taking the next step. The door to Mel's bedroom was closed, but luckily the handle was a lever sort. I kind of backed up to it, rose up on tiptoe, and eased it down.

Sometimes, having a strongly defined backside comes in handy.

"There you are! Girls, you remember my sister, Maggie, don't you?" Mel said as I backed into the room, deftly avoiding the door as it bounced back. There were a number of DVDs already fanned out across the bed, waiting for a selection to be made. I took a glance at the covers as I drew nearer. Mostly cookie-cutter romantic comedies featuring flavor-of-the-month abworthy hunks. Chick-o-rama. "Maggie, set the trays down over there. I just sent Jenna and Courtney back into their room to play, so if you could keep them entertained and quiet, that would be great."

Under normal circumstances I might have protested being relegated to the role of slave babysitter while the rest of the grown-ups played, but considering the company I would otherwise be expected to keep . . . I set the trays down on the small round table between Margo and Jane.

"There's one more girl who's running a little late," Mel said. "If you could listen for the doorbell . . ."

"Sure."

I hurried to close the bedroom door before she could think of anything else to ask. Mel was completely in her element today, that much was obvious. While I had gotten busy in the kitchen so that Mel could play hostess with the mostest, she had set about freshening herself up—as if any further primping was needed—and now her makeup was flawless, a fresh nightdress crisp across the mound of her belly, not a shining hair out of place. Perfect. She looked like a queen, surrounded by her loyal subjects.

Just the way she liked it.

I headed down the hallway toward the singsong sound of the girls' voices coming from their room. Giggling, loud whispering that wasn't really whispering at all, and squeals reached out to me. A lovely, sweet sound. I tiptoed up to the door, wanting to catch them unawares in the act of being themselves. There was something so innocent about it.

"No, Courtie. You can't do that with your Barbie. Barbies don't like their heads pulled off and stuffed under the pillow. It's not nice." Jenna, as usual. There was a pause filled with a little muffled mumbling. "Coco says Mommy used to do that to her Barbie dolls."

"I don't pull heads?"

"No, you should be nice to your Barbies. Fix their hair and make them pretty and stuff. That's what they like. See? Like this."

I peeped around the doorframe to see the two of them sitting across from each other on the little round rug in the center of the bedroom. They'd made a circle of their dolls around them, sitting as though they were a part of a camp sing-along. Jenna was looking up at a place on the ceiling. Little Courtney held her headless Barbie up and rocked her back and forth, making her dance.

"Coco says she never had a dolly that could dance so pretty. I want to be a ballerina, don't you?" Jenna rose to her feet and lifted her hands above her head, doing a whirling-dervish of a pirouette. "They have pretty shoes, and pretty dresses. I want to be pretty. Like Mommy. Right, Coco?" The two girls smiled up at the ceiling again.

Aw, how cute! They shared an imaginary friend. Once upon a time, I had an imaginary friend that kept me company while I rampaged around the countryside, hung out in trees, buried myself in the haymow, and talked to the animals. Her name was Anna, and she always visited along with a funny purple elephant named Ethan. Ethan liked to chat even more than Anna, and sometimes he could be very opinionated. He was also partial to Grandma Cora's raspberry pie. Together the two of them would whisper to me about the stars and the moon, the wind and the rain, and everything under the sun.

Funny, how wild imaginations seemed to run in families.

Off in the distance I heard the doorbell ring, so I left the girls to their fun while I went to answer it. Downstairs I opened the door to a pretty young woman with long, near-black hair that swirled heavily around her shoulder blades, and a trim figure that still somehow managed to be reminiscent of the Barbie dolls the girls were playing with. "Hi there," I said. "You must be—"

"Libby Turner. Hi." The young woman was struggling

with an exquisite leather purse the size of an airline carry-on and barely looked up.

"Everyone's upstairs in Mel's bedroom. Do you need me to show you up?"

She shook her head and headed for the stairs.

The brownies I was baking smelled as though they were about done, so I went into the kitchen to remove them from the oven, then made my way back upstairs. Mel's new arrival had closed the door behind her, which was fine with me because it excused me from being friendly.

The girls heard me coming this time. "Auntie Maggie! Come and play with us!" Jenna exclaimed.

"Play!" Courtney echoed. Short and sweet, just like her.

"You want me to play?" I sat down with them, cross-legged on the floor, feeling like an overgrown pixie.

"You want a Barbie?"

"I'll take Ken." I picked up the ultraplastic male, who was dressed to the nines in a fluffy fur coat, ski boots, and skis. I have been looking for the perfect male, but, well, *hmm*. "Where has Ken been? He looks like Santa's favorite elf."

"He was cold. Mommy likes air-conditioning."

"Uh-huh. Well, it is kind of hot outside."

"I like hot."

Jenna proceeded to strip her Barbie, a tawdry superplatinum blonde who looked right at home with the extreme lack of clothing, and then began to dress her in a glittery lamé bathing suit I wouldn't have put on a dog. "Wow, that's quite the swimsuit. Where did Barbie get that?"

Jenna didn't take her eyes off her studied attempts to dress the doll in front of her. "Her name's not Barbie."

"It's not?"

She shook her head. "Huh-uh. She's Margaret."

Taken aback, I raised my brows. "Margaret, eh?"

"Uh-huh."

"What on earth made you name her Margaret?"

Jenna screwed up her face at the doll, thinking mightily. "Coco said that was her name."

Ohhhhhh. Coco. I hid the smile that threatened and tried very hard for the solemnity a serious chat with a four-year-old required. "Coco did, huh? And who is Coco?"

Jenna shrugged and went about her business. The gold lamé swimsuit with the Totally Eighties frilled shoulder was soon joined by a black pillbox hat, complete with veil, and a green faux crocodile attaché case. Over-the-knee dominatrix boots rounded out the lovely ensemble.

She held the doll up to me to show me the full effect. Disco Barbie had nothing on Margaret. "Mm. Very nice."

Courtney wasn't paying attention. Her dark head was bent over the doll she was trying to rehead. I closed my hands around hers and guided her through it. "What's your dolly's name, Courtie?"

Her response was immediate. "Poopy," she said, using her Barbie as a hammer to whack the Ken doll I was still holding.

"Ah. Did Coco name her, too?"

Jenna heaved a long-suffering sigh. "*No*, Auntie Maggie. Courtie needs to *go* poopy." She got to her feet and held out her hand. "Come on, Courtie, I'll take you."

The two of them toddled off toward the bathroom, leaving me to follow along behind like an awkward third wheel. As I was passing by Mel's room, I noticed the door was open a crack.

"So, someone actually hung a dummy out there to

threaten you?" I heard my sister ask. I slowed down and paused for a listen.

"Well, my husband. But yes. Left it right up there for everyone under God to see."

Realization struck. Turner. Libby *Turner*. Ding-ding-ding. I felt a shiver run through me at the synchronicity that somehow seemed to be present in my life of late. But at least the figure hanging from the conveyer system at the feed mill had only been a dummy. It wasn't real. There was consolation in that.

"Who does Joel think did it?"

"I don't know. To tell you the truth, it scares me." Libby's voice again. "I mean, we knew people weren't happy about the rate increases. Of course, everyone complained about the need for modern processing techniques," she said, bitterness creeping in, "but when it came to footing the bill, I guess we were supposed to just eat that cost ourselves."

"What do you expect, Libby? You're dealing with a bunch of hick farmers for clientele." Margo. Why did that not surprise me?

"I know, but . . . I mean, they're in business for themselves, too. They know what it takes to stay afloat these days. I don't understand why they can't accept that we have *all* been hit by this economy. I mean, Joel works day and night up at the feed mill, and there I am stuck at home, wishing we could've afforded that pricy security system and scared half to death that the next disgruntled farmer is going to stop at the house while Joel's at the office."

"I heard it wasn't just a dummy." That must have been Jane. She'd been so quiet, I'd almost forgotten she was there.

"What was it?" my sister demanded, excitement in her voice. "Spill! Libby, if you don't tell us, Jane will. Won't you, Jane?"

There was a pause, and a sigh of resignation. "Well. A note was found with the dummy. But Joel says it's nothing to worry about."

"And what did it say?" Margo pressed in a quiet, unassuming way. Quiet and unassuming bordering on Machiavellian anarchy.

"Margo Dickerson-Craig, you aren't thinking about whispering this into your husband's ear, are you?" I'd always thought Jane was a little out of step with the girls in Mel's circle. Perhaps she was better matched than I thought—she did seem to have a streak of the instigator in her.

Margo laughed merrily, a sound I had heard all too often in high school, and which still made me cringe in dislike. "Jane, I'm hurt. Just because my husband edits the *Gazette* doesn't mean I pass on everything I hear."

"No, you can't!" Libby exclaimed. "Joel wouldn't like it if it got out. He'd never forgive me."

"Libby. Honey. We all know Joel will forgive you anything. Don't be so modest about your powers of persuasion." Her laugh trilled again. So mocking. Didn't her "friends" hear that? Didn't it bother them? "But seriously, Libby. You and Joel need to sell. That place is the last feed mill in the county, and with all the upgrades? You're sitting on a gold mine. And then you don't have to deal with all the headaches. Just think. You could retire and spend the rest of your life traveling to exotic places. Get out of this one-horse town. I know I'd do it in a heartbeat."

"You know the mill is Joel's life, Margo. It's been in his family for generations. He's not going to sell."

"Still . . . after that and the fistfight with that Cullins man that you told us about last month . . ."

"Wait—I didn't hear anything about a fight!" Mel protested.

"Joel didn't report it. Bad for business. Besides, it was just tempers flaring. You know how men are."

"Do you really think it's wise to let something like that go? I mean, what if it was the same person this time around?"

Jenna called me from the bathroom then, so I didn't get to hear Libby's response. I couldn't help wondering if Tom knew about the fight. It wouldn't be the first time someone around here had swept something ugly under the nearest rug. Something they found embarrassing. Something bad for business. Or at the very least, bad for their digestion.

It was, after all, the Hoosier way. Or was it just human nature?

Jenna had run the sink full of water, and Courtney had her hands plunged in almost to her armpits. Thank goodness for short summer sleeves. Somehow they'd managed not to slop it down their fronts and all over the floor yet. "And what is it that you girls think you're doing?"

"Look, Auntie Maggie! They're swimming!"

"Swimmin'!" Courtney echoed jubilantly.

"Courtie, no! Margaret has to go first. She's oldest! Coco said so!" Jenna pushed Courtney's doll away. Instantly I saw a determined expression I knew only too well crop up within Courtney's round face as she stared defiantly up at her older sister. "And besides, Coco says—"

"No! No Coco. See, see." And with that she pointed a pudgy finger in my direction.

See who? Me? No, not me. *Behind me.* I turned and glanced over my shoulder, expecting to find one of Mel's guests patiently waiting to use the bathroom. Libby, maybe, or even Jane. Not Margo, though—patience was never her style. But nobody was there.

Confused, I reached over their heads and pressed the lever that would drain the sink. "All right, girls. Out of the bathroom. Come on."

"But Auntie Maggie!"

"No buts. Your mom wouldn't want you playing in here."

"Swimmin'!" Courtney said, huffing out her lower lip. "Out."

Grumbling, muttering, and casting under-the-breath chicklet aspersions back at their favorite auntie, the girls shuffled off down the hallway. When they were safely ensconced in their room once again, with Courtney secure in my arms, I said, "Now, girls. Why don't you tell me who Coco is, hm? Is she a friend?"

"Coco says you know who she is. She shouldn't have to tell you." Jenna smirked.

Great. A smart-alecky imaginary friend. What were the odds? "I would have to see her to know who she is," I countered, logicking them at their own game.

"She says you could see her if you tried. She talks to you, too, but you don't listen. You never listen."

A prickle of nervousness began in the palms of my hands and traveled up my arms. "What did you say?"

Jenna was digging through a plastic tote box for yet

another wardrobe change for Margaret. "Not me. Coco. Coco says you don't listen to her, and she wants you to."

"I don't know who Coco is. I know you're talking to her, but I don't see her."

"She's right there." Jenna pointed at a chair that had been pulled away from the little tea table in front of the window.

"There's no one there, Jenna."

"There is! She's sitting right there, and she's nodding her head."

I glanced over pointedly—nothing there, nothing and no one—then pointedly back at Jenna. And that was when I saw it. Out of the corner of my eye, as my gaze shifted over, I saw a shimmer. A miragelike shimmer in front of the sheer white curtains, with a few tiny, silvery, flickering sparkles of light twinkling here and there for the space of a second. The briefest of visions . . . and then it was gone.

My mouth had fallen open. I snapped it closed, and bit my lip instead.

"Cee Cee!" Courtney cried, pointing at the closet. The deep, dark closet. The door had come open about six inches. "Cee Cee, Cee Cee, Cee Cee, Cee Cee . . ."

Realization struck. Cee Cee, not See, See. As in a name, not a verb. "Cee Cee's in the closet?" I whispered, because I didn't have breath for anything more.

I rose to my feet, Courtney's repetitive chant reverberating in my brain as I made my way on tiptoe, between clear plastic tote boxes, Barbie paraphernalia, and stuffed animals, over to the closet. All the while thinking: *This is a new house, only a couple of years old. It can't be haunted. It really is just an imaginary friend or two. Kids have had imaginary friends forever. It's nothing to be afraid of. Nothing to be afraid of. Nothing. To be. Afraid. Of.*

Closer and closer I crept, while the fine hairs on my arms rose to attention. Courtney kept babbling about Cee Cee, but at least it was at a more manageable volume. I blocked the sound by sheer dint of will and stretched my fingers out to touch the door.

I'll prove there's no one there. No monsters in the closet. No boogey . . . women. Just clothes and shoes and . . . dead space.

At the exact moment my fingers connected, the door to the hall slammed closed behind us. Three voices rose in a shriek of surprise loud enough to raise the roof. One of them sounded awfully familiar.

Oh, yeah. It was mine.

Chapter 4

The girls jumped at me, and I welcomed the contact. At least it was human. Coming from the hall I heard a door open and hurried footsteps approaching. The girls' door swung inward, crashing against the doorstop behind it. Leading the charge was Lady Madonna herself. "What— on—*earth*—is going—on?"

I yanked myself back to the land of the living. "What are you doing out of bed? You know what the doctor said—"

Mel held up her hand. "Never mind that now. What was all the screaming about?"

And just like that, Madonna Mel turned into Mama Bear Mel of the snapping jowls and slashing claws. Behind her, her posse had gathered, all of them staring at me. I juggled the girls in my arms. "Melanie, go get back in bed, please. Nothing is wrong. The door slammed. It scared us. That's all."

She frowned at my brief explanation. "The door slammed."

"Didn't you hear it?"

"No. I didn't. So the door slammed, Maggie. So what? What was so scary about that anyway?"

"Well, I don't know . . . it . . . No one was near it." It sounded lame, even to me. But I hadn't been mistaken about the sudden heaviness that had crept into the room, the sense that we were not alone, and I certainly hadn't imagined the conversations the girls had held with their "imaginary" friends.

"*Ooooooooooh*. Poor widdle Maggie. The wind slammed the door and it scared widdle you?" She shook her head, her lips pressed together. "So, what is this really? Your idea of a joke?"

It wasn't the wind. The windows were closed—the AC was on. And it definitely wasn't me.

"It was Coco, Mommy."

Jenna's quiet declaration stopped us all. Distracted, Mel blinked and shifted her attention to her oldest daughter. "Coco? Who's Coco?"

"Mommy! You know. *Coco*. My friend I told you 'bout."

Mel glanced at me. I shrugged. Which wasn't easy, being loaded down with two cute yet surprisingly weighty little girls. My shoulders were killing me.

"Coco slammed the door to get Auntie Maggie's 'ttention."

If there was a universal hand symbol for imaginary friend, it was beyond my ken, and I couldn't think of any other way to tell Mel what I believed in front of the girls. Only . . . was that really what I believed? Or was there more to Coco and Cee Cee than met the eye?

Behind us there was an audible click, followed by the unmistakable hum as the TV turned on. Mel and I glanced over, certain we'd find Courtney with the remote in her hand. But the remote was on top of the TV housing. No one was near it.

And then as we watched on, the TV began to drift through the channels. When the flickering stopped, I caught my breath. On the screen was a goofy bird, bouncing off the edges of the screen, a-whooping and a-hollering: *"I'm cuckoo for Cocoa Puffs, I'm cuckoo for Cocoa Puffs . . ."*

"Oh," Mel said in a quiet voice that was not anything like her usual. All the color seemed to have drained from her face, and she began to sag against the wall.

"Oh, jeez!" I rushed over to her and jammed my shoulder under her arm for support. Margo surprised me by following suit on Mel's other side. Together we managed to get her over to one of the beds.

"Mel? Melanie? Are you all right?" I rubbed her hands between mine. "Come on, honey, wake up. Jenna, can you go get a bottle of water from the refrigerator for your mommy?"

Jane, who had been standing quietly by this whole time, stepped forward and held out her hand to Jenna. "I'll take her. Courtney, do you want to come with us?"

"I'll go, too," Libby said, taking Courtney by the hand.

Mel's eyes had rolled back in her head. "Margo," I said quietly, forgetting for the moment that she was my sworn enemy and mostly evil, "could you run and find a clean cloth, wet it with cool water, and bring it to me here?"

For once, smartass remarks and social posturing were the furthest things from Margo's mind. She scurried out.

I waited until I heard the telltale squeak of the hinges on Mel's door down the hall before turning to my sister and clearing my throat. "All right. You can open your eyes now."

My perfect, hypochondriac sister squinted at me with one eye. At least she had the decency to look sheepish. "How did you know?"

I shrugged. I had always been able to read her, good or bad. "How isn't important," I told her. "They're only going to be gone a minute or two, tops. So, what's up? Why the theatrics?"

"What's up. What's up?" She scowled at me. "First my afternoon of fun is interrupted by my children screaming their heads off, and then I get out of bed to investigate—against doctor's orders, mind you—only to find you claiming that a door closed all by its little lonesome. Of course the girls are going to follow your lead—and by the way, if you are responsible for this little stunt, you should feel heartily ashamed. And then! *Then* the TV decides to choose *this very moment* to go berserk, which, if you are responsible, was actually really well timed and . . . kind of freaky. So, everything being what it is, forgive me if I'm a little overwrought and needing a moment, because I don't think any of this is good for my already sky-high blood pressure."

I was a little irked by the fact that she still half believed I'd done it all as a joke. But then again, if I was standing in her glass slippers, I probably would have felt the same. "Mel, I know this is a little worrisome—"

"And what *about* that commercial?" she plowed ahead as though I hadn't spoken at all. "That was just too weird. *Cocoa?* What are the odds of that coincidence?"

"So, you think it's all a coincidence, then."

"Well, of course I think it's a coincidence. What else am I supposed to think?"

How much should I tell her? How much information should I trust her with? Yes, she was my sister . . . but past experience had made me leery. "The girls have been talking about their friends Coco and Cee Cee all afternoon . . . but more importantly, they've been talking *to* them. Like they're in the room with us."

"So? Lots of kids have imaginary friends, Maggie. I mean, their whole world is kind of in an uproar right now. Is it any wonder they've invented someone to help them to feel secure?"

It was certainly a possibility. And yet I also knew what I had sensed in that room. The physical feeling of someone there with us. The shiver of awareness.

"Maybe," I said softly. "But . . . I keep getting the feeling that this is something more."

"Exactly what do you mean by 'something more'?"

"Here I am!" Margo called as she sailed through the door. Spotting Mel leaning up on her elbows, she stopped. "Oh, you're up. Good. Here."

She handed me the cloth, still dripping around the edges. Without a second thought, I slapped it on Mel's forehead.

"Ugh! Wet!"

"Nice and cool," I sang, pushing her back on the bed without remorse. She did bring this on herself, after all.

Mel gritted her teeth as water trickled down the sides of her forehead into her perfectly styled hair. "I think I'm feeling much better now." She made her way back to her own bedroom.

We all followed her. "I just have to use the little girls' room," she said. We waited while she went into the master bathroom to take care of business. She didn't close the door right away; instead, she paused there as though snagged on the doorframe, her fingers frozen on the brass lever knob. "Margo?" she said, not moving. "Did you have trouble finding the fresh washcloths?"

Not seeing Mel's reaction, Margo laughed. "No, they were right in the front of the linen closet. Why?"

Without a word, Melanie released her hand from the door and gave it a gentle push. As one we leaned to the left to peer into the room.

Every drawer and door on the vanity was open, as was the medicine cabinet and the linen closet. And suddenly a chill current of air swirled around us, touching, testing . . . finally pushing up against me so hard that I took a step back for balance. Was I the only one who felt it?

"Girls?" Mel cleared her throat. "Did you go into Mommy's bathroom just now? Maybe you needed to potty and mine was closest?"

"Mel . . ." Jane stepped forward, her hands clenched together. "They couldn't have. They were with Libby and me."

"But . . . if it wasn't Margo . . . and it wasn't the girls or you two . . . and Maggie was with me . . ." Mel's mind was whirring along, trying to process it all but coming up full-stop against a wall of logic and reason. My sister didn't do intuition, you see. She'd rather do clueless and blind. It worked for her. Only a little too well, most of the time.

The current withdrew suddenly. For a moment, my ears rang hollow; and then the air filled in around me in a rush. Out of the corner of my eye I saw a *pop-pop-pop* before I heard the actual sound of the filaments bursting within the big, clear bulbs in the bathroom fixtures, followed immediately by a chorus of screams and a volley of clutching hands as everyone jammed together into a protective huddle with Jenna and Courtney at the center.

When it became obvious that there was no threat of glass spraying through the air, Mel rose to her full height of five feet two inches and thrust her fists to her gently rounded hips. "That's it. Ladies, I'm sorry. I think we're going to have to call it a day. We seem to be having . . . power issues that need to be addressed. We'll have our fun another day, okay?"

Margo and Jane left without complaint. Only Libby paused to silently reconsider the empty bathroom, frowning and gnawing her lower lip, before turning to locate her purse. While Mel returned to her bed, hugging her girls to her side, I showed the others out.

As soon as I walked back into her bedroom, Mel started in. "What the *Devil* is going on here today? It's like this house is going crazy!" At least it was all a whisper. The girls had fallen asleep already, tucked up against the warmth of their mother's body. "What were you trying to tell me back in the girls' bedroom? You said something about a feeling. What did you mean? What does a feeling have to do with anything?"

Well, if I was going to go through with it, now was as good a time as ever. I sat on the foot of the bed and took a deep breath, weighing my words. "I don't know quite how to tell you this, so I guess I should just come right out and say it. Mel, the girls' imaginary friend or friends . . . and it seems that it might be plural . . . well . . . I think they are more than that."

She looked even more confused.

"I think they might not be imaginary. Just invisible."

Mel sat up straighter in bed, her eyes never leaving me. "What do you mean, invisible?"

This was it. The moment of truth. By telling her this, I would be opening myself up to derision and more . . . but these were my nieces we were talking about. I couldn't let Mel go on, unaware of the real issue at hand. Forewarned was forearmed.

"Invisible . . . but very real." I paused a moment, allowing this much to soak in. "I think they're spirits."

She stared at me and frowned. "Spirits. You mean, ghosts?"

"Something like that. Only not necessarily a traditional haunting or anything like that. More like a being that comes to visit, to watch over the girls maybe, or because they're drawn to their energy. Or—"

"That's ridiculous, Maggie."

I had expected that. "You have a better explanation for the things that have gone on this afternoon?"

"There could be lots of other explanations."

"Or it could be spirit," I persisted as gently as I could. "But I didn't get the feeling that it was anything frightening or threatening. Probably more like a Spirit Guide, or a guardian angel of some kind." The thing in Mel's room, on the other hand . . . that one made me nervous.

"So somehow you're an expert in these things all of a sudden?" she said, reverting to sarcasm the way she always did when something made her uncomfortable. "How do you know any of this?"

I couldn't exactly take any of this conversation back, so I might as well go whole hog. "I . . . I've been studying this kind of thing lately. Because of certain things I've experienced. I'm not crazy, Mel. You know me. I might not be everything you ever wanted in an older sister, but when have I ever exhibited delusional behavior?"

"Well . . . you haven't. Except maybe when you thought you were going to marry Tony Dearing," she said, bringing up an embarrassing episode from my angsty teen years that I would love for her to have forgotten. "But . . . ghosts? I don't know . . ."

A thought occurred to me. "Wait. When I first got here this afternoon, you mentioned you've been hearing noises. Remember?"

"Well, y-e-e-es. It—it has been a little weird off and on for a while, I guess, now that you mention it . . ."

"What kind of weird?"

"Well, nothing like this afternoon. But . . . well . . . lightbulbs keep burning out. We'd put a new one in, and within a couple of days it would need changing again. Greg called an electrician to check things over, but they didn't find anything wrong. And sometimes I'd walk into a room and the TV would be on, even though I was certain I had turned it off already. Or the radio. And . . . once I could have sworn that I smelled fresh bread baking in the oven. And . . . well, you know me; I don't bake! And . . ." She broke off and lifted her gaze to mine, her eyes wide and stricken. "Maggie! *Why am I starting to believe you?* Oh my God! What am I going to do?"

"What you're not going to do is, you're not going to panic." I sat down on the edge of the bed and looked her in the eye.

"But—spirits—ghosts—"

"Are by and large benign in nature," I assured her as

soothingly as possible. "Most of them were human at one time or another. When you remember that and treat them as such, it takes some of the mystical out of the equation. People can be good, they can be bad, but they're still just people." I had learned a lot about the spirit world in my short tenure in Felicity Dow's employ. Sometimes, I even surprised myself.

"But they're around my babies."

I nodded. "But the girls don't seem afraid of them at all. In fact, they even seem playful with them."

"But you know what the nuns always said about anything *supernatural*. How can we be sure the spirits are good and not . . . evil?" she asked, folding her arms more tightly around her sleeping angels. Then she shook her head. "I can't believe I'm even considering this."

I might not always get along with Mel; we might not be the closest of sisters; but when push came to shove, when bad came to worse, when ghosts came to Stony Mill and started scoping out my family's most innocent members . . . well, blood was thicker than water in more ways than just the physical, and it was always better to err on the side of caution.

"I have friends who might be able to help," I said, crossing my fingers that it was the right thing to do. "Friends who are . . . more experienced in this kind of thing. They've been . . ." Wait. Did I really want to tell my Gossip Queen sister about the weirdness in Stony Mill? So far, the paranormal disturbances had flown under the radar of the bulk of Stony Mill's conservative contingent. To bring it to the light of day . . . was that smart at this point in time? I made a quick reverse and change of approach. "They are experts who investigate claims of supernatural occurrences, and who try to help both the people and the spirits who might be involved."

"Skeptical" did not even begin to cover the doubt twisting Melanie's features. "You mean, like the Ghostbusters?"

"I guess you could say something like that."

"And these are friends of yours?"

"Yes."

"Hm. You have just become almost interesting, Maggie. Congratulations." She smirked. "Bet you Mom doesn't know."

I raised my brows at her. "And she's not going to. Or you can deal with the invisible friends yourself."

"Kidding! Sheesh." She paused then, considering me thoughtfully. "Is your boss involved in this with you?"

I froze. "Why do you ask that?"

"I don't know. You've been . . . different since you've worked there. I can't quite put my finger on it. And your boss . . . she has that air around her. As though she's somehow above this world." She made a wry face. "I'm probably being silly."

Hm. Maybe Mel did intuition better than I thought. "Well . . . yes. Yes, Liss is involved. But it's nothing to be afraid of, you have to trust me on this, okay? We'll figure things out."

She nodded, looking down at the shining heads of her daughters, her gaze softening in a way that made the gears in my heart ping with a longing that I would rather ignore for now. Talk about a ticking biological clock. Oy. She leaned down and kissed each daughter gently on the forehead.

"Don't worry, Mel," I told her softly. "The girls will be fine."

She looked up at me, and I could both feel and see her uncertainty. "They had better be. They'd just better be."

Chapter 5

I was exhausted when I was able to leave at last. Greg had stayed out far longer than Mel or I had expected, citing a dead cell phone battery when Mel asked him why he hadn't called. Which led to a discussion about priorities and a lack thereof. Which led to a discussion about why it was that hormones run so fast and furious in pregnant women. Which led to a bona fide argument about . . . well, I didn't stick around to find out.

Once home, I fell onto my bed and pushed my shoes off with my toes. They dropped to the carpeted floor with a plop. It was the last sound I heard until I awoke early the next morning, eyes gritty, mouth dry, and goose bumps covering my entire body despite the oppressive heat outdoors. Groaning as I recognized the muscles I had strained by cleaning on my hands and knees the food spills and tracked juice trails on Mel's kitchen floor, I resolutely shut my eyes and drew the soft pink comforter around my body.

The moms of the world, I'd decided, were unsung heroes in my book. I had no idea how they did it, making a mental note to call my own mother and give her kudos for making it through raising me, Mel, and my brother.

But I had another task to accomplish today in between my usual Monday morning busyness at the store. Family duty would be at the top of my list.

Sighing, I rose and went to the bathroom, flipped on the light over the sink, and turned the water in the shower on full blast until steam started to rise. Water, the great purifier, healing and holy. Water, beloved of the Goddess. Water, bringer of life. Shower time was usually meditation time for me, a necessary morning ritual for my peace of mind. It woke me up, it refreshed me, it centered me before beginning my day, and it got me going. Not a bad bargain, for something most people took for granted.

Today, though, there would be no lingering. I was in and out before my muscles even had a chance to unkink. One pair of lightweight capris, a ruffle-edged T, and a pair of ballet flats later, and I was out the door. I didn't even stop to make a PB&J for lunch.

Enchantments was my home away from home, and the longer I worked there, the more I appreciated it for the blessing it was. The store was located on River Street, one of the oldest parts of Stony Mill, where a stretch of old-style warehouses had been turned into picturesque, Rockwellian-style storefronts, primarily antiques and collectibles, with a few others interspersed throughout. My boss, Felicity Dow, had purchased one of the old warehouses when she moved to town ten years ago with her late husband, and had proceeded to turn her gift and antiques business with its popular tea and coffee bar into one of the most thriving of the bunch, thanks to her keen eye for presentation and her insistence upon serving only the highest-quality goods to her customers.

But unbeknownst to the somewhat stuffy matrons of Stony Mill society, Enchantments served a higher purpose. Behind the scenes, the store was also a witchy emporium, one of the largest metaphysical storefronts in Indiana, which meant some of our customers traveled long distances to browse our secret merchandise in the upstairs Loft. Of course, not all of the metaphysical stuff was hidden away. Few Stony Millers would suspect that the leaded crystal etched with a sprinkling of stars and a crescent moon was actually the work of an artisan of the Craft hailing from Ireland, nor that the photographic prints of stone circles and other pre-Christian locations such as Glastonbury Tor were the vision of a Gardnerian High Priestess better known for her work in the fashion world. Witches and mundanes shopped side by side without friction . . . possibly because the regular folk didn't realize the other group existed. Or maybe I was underestimating the tolerance levels of our town populace.

Eh, probably not.

I parked Christine, my beloved VW Bug, in the usual spot, but I didn't bother to lock up. We didn't have a lot of petty crime here in Stony Mill, and we were right around the corner from the shared space of the Police and Sheriff Departments, which was right across the street from the Courthouse. I wasn't the only one in town with terrible lock-tight habits. There was an unspoken level of trust in our town, one we all took very seriously. Making concerted efforts to lock your house and belongings might be viewed as distrust of your neighbors. Even with three recent murders, that level of trust hadn't been affected. *Yet*.

Old habits do indeed die hard.

It was a relief to step out of the heat and humidity into the aggressive air-conditioning of the store. Christine had been made in a time when AC wasn't considered standard. Though come to think of it, her heater rarely did the trick either. As soon as I stepped over the threshold, the lenses in my sunglasses fogged up so thickly that I could have been facing a hundred ghostly faces and I wouldn't have seen a one.

But there were no ghosts staring me down from the store office. There never were. No wraiths, no h'aints, no ghostly voices. Not even the odd shadow figure. The store was one of the few safe havens in my life, and a welcome one.

My boss breezed in through the purple velvet curtain that separated the storefront from the dark little office and storage space. She stopped when she saw me and glanced at her watch. "Goodness, is it that time?"

I smiled at her. "You've been busy, I take it?"

She shook her head, her silvery auburn waves swaying gently about her jaw. "Only a bit of meditation in the Loft. I lost all track of the hour."

"I'm not late?"

"No, no. Unless my watch has stopped, you're right on schedule." She chuckled. "You seem a little out of sorts. Was your Sunday that bad? Or that good?"

"Well," I said, trying for irony, "considering that I spent the whole of it at my sister's, tending to her every need, her every whim . . . I'll let you guess."

"Oh, dear. That good?"

"Better. Infinitely. The doctor has put her on bed rest, and she's kind of running my mom ragged. I promised I'd help out."

Sympathy and understanding were two things Liss was very good at. "My, you will be busy, won't you. Poor thing."

My boss, Felicity Dow—Liss for short—was my personal savior and mentor extraordinaire, and a delight to work for. She was also a witch. The good kind, not the euphemism for someone far less desirable. She had come into my life eight months before, at a time when I had desperately needed a good flashlight to help me find my way through the darkness. A talented witch with intuition to spare, Liss had done that, but then she'd done me one better. She had taught me that I could be my own flashlight, so that I'd never have to feel lost again.

The Darkness would never be the same. Thank goodness. Oh, I wasn't an expert yet by any means, but I was at least starting to get the hang of this empath thing. Experiencing the emotions and private motivations of another person might never be truly a comfortable thing for me, but because of Liss I was learning the inner tools I needed in order to feel at ease with myself. Even more importantly, I was beginning to discover that things were never cut-and-dried as far as intuitive abilities were concerned.

Liss was the person I wanted most to be when I grew up at long last. Educated, elegant, and with a personality that was both calm and compassionate, she was exactly what a girl should aspire to become. And of course, her posh British accent didn't hurt. She'd once told me she had relatives in Scotland, including a nephew who had made a career out of studying topics paranormal, but if there was any Scotland left in her accent, it appeared only occasionally. Which was too bad, really. The more European accents surrounding me, the better. Accents made the world seem smaller somehow, and yet also more exotic. It made me feel better to realize that life wasn't confined only to this tiny corner of the planet.

Liss also had a sense of style that was uniquely her own. It didn't matter what anyone else was wearing; if it suited Liss's whimsical nature for the day, then it was a go. I had never actually seen her closet, but it must be huge, because I couldn't remember ever seeing her in the same outfit twice . . . and yet, I knew I must have. Excess was *not* Liss's style.

Today she was wearing a khaki linen safari suit, complete with belted short-sleeved jacket, and a tall pair of riding boots polished to a smart sheen. All she needed was a pith helmet and she'd be ready for her next journey into the nearest jungle. Or at least the next foray into the great beyond. Whichever came first.

"On a happier note, I hope," she said, "how was your date with Tom?"

Yet another sore subject. "Woefully interrupted by a dummy at the local feed mill. *Literally* a dummy, as in meant to resemble a human being, which some jackass strung from the conveyer system," I grumbled.

Liss was shaking her head and trying not to smile. "So . . . want a cuppa?" she asked. "It'll cure what ails you."

Well, I wasn't so sure it would cure any of my problems, but I nodded all the same. I would need one before I embarked on the full story of my weekend. "I'll pour."

We made our way to the coffee bar at the front of the

store. Normally it was my job to fill all the pots and vessels with water, readying them for the droves of regulars we would have throughout the day in need of their jolt of java. Or tea, as the case might be. We served both at Enchantments, though rarely your everyday cup. Our teas and coffees were as gourmet as they come, from many foreign destinations. In fact, our customers often claimed that the coffees and teas we served seemed to transport them to distant lands, and it was that lovely dreaminess that kept them coming back for more. I'd often suspected that my wonderfully witchy boss might have a little something to do with that—a choice selection of words of power spoken over the crates perhaps? Or maybe it was the organic honey we sweetened it with, collected by a commune of bee charmers in northwest Michigan. They, too, were neo-hippie pagans, and who knew what spells were spoken over the sweet stuff up there. I've heard tell those Michigan pagans are a wild bunch.

This morning, all the receptacles were cleaned, filled, and ready for business. Liss wasn't being quite truthful when she said she had only been meditating, but I loved her for it. All that was left was placing out the trays of filled pastries and other mouthwatering confections from our favorite café in town, Annie-Thing Good. We'd started placing a regular order with Annie because the trial run had been so successful. On second thought, though, I wasn't so sure it had been a good idea. Can you imagine what happens when you stare at delectable, de-lickable, mind-alteringly good pastries all day long? My thighs would never be the same.

I chose a good strong cup of coffee—black and unsweetened, in light of the yummy stuff I was sure not to be able to resist at some point—and made Liss her usual cup of English Breakfast, heavy on the cream.

"It wasn't only my sister that made the weekend so interesting," I said as I worked.

"Do tell."

"Well. My sister's house seems to have attracted something."

"Termites? Wooly worms? A bevy of men in white oxfords, black pants, and ugly shoes trying to sell her their church newsletter?"

"Try a couple of spirits or entities."

She stopped and looked at me, suddenly serious. "Really? All of a sudden? She hasn't noticed any activity before?"

I shook my head. "The house is only a few years old. It's only lately that she's been hearing strange sounds. Lightbulbs breaking, the radio or TV turning off or on. That sort of thing. But while I was there . . ." Briefly I described what had happened between my nieces, and then the weirdness in Mel's bedroom as well.

"Interesting," Liss said, that familiar light of intrigue in her eyes. "And the girls . . . have they ever demonstrated abilities before?"

It was a fair question, one that I was ashamed not to have an answer to. I'd realized something as I'd played with them Sunday afternoon. How much of their lives I had missed out on by avoiding my sister whenever I could. It seemed only yesterday that Jenna was a baby with the biggest blue eyes I'd ever seen. "I don't think so."

Liss nodded. "Something to keep watch for, then. Children as a rule are more open to spirit activity. They haven't yet built walls in their minds against it, so it doesn't occur to them to question what they are seeing and hearing as not being a part of this world, this reality. Your nieces can still build those walls . . . or they might accept the gift and retain it. Only time will tell."

The gift. I'm not so sure Mel would agree with Liss's description.

"What about the activity in Mel's bedroom?" I asked her. "I could be wrong, but . . . it felt different, somehow, than what the girls are experiencing. Separate from that. It felt . . ."

Just as I was about to go further into what I had felt standing in Mel's room, all hell broke loose in the store.

Three trucks attempted to deliver at the same time, somehow all managing to get stuck in the alleyway, unable to navigate the narrow passages. One of Stony Mill's finest stopped by to direct traffic, and somehow messed it up even worse for a time. Pedestrian traffic was unusually heavy, dodging this way and that in between the snarled cars, trucks, and even bicycles as they made their way toward the stores for a bit of summertime antiquing. Despite the fact that one of the deliveries was for us, Enchantments suffered little from the stoppages. Heavy foot traffic always boded well for a smashing good day, saleswise, and today was no different. We were well and truly swamped.

Lunch went forgotten in the middle of all the chaos. My cell phone rang around one o'clock. Caller ID showed Mel's number, so I answered it quickly.

"Maggie? It's Mel." Her voice was scarcely more than a whisper.

"What's wrong?" I asked, keeping my eye on the customers traversing the aisles. "Why are you whispering?"

"I don't want Mom to hear. Listen, do you have any news yet about my . . . *situation*?"

"Not much, Mel, sorry. It's been incredibly busy here today."

"Oh. Okay. I've just been dying here all morning."

The receiver went airless in my ear, and for a moment I thought I heard muffled voices speaking in the background, as though she'd covered the mouthpiece with her hand. "Someone there with you?"

"What? Oh! No. No one. Listen, Maggie, I'd better let you get back to work. Say hello to your boss for me. What was her name again?"

"Felicity," I told her, getting a funny feeling again. "Felicity Dow." I'd almost forgotten Mel's singularly spot-on moment of intuition last night.

"That's it. Tell her hello from me, and I guess I'll see you when you get here, unless the two of you come up with something before then?"

"Right. Bye, Mel."

I didn't have time to dwell on the call too long. The rest of the afternoon was as busy as our morning. But by the time four o'clock rolled around, the crowd at the store was finally thinning, we'd gotten our delivery and could maybe-kinda-sorta start to see the light at the end of the tunnel as far as maybe-possibly-hopefully being able to go home at the end of the evening. My feet hurt from standing too long, I was starting to glaze over, and my cheeks ached from smiling all day.

By six o'clock, Liss and I were sitting on tall stools behind the counter, resting our tired tootsies. She rolled her head around on her shoulders, stretching her tense muscles, then looked over at me and smiled. "It's only been a day, and already I miss those girls."

Those girls were Evie and Tara, our two teenage protégés and part-time helpers. They, too, were members of the N.I.G.H.T.S. and were quite special and talented in their own right. Normally at this time of day they'd be lolling about on the stools with us, chatting about the latest spirit investigations just as easily as they would about boyfriends and movies and the latest fashion mags. This week was special—they'd be gone through next Sunday. Evie had talked Tara into going along with her to camp, for company. Tara immediately had visions of midnight cemetery jaunts and streaking naked through the woods, and leapt at the chance. By the time she'd realized it was church camp, it was far too late to turn back. I couldn't wait to hear all about it.

"You should just go home," I told her, taking in the weariness lining her eyes. "You look exhausted. I can handle things for the rest of the evening."

She shook her head. "Impossible, I'm afraid. I'll be here late tonight—I have a couple of people scheduled to come in. One of them designs beaded handbags using antique frames. They're gorgeous, absolutely gorgeous. And then the second is a friend of Marcus's. She's interested in starting up a metaphysical store over the state line in Ohio, and Marcus was hoping I could give her a few pointers."

Inadvertent though the mention was, she'd gotten my attention. I couldn't help myself. "Her?"

She stopped, and reached out and covered my hand with her own. "Oh. Don't worry, dear. I'm sure it's just a friend of his. I didn't get the feeling of any stronger connection between them."

I shook my head. "No big deal. It's not like we have anything . . . you know . . . Tom and I . . . I mean . . ." I didn't know what I meant. As far as anyone was concerned, I was a single woman. Single, semiunattached, and free of true mutual arrangements of any kind. Emotional attachments, well, they were a little more difficult to define. And I didn't know whether Tom would agree to the semi-unattached label either. I didn't know anything.

Why did finding true love have to be so darned confusing?

Sympathy shone in her eyes, but Liss had the sense to leave well enough alone for now. "Well. Be that as it may . . ."

She was about to say more when the brass bell attached to the front door tinkled. Another customer. Whatever reassurances she had meant to give me would have to wait for another time. Which was all right with me, since they embarrassed me just a little. Liss was able to read my mind a bit too clearly for my comfort. Sometimes I wished I could hide my thoughts better. At least until I was ready to expose my innermost neuroses and ultimate humiliations to my nearest and dearest. That wasn't too much to ask, was it?

"If you wish to control it, you have to learn to shield a little better. And maybe faster," Liss whispered helpfully, rubbing my shoulder. "You're an open book, and you know I can't help riffling the pages." Smiling, she turned to welcome our customer. "Can I help you, my dear? Are you looking for anything in particular? Or just browsing?"

"Um . . . oh . . . well . . . A-Actually I was hoping to speak with Maggie there . . . if that isn't against the rules . . . ?" A soft voice, almost timid, and somehow familiar.

"Of course not," Liss said. She swept her arm out to reveal me standing behind her.

Libby Turner was standing in the main aisle, as tiny and birdlike as ever. In light of the weather, she was wearing a plain tissue-weight T and a pair of skinny-cut linen Bermuda shorts in colors of sea and sand. The aqua of her shirt contrasted beautifully with the smooth sheen of her dark hair. An obviously expensive bag—different from yesterday's—and a pair of cork-wedge sandals that added an additional four inches to her petite frame completed her quietly fashionable look, but what intrigued me the most was the weight of fear hanging about her shoulders. I sensed it there, heavy and black and thick enough to reach out to me. Not this time, though; I hastily strengthened the invisible boundaries crafted of my own energy that helped me to deal with others without absorbing theirs. But I saw the shadows of it in her eyes, and her fingers were clenched tightly around the bag's braided handle.

I waved at her, pretending I hadn't just glimpsed something I wasn't meant to. "Libby. What a surprise to see you here. Are you in the market for something? A gift, maybe?"

She shook her head so hard that the long layers in her hair swung crazily about her jaw. She glanced at Liss, then back at me. "No. I have a question for you . . . if you don't mind."

Liss began to pull back her energy in a quiet retreat.

"I'll get out of your way, ducks. I have a few phone calls to make before my evening appointments arrive, and—"

"Actually . . ." Libby had reached out with her hand, but she pulled it back just as quickly, as though she had been about to put it into something dangerous but caught herself in time. She cleared her throat. "Actually, if what Melanie says is true, then perhaps you had better stay, too. I don't mind. I could use as much information as possible, for my own peace of mind."

"Melanie?" I frowned. "What about Melanie? She's all right, isn't she?"

Liss paused in midretreat, watching the dark-haired young woman.

"Mel's fine. I just left her house a little while ago. She's . . . well . . ." Libby winced, hedged, grimaced, sighed, and winced again, then summoned her courage up around her to fumble on in a rush: "Is it true, what she said, about you all doing spirit investigations?"

Mel-a-NIEEEE! I felt my stomach drop and hit the floor with a dead thud. Emotionally speaking, of course.

My mouth had fallen open. I closed it and cleared my throat. "Well, that depends," I said as calmly as possible. "What—*exactly*—did Melanie tell you?"

Libby took a deep breath. "She said that you hunt ghosts and that you have a lot of experience, and that they, meaning she and Greg and the girls, have at least one in their own house, and how can that be when their house is only a few years old, that's what I want to know, and she said that if we or anyone we know is having trouble, we know who to call, meaning you two, so I guess you all consider yourselves to be Ghostbusters or something, huh?"

The words had come out all in a rush, and now she looked at us expectantly, her big dark eyes opened wide with a blend of hesitation, curiosity, and . . . something else. Something shuttered off behind the windows of her eyes. I knew she was afraid of Liss and me—that much was clear the moment she walked in the door—but there was more to it. Something had her spooked, big time.

Liss glanced at me. I wondered what she was thinking. I knew it had been a mistake to reveal the N.I.G.H.T.S.' activities to Melanie, but sisterly concern had gotten in the way of logic. I had just wanted to help, and now it appeared I had let the black cat out of the magickal bag of tricks.

"Well, now, dear," Liss said, taking Libby by the arm and steering her ever-so-casually toward the office—away from the few stragglers still milling through the aisles. "What exactly are you here for? Why did you come to us?"

I plopped a BACK IN A MOMENT placard on the counter by the cash register and hurried to follow in their wake.

Once we'd stepped past the purple velvet curtain into the office, her eyes grew wider still until they adjusted to the dim light filtering in through the pair of small windows someone had installed high off the ground for security. Too high up for a person bent on theft to attain easily, too small to allow adequate light through. As windows went, they were pretty useless, when you thought about it.

"Here. Sit."

Liss scooted a chair out for her. Libby took it, but kept her bag clutched to her body on her lap. "Thanks." She glanced back and forth between me and Liss. "I guess I came on a little strong back there. I do that sometimes when I get nervous."

Liss patted her on the hand and gently prompted, "You were about to tell us why you sought us out. Am I wrong in assuming you're having trouble of the paranormal kind?"

The cat was out of the bag, so I guess there was no need to keep it in velvet mittens. Libby bit her lip. "Well, I—I'm worried that there might be . . . there has to be some reason all of this stuff seems to keep happening to us. There is a . . . black cloud hanging over my husband and his business. Things keep happening there. Minor accidents, personal attacks against my husband and the property itself. I mean, it could be something . . . demonic . . . couldn't it?"

She said it almost hopefully, and I had the sense that she wanted it to be true. I thought it odd; but then, who knows. Maybe in some twisted way it was easier for her to accept something like that than to accept the more likely explanation: personal liability. Meaning, sometimes a black cat was just a black cat. Sometimes a person needed to take responsibility for their own actions and the cause and effect they will have on others. Human frailties were so common that a paranormal reason for something like what Libby was describing was almost overkill.

"Well, now. That does sound trying." If Liss was feeling as skeptical as I was, she did not show it. "Has there been anything else?" Anything that couldn't be explained, is what she meant.

Encouraged, perhaps, by the fact that no one was laughing at her, Libby relaxed her fearful edge just a bit. "You mean, have I seen anything? Shapes and shadows and energy distortions and the like?" I raised my brows at her use of the lingo. I couldn't help it. Seeing my reaction, Libby hurried to explain, "I was reading up on it this morning. After Melanie's phone call last night, I didn't sleep a wink. It was all I could think about. You understand, don't you?"

What I understood was that Melanie had opened her big mouth and scared the bejeebers out of this woman for no good reason that I could see, other than the sheer joy of being the one to drop the stinkbomb on an unsuspecting audience. And it was all my fault, because I'd just fed into her almost pathological need to be at the top of the gossip chain. I'd forgotten the number one rule: With Mel, it was *always* "Have Gossip, Will Spill." And it was all downhill from there.

I made myself push all that aside for the moment. "Of course we understand. It's normal to focus extrahard on things we find disturbing. Have you experienced anything like the things you mention, then? Anything out of the ordinary?"

She bit her lip, but shook her head. "No. Well, I don't know. Maybe. I mean, there have been weird sounds and all, but at the time . . . I guess I just never thought it was possible for it to be anything like . . . this."

Liss patted her hand again, the soul of sympathy. "If you will accept my reassurances, there is no reason to suspect anything paranormal as yet. In these things, it's always best to rule out all ordinary explanations before making the leap to the dark side," she said with a wink.

It was meant to alleviate tension, but at this suggestion, Libby's gaze flew to hers in alarm. I opened my mouth to change the subject in hopes of easing her apprehension, but Libby beat me to the punch. "Do they . . . do people—*spirits,* I mean—hang around when we die, then? Is that what you believe?"

"Some do," Liss told her gently. "And some move on instantly, as we are all meant to."

"Why?" Libby pressed, leaning forward with a curious glint in her eye. "Why do some stay?"

"I'm afraid it's a complicated issue, my dear," Liss explained. "It has been my experience that some stay due to a state of confusion. Perhaps they passed quickly and do not realize they are no longer alive. They cling to whatever familiar things and people they can find because they are lost in the mists of time and space. Others stay in fear of passing completely to the other side. They have convinced themselves that they are unworthy of the goodness of the light, and are suspicious of those who beckon to them from the other side. Still others . . ." A shadow crept over Liss's fine-boned features, one she tried very hard to disguise. "Still others are not ready to pass. They want more of the very thing that has been stripped away from them . . . *Life.* They act out against those who come into their sphere because of that very desire."

Libby's eyes had gone wide. "I was just thinking of those poor people whose lives were . . . who were . . . murdered. This year has been terrible for Stony Mill."

She could say that again.

"Terrible," she repeated, following my thought processes to the letter. "I don't know what made me think of them, but . . . when you said that, I couldn't help thinking that they could be hanging around right now bent on . . . revenge. Don't you think?" she asked, her eyes intense.

"Unfinished business," I mused, nodding. "There is that." Only I couldn't help thinking that revenge was the least of Stony Mill's problems. There was something else there. Something else underlying us all. And if I thought about it for too long, it scared the crap out of me.

Libby fell silent, lost in thought. The only sound to be heard was our breathing and the occasional rustle from the front. I exchanged a questioning glance with Liss, who seemed to be as bemused as I was feeling.

"Libby," I said at last, edgy after several long minutes of watching her chew on her lower lip, "if you are experiencing something . . . well, even if it turned out to be nothing, maybe we could come out to do a clearing of the site for you."

She looked up at once. "You can do that? Will it send away anything that might be there?"

I nodded. Well, I myself had never done one, but I knew it really was simple in theory, and I knew without a doubt that Liss and the N.I.G.H.T.S. would have my back. Besides, it was about time I learned. At the very least it might make her feel better.

Libby jumped out of her seat, nearly startling me out of mine. She scrabbled at her bag. "I have to run now," she said. "I have to get home before my husband does."

She was out of the room so fast that the air didn't quite seem to have a chance to close in on the space she had been occupying.

"Well, now," Liss murmured. "How very interesting."

"Quite," I said, imitating my boss's posh accent. She raised her brows at me, and I dissolved into giggles.

"Such cheek." Liss grinned. "Hm. She didn't say

whether she wanted a visit from us. What were your impressions? Everyday situations or paranormal?"

I frowned. "I don't know. She really didn't give many details, did she. It could be anything at this point. But . . . there was something there, in her voice. In her face. In her energy." I looked her in the eye. "Fear."

Liss nodded. "Yes. Fear."

My cell phone started chiming airily away in my purse. No longer the "1812 Overture," thank goodness—I had figured out how to change it at last, despite being *slightly* low-tech by nature—but I wasn't sure this canned fairy twinkle-toes selection was any better.

I grabbed my bag and did the usual dive-and-scramble to dig through the flotsam that always accumulated at the bottom in order to find that tweedling bit of technology that was quickly starting to run my life. I've never been able to ignore a ringing phone. Somehow a cell phone call seemed even more urgent than usual.

My fingers closed around cool plastic that buzzed as I touched it. *Success!*

I flipped open the case. "Hel—"

"Maggie!" The voice of my sister cut off my greeting without a by-your-leave, but I was used to that. What I wasn't used to was the sense of terror that came sizzling across the airwaves. "*OhmyGod!* Maggie, you've got to come now."

"Mel, what's wrong? Is it one of the girls? Are you hurt? Where's Mom?"

"No, not the girls! We're okay, but just come, Maggie! I think I did something stupid. Really stupid. Maggie, come over! Please! Now!"

The phone went dead, empty air space echoing in my ear. "Melanie!"

Liss mobilized into immediate action. She picked up my bag from where it had fallen to the floor when I jumped out of my chair—I hadn't even noticed—and handed it to me. She even found my ring of keys for me, and pressed them into my hand.

"Go," she said.

By the time my feet crossed the threshold, the urgency in Mel's voice had started to hit home even harder. I toyed with calling the police—my fingers clenched reflexively around the case of my cell phone more than once—but something stayed my hand. She'd done something stupid, she'd said, without elaborating. And she'd called *me* to fix it. Not Greg, not Mom, not even Dad, but me. This had to be a first. I was worried, but my intuition was telling me there was a reason for it. So instead I left the parking lot with a roar of the ancient motor and a spit of limestone gravel, and began the short trip across town.

At top of the hill, where River Street crossed Main, I was forced to stop for a red light. Not the easiest thing to do on a hill when one was driving an old manual shift clunker—er, antique beauty—with an iffy clutch. While putting the majority of my focus into not backsliding down the hill and trying not to worry about what was going on at Mel's place on the other side of town, I happened to catch a slight movement out of the corner of my eye—a flash of aqua and a sense of the familiar. Distracted, I flicked my gaze in that direction. Libby Turner had stopped at the old pay phone on the corner. Her back was to me, but between the outfit and the sheen of her dark hair, there was no mistaking her. She looked as tense as she had in the office minutes ago as she tapped her fingers in a sharp, never-ending staccato against the glass wall. Didn't she have a cell phone? I wondered. Why hadn't she just used the phone at the office? It would have been much quieter and far more private. But then, perhaps she hadn't wanted to impose. Perhaps the need to call had come up as an afterthought. Who knew why people did the things that they did?

The light ahead of me changed, bringing me back into the moment and reminding me of the need for speed. From there, I made it across town in ten minutes flat, in spite of all the inevitable afterwork traffic choking the two-lane state highways and residential byways that made up the bulk of Stony Mill's road system. When I arrived moments later at Mel's taupe split-level modern with its stylish eggplant-hued shutters, I was a little taken aback to find several cars there ahead of me parked along the curb—she hadn't mentioned that she had company. What on earth could have panicked her so much when she was surrounded by friends and—yep, Mom's old sedan was there, too? Moving forward a bit slower now that I knew she wasn't alone and helpless, I switched off the engine and crossed the lawn, bypassing the tastefully curved granite pathway for the more direct route.

I let myself in. "Mel?" I called.

No answer.

The quiet disconcerted me, I had to admit. Especially following on the heels of the panicky phone call. What. The. Heck? Where was everyone? Where was my mother?

I tried again, making my way toward the kitchen. "Hello?" I called, peeking around the corner. "Mom?"

Nothing. No one. Not there.

My heart started beating faster, a tattoo of worry combined with the sudden sense that the quiet was *too* quiet. There were no clocks ticking, no hum of the refrigerator, no sound of cooling air rushing through the ductwork. My hand reached automatically for the switch on the wall.

No lights. No power. Power outage.

A rush of relief swept through me. At least there was an explanation for that much. The early heat wave must have pulled too much through the circuits in that part of town. Breathing a little easier, I passed through the kitchen and made my way for the stairs. But every step that I took, the heavier the air felt.

Spirit heavy.

But this didn't feel like the girls' invisible friends' spirit energy that I had felt the day before. Invisible friends don't make your chest feel like it's caving in on itself because the air around you has turned itself inside out. Invisible friend energy didn't get in your face and make you feel like turning right back around and getting the hell out of Dodge.

"Well, well," I said in an undertone from my position on the fifth step, where I'd stopped to reassess. "What—or should I say, *who*—do we have here?"

The air billowed up against me, crowded around me, questioning, testing . . . and then in an instant, it withdrew.

I took a careful breath, but it was gone. Full retreat. Or maybe it was just strategizing. Looking for the right opening.

The right opportunity.

I didn't like the thoughts that were springing into my mind. What on earth was going on? Where did *this* spirit come from?

What had the girls let in?

Chapter 6

Putting one foot in front of the other, I made it to the top of the stairs and tiptoed down the hall's thick carpeting. The house was utterly, coldly still. All the doors to the bedrooms and bathrooms off the hall were closed. Melanie's was the nearest to the stairs, so I headed there first.

I rapped my knuckles lightly against the wood panel. "Mel? You in there?" I tried the lever knob. It wasn't locked. The door opened easily beneath my hand. For a moment. Then in the next, it pulled out of my hands and swung sharply inward, ricocheting off the dresser behind the door and slamming shut again. Before it did, I had the briefest glimpse of the pale and frightened faces huddled together on Mel's bed on the opposite wall. They were all, every last one of them, inside this room. I heard the smallest wail coming from within, a muffled sniffling cry.

My heart leapt to my throat. *Little Courtney . . .*

And that was all it took, because when faced with the

urgent need to protect those we love, we never even stop to consider the risk. We just act.

I felt the energy within me rise, adrenaline mixed with something inherent that emerged from the very core of me, rushing upward and outward as I closed both of my hands around the brass lever, pressed downward, and shoved with all my might. The door resisted, but I pushed harder, steadier, mightier than the force that was opposing on the other side.

And then the resistance was gone, as if it had never been there at all. The door crashed inward again, but this time it stayed open with the slightest pressure of my hand. The action also seemed to relieve the fear holding Mel's friends in position. Suddenly the utter silence lifted and the air was filled with a flood of female voices, agitated chatter, and frightened sobbing. The room, so still before, became a flurry of movement as—I should have known—Margo Dickerson-Craig and Jane Churchill scrambled off the rumpled bed and dove for their purses and car keys, their white faces giving testament that something had indeed scared the living daylights out of them.

And I think I knew what that something was.

A Ouija board sat in the middle of the duvet, pushed slightly to one side by Mel's legs when she had drawn them up as a protective measure for herself and the girls, who were cowering at her side. My sister's eyes were huge, her face pasty. The girls still hadn't pulled their faces out from their hiding places beneath their mother's arms. When they finally realized that the Big and Scary Whatever was gone, at least for the moment, they withdrew from their mom and slid off the edge of the bed, launching themselves at me as one.

I held them to me, Mel's babies, and pinned her with a pointed stare. "What's been going on, Mel? Where's Mom?"

Her gaze had not moved from the board at the end of her bed. The pointer lay on the floor, halfway across the room.

"Mom?" she parroted vaguely.

I stalked across the room and picked up the pointer. Mel flinched when I set it back on the board.

"Yes, *Mom*. You know. Medium height. Gave birth to us. Likes to go to church. A lot."

Melanie just shrugged and looked confused.

"What's this all about, Mel?" I hissed at her. "What's with the board, and the friends, and . . . please tell me you didn't use that thing."

She blinked. "We . . . It was supposed to be for fun. To see if we could talk to the ghost that you felt was here. Find out a little bit about him. Margo said she'd used a Ouija board when she was a kid, and since she knew how it worked . . . it was supposed to be safe. It's just a game." She lifted her gaze to mine, pleading for me to understand. What she really wanted was for big sister Maggie to fix things for her.

My sigh was heavy with resignation, perhaps even a teensy bit of fear. That was no game she had been playing, and the result was not a fun little spirit sprite who would entertain and tease. The energy I had felt a moment ago . . . well, I wasn't sure it had ever been human. It had reached out to me, its only purpose to size me up and, perhaps, intimidate. And it had accomplished its goal only too well. I knew enough by now to temper my fear, to shelter it behind the personal shields I had been learning to erect and strengthen with each breath I took, with every beat of my heart. But the fear was still there. I would have to deal with it sooner or later.

I chose . . . later. With backup. Lots of backup.

Sometimes procrastination was the only real answer.

But right now, there were more important things at hand. I bent down to my nieces and curved my arms around them. "It's all right, girls. Why don't we go downstairs and get you both a snack, and maybe you can help me find Grandma."

"She's in the basement," Jenna said with a sniffle as she wiped the back of her hand beneath her nose.

I looked into her eyes, so clear and blue. "In the basement? Why would she be in the basement?"

"She's locked down there," she said, her eyes brimming with tears again. "Coco says *It* didn't want her to interfere."

It. I was about to question her further about the hows and the whys, but I saw the look in her eyes, and I knew there was no mistaking what was there. Intelligence and understanding beyond her years.

Jenna *knew* things.

And Melanie was not the type of mom who would understand.

Instantly I snapped to a decision. Jenna needed protection. She needed someone to watch out for her, to guide her through. Maybe if I had had a mentor when I was growing up, someone who understood me and knew what I was feeling and experiencing, someone who didn't make me feel like it was all my fault, maybe, just maybe, I wouldn't have grown up to be the neurotic mess I sometimes was. It didn't have to be that way for Jenna. She had me.

I took the girls by the hands and led them toward the door. "Come on. Let's go get Grandma." I glanced back at Mel. "Does Mom know what you were up to?"

Her eyes still on the Ouija board, Mel shook her head. "I don't think so."

"Good. Hide the board. I'm going to get Mom." I issued her a warning glare. "*You* stay there."

She opened her mouth as though she might try to object. I closed the door behind me before she could gear up the engines.

Courtney tugged on my hand. I looked down into her dark eyes that communicated with me so soulfully. "Don't wike that. Bad thing."

I squeezed her fingers to reassure her. "I know, honey." The Ouija wasn't exactly the most reliable of tools for communicating with the spirit world. The gate it opened was just too indiscriminate. It was like giving a party pass to the *Spring Break* filming crew. Forget sex, drugs, and rock 'n' roll. The kind of crew the board was liable to bring in was more likely to include spooks and dark entities, getting their buzz on, wild-style. H'aints and imps and shadow creatures, just hangin' with the homies. And good times would be had by all . . . all except you, the clueless person with the fingers on the pointer, that is.

What had Mel been thinking? I fussed as I followed the girls down the stairs. Using a Ouija board with another consenting adult might be ill advised, but at least both persons involved had a choice in the matter. Having children present, with their beautifully open minds and their life forces so shiny bright and new, was like hanging a Welcome sign on their psyches for all earthbounds in the vicinity. Those souls who were either too confused, too angry, or—and these were the most worrisome—too fearful owing to their immoral, unethical, or downright cruel activities here on earth, to move on. Talk about an invitation for disaster.

The basement's only access was through the garage, a design flaw that Mel had always complained about. Mel and Greg had discussed what it would take to hire a contractor to remedy that situation, but hadn't taken the financial plunge as yet. If Mom was locked down in the basement, that would explain why she hadn't heard me calling. At least, I hoped that was it.

Sure enough, the deadbolt was engaged on the door to the basement stairs. I unlocked it, feeling the thunk of solid metal as it slid back. I opened the door. "Mom?"

I heard a scurry of footsteps down below, where no lights shone. A pale face floated into view at the bottom of the steps. "Margaret? Is that you?"

"That's not Margaret, Grandma," Jenna piped up, her high-pitched voice echoing down the stairs. "That's Auntie Maggie."

"Auntie," Courtney chimed in.

"Oh, thank the Lord," Mom said, stumbling up the steps. "I thought I would be down here until Greg got home."

"What happened?" I asked, giving her my hand as she mounted the last of the steps. "Why were you sitting in the dark down there?"

Mom shook her head. "It's a long story, and I need a cup of coffee."

Her hand was trembling within mine. I gave it a squeeze. "Come to the kitchen and I'll fix you a cup. Girls, take Grandma's hands."

The kitchen was blissfully bright and calm and ubernormal, with no trace of unwanted entities hanging around. Mom had made fresh ginger cookies that day, despite the heat wave, so I sat the girls down at their little table set in the nook with a snack of cookies and milk before settling into the familiar task of making fresh coffee. Mom sat perched on the edge of a stool at the counter, looking dazed and a little fragile, but no worse for the wear for her ordeal, I noted gratefully.

With the coffee bubbling away, I sat down next to her. "So? What happened?"

She sat back in her chair and shook her head. "I . . . I'm not sure. I went downstairs to transfer the laundry over to the dryer. The next thing I knew, the lights went out, the dryer stopped working, and I was completely in the dark. I tried the fuse box, but it didn't seem to make a difference. They simply wouldn't come back on."

"And the door?"

At this she seemed even more agitated. "I don't know. If the girls hadn't been upstairs with your sister, I might have thought they were playing a joke on their old grandma. Maybe the lock turned when I twisted the knob and I didn't realize it. I guess it must have. I thought I had propped the door open, but . . . it must have closed itself. I called, but they couldn't hair me upstairs."

I didn't tell her it wasn't the lock on the knob, that it was the deadbolt itself that had been engaged. A deadbolt that was wholly separate from the doorknob assembly, and that could only be engaged by purposeful intent. I couldn't see Margo or Jane coming downstairs to lock Mom away for the duration. I didn't much like them, but I knew better than to take my personal prejudices that far.

"I'm glad you came when you did, though," she continued, with a nervous little laugh. "The darkness was starting to get to me. I kept imagining I was hearing things.
Awful things." She shuddered.

I peered at her, curious. "What kinds of things?"

She shook her head, but I noticed that her hand had
crept to her bosom, where I knew she wore a crucifix beneath her simple, short-sleeved blouse. "Just the house settling, I guess. You know how imaginations can run wild in
the dark."

Boy, did I ever. Unfortunately, I also knew that it wasn't
always one's imagination that was causing the problem.

I poured her coffee for her, and we sat in comfortable silence for a while, listening with half an ear while the girls
chattered. Soon enough, the chatter turned quiet enough
for it to register with me.

"No, Courtie. Coco says you shouldn't tell."

"Yes, Jen-NA!"

"Coco says Grammy can't know," Jenna hissed. "Not
yet."

Coco again. I let my gaze drift toward the girls as in-
conspicuously as possible, but the two of them had already clammed up and were sitting on opposite sides of
their table, arms crossed stubbornly over their chests, their
rosebud lips huffed out in the prettiest little pouts. Mom
hadn't noticed the exchange. She was still staring off into
space with her hands curved around her coffee mug.

Mom pushed to her feet and set the mug down on the
counter, for the most part untouched. "If you don't mind,
dear, I think I'll head for home."

I nodded. I couldn't say that I blamed her. If I had been
locked in a basement by a thing that I couldn't see, a thing

that promptly turned off the lights and made noises, I'd have already been out the door. Of course, she believed it to be an accident, at least on the surface, but it appeared to have been no less unsettling, however one defined it.

With Mom gone, I escorted the girls back upstairs. Courtney dug in her heels as we approached Mel's closed door.

"Don't want to!" she said. "Bad thing! Cee Cee don't like it."

"It's okay, Courtie," I told her. "The bad thing is gone. Cee Cee chased it away."

Jenna looked sideways at me, and I could see the hesitation in her eyes. She didn't believe me for a minute.

"All right," I said, relenting. "If you girls promise to be good, you can go on into your room and play with your dollies. I need to check on your mommy, but we'll leave both the doors open. Will that be okay?"

They nodded in tandem, big-eyed and grave.

There was no reason to worry with the doors open, I reasoned. And until I could discern exactly what the issue at hand really was, perhaps it was best to keep them away from the scene of the crime. Keep them where they'd be safe.

"Be good and stay here, 'kay? I'll be right back."

Mel's door was still closed, so I knocked lightly before turning down the lever and sticking my head in. "You okay?" I asked.

She looked up at me and bit her lower lip. She hadn't moved from her nest at the head of the bed except to draw the covers up around her neck like a tent. The Ouija board had fallen to the floor when the duvet slid out from beneath it. It lay facedown on the carpet, nonthreatening and forgotten. Or at least it would have been, had there not resurfaced an indefinable something that lurked there, on the fringes of the bubble of energy and human existence that filled the room. Melanie's life force was as strong as her personality, but she had been playing with things she had no understanding of. And I, I had been mistaken to think *it* had left so willingly.

Wishful thinking, that.

"Take that thing away, would you?"

Without a word, I picked the board up from where it lay and placed it on the table by the window. Instinct told me to leave it facedown, so I did. It felt less of an open invitation that way, for some reason.

"It's still here, isn't it." The question Melanie posed already had an answer in her tone of certainty. "It hasn't gone at all. It's just waiting for me to let down my guard."

"Mel . . ."

"It is. I don't know how I know it, but I do. I—I feel it. Is that crazy?"

I sighed deeply and shook my head as I sat down on the end of her bed. "A Ouija board. Did you have to use a Ouija?"

Her composure, hard-won, cracked beneath the strain of her fear, and her face crumpled. "I didn't know! It was supposed to be just a game. That's what everyone says, don't they? God! I thought Margo was being her usual pushy self when the pointer moved. It would have been just like her. I mean, she is my friend and all, but facts are facts, plain and simple." She swallowed hard. "But when I saw her face . . . and Jane's, too . . . I knew they weren't doing it. I only wish that they were."

Wishes were all well and good, but prudence worked

much better, in hindsight. Prudence, and humility, and respect, especially when it came to those forces in the universe that most of the time went unseen and undetected. Forces most people had forgotten even existed. Some of us learned things the hard way.

Mel lifted her head suddenly. "Maggie . . . where's Mom?"

"Home. Somehow she locked herself in the basement," I told her, avoiding her probing stare.

"Somehow?"

"The deadbolt was turned."

"That's not possible."

"I don't suppose Jane or Margo left the room?" I asked hopefully. "Or maybe one of the girls?"

Mel shook her head, and her eyes met mine. "No one. You know what that means? *Jesus* . . . If it can do something like that . . . *what else can it do?*"

I didn't think we really wanted to find that out.

She looked really frightened now. "What am I going to do, Maggie?" she wailed.

Well, I knew one thing for sure. There was no way in hell I was going to let my baby sister and my beautiful nieces swing in the breeze while some unknown entity was swimming the astral beneath their dangling feet. Liss was right. Blood *was* thicker than water. "*We* are going to get rid of it, that's what," I said with a firm defiance I was doing my best to feel. "The last thing you need right now is to worry about . . . intruders. But I might need a little help."

"Your friends?"

I nodded, my mouth a grim line. "My friends."

"They'll know what to do?"

"I hope so. Between the lot of us, at least, we'll figure something out."

"Good. How soon are we talking here? Because Greg's going to kill me when he figures out what's going on. *If* he figures out what's going on. It's not like he's been spending a lot of time at home lately," she said, her mouth making a small moue of annoyance.

"I'll call Liss and let her in on your little problem. We'll see what she says."

She sniffled and nodded, but I could tell that her relief over a possible solution to the spirit problem was working to diminish her fear. Still, she asked me to get her crucifix and prayer beads from her jewelry box. As an afterthought, I brought her a flashlight and double-checked that she still had her cell phone as well, just in case.

Liss, bless her heart, was ready in an instant to cancel her last remaining appointment and come straight over to assess the situation. Since she was unfamiliar with the twisty and turny maze of the extensive subdivision, I offered to drive to the store and bring her back with me.

"You'll be okay while I'm gone?" I asked Mel. The girls had been exhausted and had gone to bed early after a quickie supper without a single complaint.

She nodded. "Just hurry, would you? I feel a little weird being alone right now."

Once at the store, Liss and I decided that it would be easiest for me to drive rather than take two cars, as I had to drive back downtown on the return trip anyway. We were back at Mel's in no time. Greg was still a no-show.

Since Melanie was confined to bed, I let her know quickly that we had arrived, and that I would be giving Liss the N.I.G.H.T.S. version of a guided tour along with all the background information I could remember. I showed her the basement first, explaining what had happened to my mother. Her expression remained neutral throughout. The kitchen and downstairs living areas didn't give her pause, so we quietly moved on to the bedrooms upstairs. In the girls' room she smiled once, closing her eyes, then backed out of the room with a satisfied nod. But when we approached the open door to Mel's room, I saw her hesitate. Only for a moment, but it was enough to worry me.

I went in first. Mel had been craning her neck from the bed to see what we were doing. Liss barely acknowledged her presence as she walked through the room, her fingers trailing over surfaces, her eyes touching everywhere. Curiosity burned in my sister's eyes, but her face showed disappointment. Had the situation been slightly less dire, I might have laughed. Perhaps she had been expecting something a bit more . . . exotic? Of course, she didn't know that Liss didn't need all the bells and whistles to sense . . .

"Strong one," Liss whispered.

My head came up. I had been lost in thought, not paying complete attention. Liss was standing at the dresser, gazing into the mirror with eyes that were not quite focused. I glanced at Mel. The disappointment she had shown only a moment ago had gone. Now her eyes were fever bright and following Liss's every move.

Liss turned to my sister. "Well. I don't know what you girls were doing, but you seem to have picked up a little more than you bargained for."

"What is it?" I asked her. The room had felt heavy, the air thick, from the moment we walked in. I realized I'd been holding my breath—not with anticipation, but because it felt easier, better somehow, to go without.

"Is it . . . demonic?" Mel asked, her voice ending on a squeak. Her hand was in a tight fist, from which her prayer beads overflowed.

Cocking her head to one side, Liss stood quietly a moment. "No. No, I don't think so. It's not of the light, but not what I'd call of the darkness either. It is of the in-between places."

The In-Between. "Human?" I asked her. My ears were burning. On fire. The top of my head was prickling uncomfortably.

"Hmm. No. No, it feels more . . . interdimensional to me. Very assured. As though it goes wherever it wishes, as it wishes."

Interdimensional sounded ominous somehow. Powerful. Capable of just about anything.

"I'm not sure I like the sound of that," Melanie quavered. "How do I get rid of it?"

Liss was about to answer when we heard the front door slam downstairs, followed by heavy male tread coming up the carpeted stairs.

"Melanie?" Greg's voice preceded him, but only by a moment or two.

"In here," Mel called back, tucking her crucifix under her covers and holding her finger to her lips to warn us not to say anything to him. "Maggie's here, and—"

He paused in the doorway as he caught sight of Liss and me. "Oh, hello," he said, his brows quirking in mild surprise. He smiled politely at Liss. "Friend of yours, Maggie?" He seemed oblivious as the energy pulled itself back to more manageable levels with his sudden appearance. *Interesting*.

Clearing my throat, I stepped up to make the introductions. "Liss is my boss at Enchantments," I explained.

"Ah." He looked at us expectantly.

"Well, we'd best be getting out of your hair now that you're home," I said, edging toward the door. "The girls are in bed, Greg, and you have a little something waiting for you in the fridge." To Mel, I said, "I'll talk to you tomorrow, sis. We'll chat more about everything then."

"A pleasure, Greg," Liss inserted, holding out her hand. "Melanie, my dear, be well."

Easier said than done when you had a potentially interdimensional, not-dark-not-light something-or-other from the in-between places in your home.

Oy.

Over our heads, the half-moon glowed from behind a haze of condensation and cloud cover, but the night seemed otherwise calm. Liss and I ensconced ourselves in Christine's worn but comfortable interior before continuing the conversation.

"Interdimensional?" I prompted.

She smiled at me, hearing the concern in my voice. "It was a very strong, very assured energy. Powerful. Bigger than your average spirit. Not all who visit are from earthly dimensions, you know."

Unfortunately, I didn't. "Is it something to worry about? I mean, I know you said you didn't think it was demonic, but . . ." I risked a glance at her. "What kinds of entities are we talking about here?"

"Well . . . angels are interdimensional, obviously—they

can appear anywhere at will—but I didn't exactly get 'angelic' in there, did you?"

I thought of how it had bumped up against me, testing me. Perhaps even challenging me . . . "No."

"Entities from other planets certainly are a possibility."

"Other pla . . . *aliens*?"

"Or even the Fae. Though if so, this one I would have to say existed on the darker side of the faery realm."

I had an image of a teensy, tiny little flickering light the size of a hummingbird, complete with glitter and sparkles. "You mean, like Tinkerbell?"

Liss laughed. "Hardly. I rather meant the feral kind."

This was not sounding any better. "Anything else it might have been?" I said as I pulled from the subdivision entrance out onto the main drag.

"Hmm. Shadow men are, I believe, considered interdimensional," she mused. "As are vampires and werewolves, though I don't think we really have to worry about those," she said with a twinkle.

I didn't understand how she could be twinkling at a time like this.

"If your sister wishes to be rid of it—"

"She does. Trust me on this."

"—then let me consult with Marcus, and we'll see what we can come up with. No promises, however. Sometimes these things can be very sticky. They don't always want to leave. Oh . . . I wonder what that is just ahead."

The "just ahead" turned out to be a train that, for some inexplicable reason, was stopped on the tracks, barring the street. Quite a number of cars had lined up on the road ahead of us, trapped by their bumper-to-bumper proximity. Some of the drivers had thrown their vehicles into "Park" and were actually standing on the road outside of their cars, discussing the situation in particular and shooting the breeze in general. Nothing was moving.

I made a last-minute decision and turned off onto a side road before it was too late. "Let's see if we can find a way around that mess."

The only possible way around that I knew of, without going several miles out of our way, was cutting across the tracks that ran beneath the largest spill chute at the feed mill, assuming that the stopped train did not venture out that far, so that's the way I headed.

That decision would prove the last straw in a haystack already prepared to tumble.

Chapter 7

At first I thought my quick thinking had saved the day. We left the town limits and circled around via bumpy and narrow country roads whose edges were already choked with weeds. Hitting Mainline Road, I zipped toward the feed mill, whose towering silos, conveyer systems, and chutes loomed like a cityscape in miniature on the horizon ahead with a dazzling array of security lights bright enough to light up the writhing mists high above. *Almost there . . .*

Success was nigh.

And that was when I came around a bend and saw the rotating series of red and blue police strobes lighting up the road ahead, determined to spoil my brilliant plan. "What's this?" Liss mused, staring off into the distance.

"An accident maybe?" I slowed Christine to a crawl. The choke-up seemed to be right at the tracks. Phooey! Foiled again. Only this time there was no turnoff, the road was blocked with both barricades and flares, and like most county roads, it was far too narrow to manage a three-point turn. So much for brilliance. It appeared our only option was to wait for someone to approach and hope that they would allow us to turn around in the feed mill's parking lot.

A patrol car was stopped across the roadway behind the barricades. I couldn't see past it or the cars just beyond in order to figure out what the holdup might be. A lone officer stood with a large flashlight in front of the cruiser, the popping red and blues silhouetting him from behind with an unearthly glow. He walked toward us as we crept near and motioned for me to roll down the window. I recognized him from my few times visiting the department to see Tom. *Johnson*, I thought. *Something Johnson.*

"Ma'am, if you could just—" he began in the usual clipped tones of policespeak in the moments before recognition struck. "Oh, hey there, Maggie. Sorry you had to happen upon all this. Your bad luck, I guess. We'll be here awhile. There are some things that are gonna have to happen before I can show you where to go to get outta here."

Mike, I remembered suddenly with relief. "Hey, Mike. Good to see you. What happened? Someone run off the road?"

"Nah. Nothing that easy. Just a freak-ass accident, I guess. One of the owners fell down from the top of that silo there"—he indicated the largest, tallest, most impressive of the bunch—"and crushed his skull in. Broke a lotta bones in the rest of him, too, but I don't guess he felt anything by then. Already gone."

I blinked at him, my stomach wobbling around queasily. "One of the owners, you say?"

"Yeah. One of the Turners. He's lucky, too—well, at least his family is lucky. He bounced off the hopper that was lined up there for pickup by this here train, and fell right onto the main tracks. Coulda been chopped into bits by the wheels of the train if his brother hadn't come across him lying there."

One of the Turners, dead.

"You wanna just pull over as far to the right as you can, Maggie, and I'll let you know as soon as I can get you outta here."

"Yes, of course."

I switched the engine off and turned on my four-way hazard lights. Liss was surveying the action ahead of us, not saying a word. An ambulance had arrived through the main feed mill entrance and had wended its way back around through the maze of silos and tractor trailers and waiting semis.

"It's happening again, isn't it?" I murmured.

"What is, ducks?"

"All the weird deaths we've had in town." One of which had been Liss's own sister.

"The officer said it was an accident."

"Maybe." I turned to look at her. "Is that what your instincts are telling you?"

Her enigmatic half-smile answered my question quickly enough. "Perhaps. Perhaps not."

That's what I was afraid of.

Damn.

I opened Christine's door and let myself out. It was too hot inside the car to stay there for long anyway. Outside it wasn't much cooler, but at least there was the pretense of a breeze teasing us on occasion. I leaned back against my closed car door, watching the scene unfold. One of the Turners, Mike Johnson had said. *One* of them. I took that to mean that Joel Turner had brothers or sisters. Which Turner was lying out there, about to be scraped off the ground by the trusty boys in blue and tan? And was it just me, or did this whole thing feel just a little surreal?

I saw a uniformed officer coming toward me. Good— maybe he was going to share with us how to get out of there. But as he drew near, I realized I was about to be shared with, all right. Big time. Just not in the way I'd hoped.

"Maggie. I should have known. I don't suppose you can explain to me how it is I continually find you smack in the middle of yet another . . . incident?"

There was no mistaking the voice, just as I'd recognized the walk. I held up my hand and gave a weak little wave. "Hi, Tom."

"Well?"

"Well, what?"

"How did you come to be here this time?"

There was no explanation, really. Instinct had guided me away from the logjam of cars on the main road through town. "Just lucky? I guess?"

"Luck. Hm." He was in full cop mode, but I'd have expected nothing less from him at a time like this. Actually I was feeling a little guilty for the intrusion, even though it had been completely unintentional on my part.

"Liss is here with me," I said as a small measure of defense.

"Oh, that makes me feel so much better," he muttered under his breath. I shot him a dirty look, to which he responded by leaning down and waving at her through the windshield. Liss gave him a gay wave in return, one that was far more sincere than his own mocking version. "Is

she the only one, or do you have more of your friends
hidden away in there?"

I got the impression that he meant one friend in
particular—a friend of the male persuasion, in fact—more
than any other. "No, it's just the two of us."

He nodded, satisfied for the moment.

I indicated the scene ahead of us with my chin. "Who
is it, then? I heard it was one of the Turners themselves."

He pressed his lips together. "Johnson has a loose
tongue. Yeah, it's the owner, actually. Joel Turner. His
brother found him. Accident. These things happen."

Joel Turner himself. Libby's husband. Only the other
day he'd been stalking around the feed mill like an angry
lion protecting his pride. And maybe he had been, at that.
I shook my head, wondering at the ways of a world where
synchronicities and coincidence reigned supreme. How
else could you explain the strange incident at the feed mill
the other day, followed by the odd coincidence of meeting
Libby herself, followed by . . . this? Was it prudent to write
it all off as being in the wrong place at the right time? Was
that even possible?

I no longer could know that for sure. *Something* sure
seemed to be affecting the natural order of things in Stony
Mill. I just wish we knew what that something was. At
least then, maybe, we could confront it head on before it
could do more damage.

"What?" Tom said, seeing my face.

I frowned at him. "Don't you see? First the dummy,
and now this . . . accident? Doesn't it all seem a tad bit
coincidental to you?"

"Well, I admit that the Turners have had a run of bad
luck lately—"

"In light of what has happened here tonight, that's a huge understatement, wouldn't you say?"

"—but there's no reason to leap from that into full-blown suspicion of there being more to this than meets the eye. Come on, Maggie. Sometimes an accident is just an accident."

Maybe.

The silo caught my eye, lit up in all its newly sinister glory. "So he fell from up there?"

He nodded. "From the maintenance walkway."

I gathered he was referring to the half-caged-in ladder and catwalk that spiraled steeply up the silo until it reached the uppermost level. From there the conveyer connected in from what looked to be an extremely complicated system of moving grains and whatnot around the complex. I looked up at it, wondering where he might have fallen from.

"Quite the drop, eh?" Tom said quietly.

"I'll say. You think he fell from all the way up?" Yikes. A shiver crept up my spine, despite the trickle of sweat creeping down it.

"He'd have to have, with the amount of damage there is to his head and body. He's pretty beat up. Of course, this is off the record. The county medical examiner will want to have his say, I'm sure."

"I'm sure." Secretly I hoped he was right about the whole coincidence thing. Maybe the notion that it all seemed a bit too happenstance was just fear and suspicion having its way with me. My sensitivity to all matters mysterious was, shall we say, cranked up to High—with good reason, granted—but maybe that was part of the problem. Lately anytime anything out of the ordinary happened, my mind immediately leapt to the esoteric. Tom was right; there was a real chance that this was an accident. Best to leave well enough alone unless there was a reason to suspect. The Turner family would have enough hardships to deal with in the coming days without rumors adding to the mix.

Tom gave me a halfhearted salute and went back to the scene. Liss got out of the vehicle and joined me in my vigil.

"Tom said it was an accident."

She nodded. "I heard."

"But you don't think so either."

Liss gave a great sigh. "It's a feeling, more than anything. Who knows. Maybe we've both had a bit too much happen over the last several months, eh? Such closeness to death—it's enough to affect anyone's perception. I hope"— she paused, reflecting—"I hope that Tom is right. It would be lovely to have this part of the town's history over and done with."

Her choice of words spoke volumes. *This* part. Not *that* part. Semantics? Or Freudian slip?

The roar of an engine to our left drew our attention in that direction. A sporty green car peeled into the feed mill's main driveway, sliding sideways across gravel as it came to a sudden stop. The driver, a woman, left the car at a run, narrowly missing coming into the path of the F350 pickup that had been following on her bumper. It didn't even faze her. She kept up her flailing headlong trajectory toward the collection of emergency vehicles situated around the base of the giant silo. Even from here I could hear her wild sobbing.

It was Libby.

The driver of the F350 caught up to her before she managed to reach the accident scene, catching her by the elbow and spinning her back into his arms. Holding her there when she would have pulled away. Turning her face away when she would have looked. She beat on his chest with her fists, but he held her fast, protecting her from her own desperate need to see her husband.

I found myself leaving the relative anonymity of the sidelines and walking toward the two of them. Someone else had left the circle of officials around the body and was also on an intercept path with the crying woman and her erstwhile protector. He reached them before I did.

"Libby," the second man said, his face shadowed beneath the brim of a white straw cowboy hat, "what are you doing here, girl? You should go home."

Libby leaned back within the circle of the first man's arms, her hands and a thick sheaf of mussed hair covering her pretty face. "I c-can't!" she wailed. "That's Joel lying out there, Frank! I—I can't believe it. I can't believe this is happening!"

The second man—Frank, she'd called him—stood to one side and reached out a big, work-calloused hand to pat her roughly on the shoulder. He resembled Joel Turner quite a bit, from what I had seen of the man the other day, though he was perhaps a little older and significantly less polished. With his sleeves rolled up to the knotted muscles above his elbows and his baggy overalls, he looked as though he was used to hard work and manual labor. Libby's protector, too, had the family resemblance, but he was dressed more like an accountant, and though he drove the enormous F350 truck, not a cowboy hat was in evidence. Brothers of Joel, both of them, that was my guess.

The younger of the two caught sight of me as I stood there, watching them. He lifted his chin in acknowledgment of my presence. "I think there's someone here to see you," he said, putting his hands on Libby's shoulders to turn her in my direction.

Sniffling back her grief, she wiped her cheeks with the palms of her hands, then looked over at me. For a full ten seconds, I thought for sure she didn't recognize me. Then her face crumpled again and she launched herself at me, throwing her arms around my neck and burying her face against my shoulder. I was a little taken aback by the familiarity—I'd been wanting to offer her my sympathies, but never once did I expect this. As I would have comforted one of my nieces, I rubbed her shoulder while she sobbed and sobbed and the men watched on in obvious discomfort. Ordinarily, when faced with someone in so much emotional pain, I would be overwhelmed myself; so much that I would be choking on it. I hoped that meant I was getting better at shielding, because at the moment mine seemed to be holding.

Gently, I extricated myself from her grasp and set her back on her own two feet. "Here, now. Why don't we go into the office over there and make you some coffee? You don't need to be here to see all of this, Libby."

"I think that's a great idea," Frank said. I saw his relief in the set of his big shoulders. "I'll stay out here and wait to hear—"

Libby turned to him, almost desperate. "No. No, come with us, Frank, please. I need to have you both with me. Please."

Frank hesitated, but the pleading in beautiful, young Libby's eyes worked magic on the man. "All right."

The younger brother put his arm around Libby's shoulders. "Come on, Lib," he said in a gentle-gruff voice. "We can't do any good out here anyway."

He guided her toward the freestanding office building, leaving me to follow along in their wake like some sad kind of third wheel. With the brothers taking charge of the situation, there was really no reason for my presence . . . and yet I felt myself being pulled along with them by some internal guidance I didn't understand and couldn't explain. Confused, I glanced over to where I could see Liss standing beside Christine at the side of the road. I held up my hand and waved to her, glad now that I'd left my keys there with her.

I followed them into the office, wondering how I could extract myself and give them their privacy.

They had flipped on the lights before I stepped over the threshold into the icy cold of the office. It was like stepping from the shower into a meat locker. A shudder started at the base of my spine and worked its way up.

"Who left the AC turned down so low?" Frank said. "Noah, check that, would you?"

The younger brother, Noah, went over to the thermostat on the wall. "Nope. Everything looks okay. It's set on seventy-eight, just like it always is. You know how Joel hated waste like that."

"Well, it's sure as hell not seventy-eight in here right now. We'll have to arrange to have someone come out and take a look at it in the mor . . . when we reopen," he revised quickly, stricken by his unintentional gaffe.

I crossed my arms and rubbed at the goose bumps that

were raised there. The hairs were lifting at the nape of my neck. Criminey, it was cold. More than cold. It felt like it was getting colder by the minute—I put out a hand, testing the air, waving it back and forth slowly—yes, right here. I looked up. No ceiling register blowing down on me. The floor? There was nothing that broke the tile surface that I could see. Worse yet was the feeling that crawled over my skin the longer I stood there. Strange. Uncomfortable. As though I was an intruder in the space. *Just my discomfort at being a part of their private moment,* I told myself.

"Brr. It's freezing in here! Leave the door open, would you, Frank?" Libby said.

I cleared my throat and indicated the coffee bar over against the far wall. "I'll just make some coffee."

Libby sat down with a sigh on the only sofa in the sparsely furnished lobby. "Thank you, Maggie. Thank you for being here. I appreciate having another woman present to balance things out. Frank and Noah are a blessing, but . . ." She sighed again and clasped her hands in her lap. "I—I just can't believe that he's gone. What's going to happen to the feed mill without him? It was his baby. He wouldn't let anyone else near it. Well," she said, glancing over at Frank, "not really. I mean, Frank worked with him here, of course, but Joel was the one in control, wasn't he. Always." She sighed. "I just don't know what's going to happen to it. I just don't know."

Noah sat down next to her and patted her clasped hands. "We'll think of something, Lib. You don't have to worry about this now. Actually, you don't have to worry about it at all. Frank and I, we'll take care of everything. Won't we, Frank?"

Turning away to give them their privacy, I filled the

water vessel and measured out the coffee. Nothing gourmet here. Just plain old preground coffee that they probably bought cheap at the local grocery store. It didn't matter—it would do the trick. Anything to jolt reality and inject a little bit of normalcy into the situation.

With the coffee on and the water heating through, I began to drift along the fringes of the office in an attempt to find something to distract myself with from the awkwardness of finding myself a part of the strange proceedings. The big desk in the corner had a number of photographs on it, so I wandered over.

One of them caught my eye: a smiling, happy couple sitting on a park bench. It was Joel as he'd not come across in my only meeting with him—relaxed, in love, on top of his world with his woman by his side. Nowhere in this picture did I see evidence of the anger and tension I'd seen in him the other night. It was almost like looking at two different people. I touched the frame, and shivered.

"I'd forgotten he had that picture here." Startled, I yanked my hand back as Libby appeared at my shoulder. With an eerie sense of calm, the kind that often descends right after a sudden death, she reached out and picked up the picture. "It was one of our first candids as a married couple . . . one of his favorites of us. Joel always said it made him look ten years younger."

There *had* been an obvious age difference between the two of them. Remarkable, really. Ten to fifteen years seemed most likely. Was it something he had felt acutely, the older he had gotten? In the photo he looked like he hadn't a care in the world but the young woman beside him. So different from the man I'd encountered. What a difference a few years made. Was it the stresses and challenges of business ownership that had settled the weight of the world in his aura? Call me nosy, call me a student of human nature, but a part of me couldn't help wondering what it was that had wrought so much change in him.

Frank was staring out the window at the proceedings, his spine stiff and his shoulders hunched, his hands clasped behind his back. "They're putting him in the ambulance now," he said quietly.

Setting the framed picture down, Libby went to stand beside her stalwart brother-in-law, her arms tightly hugging herself as she gazed out the double-paned window. Noah remained in his seat, watching his brother and sister-in-law, before putting his head in his hands and dragging his palms down his face, then gathering his hands together in front of his chin.

I didn't belong here with them. I felt that so keenly, and yet there I was anyway.

Desperate for some distraction, I checked on the coffee, but it was only midway through the pot. I set out a couple of cups and located the ubiquitous artificial creamer and sugar packets, but that took only a second. I needed something, anything, to occupy my attention. The office was fairly Spartan. Most of what could be found along the walls pertained to some new chemical field additive for weed control, or a new and improved kind of fertilizer that wouldn't burn the plants when topically applied. Snoozeville, big time. A pile of books on top of a credenza-style filing cabinet proved to be nothing more than a selection of farming catalogs. A large, utilitarian bulletin board was filled with a plain calendar, bits and pieces of papers, clippings, and various ephemera found in any office. The ephemera was, as expected, just a jumble of things that meant something to

Joel but little to me. Business cards, carbon copies of packing slips, pages torn out from hunting magazines, a clipping for Rogaine—hmm, wonder if that was why he had worn a cowboy hat—tucked back behind an advertisement for a fairly effective-looking handgun.

Behind me, a great, hiccupping sob emerged from Libby, and she turned from the window and ran down the hall. The slam of a door followed, but it didn't mask the weeping that issued forth from within. Frank and Noah looked at each other, then Noah clapped his older brother on the shoulder and went off to do his brotherly duty.

My shields had held for Libby; but it was Frank that proved their undoing. Bewilderment, sorrow, pain threaded in, bit by bit. I tried to push them back out, but once in, they grabbed hold and wouldn't let go.

"Why?" Frank murmured, as though he had forgotten I was there. "Why was he up there? Jesus."

The coffeepot stopped burbling a moment too late for Libby, but maybe it could do Frank some good. I poured him a big, steaming mug and carried it over to him. Unfortunately as I passed the desk, my hip bumped a stack of papers on the corner. They swept to the floor, taking with them the picture frame Libby had set down beside them. It fell to the tile floor with a clatter that made me cringe.

I stood among the wreckage of strewn papers and bit my lip. Frank turned around. "I'm so sorry," I said, feeling terrible. "I must have bumped it as I walked past." I set the coffee down on the desk and immediately knelt to assess the damage.

Frank bent to pick up the papers, which had caught invisible air currents and floated in all directions. I gathered the nearest ones together, then, cringing, I reached for the photo frame. My heart sank. The glass was broken. A jagged, lightning bolt line separated the two lovers in the photo down the middle. A second line reached from the center and spider-webbed over Libby's face. "I'm so sorry!" I repeated. "The glass is broken."

Frank knelt down and took the photo from me. "No harm done. It's just the glass, see? The photo itself is fine. Don't you worry about it."

Between the two of us we got the rest of the mess picked up. I was about to get to my feet when I spotted one last thing lurking half under the desk. I slid it out. It was a cheap desk agenda, notebook-style, held open with a rubberband to display the month of June. A couple of pages had wrinkled in the fall. I smoothed them out, running my palm over the paper. Absentmindedly I noticed there weren't a lot of entries on it. A couple of doctor's appointments marked there in a heavy black scrawl— one on the fifteenth, just past, 2 P.M.; and another coming up on the twenty-ninth. Joel would be missing that one. The poor guy must have had some sort of recurring medical issue he had been taking care of. "Someone will need to cancel his appointment with Dr. Dorffman," I murmured, half to myself.

"What's that?"

I held up the agenda. "This fell, too. Sorry for being such a klutz."

Frank took the agenda and dropped it on the big desk beneath the lamp, then held out his hand and helped me to my feet.

Just in time, too, as Libby and Noah emerged from the bathroom. Libby's cheeks were damp, her eyes red. Poor thing. I hurried to pour cups of coffee for her and Noah.

Libby had opened the door and stood there, looking out at the scene.

"What was that?" she asked suddenly. "Over there by the pig barns. Did you two see that?"

Noah frowned and leaned closer to the glass. "What did you see?"

"A shadow of some sort . . . and then it moved. Like a person. Didn't you see it?"

"Where?"

"Over there"—she pointed—"by the pig barns."

Frank turned away from the window. "I didn't see anything," he grunted dismissively. "Probably just one of the emergency workers."

I looked out the window, too, once the rest of them had moved away at last, and immediately a chill ran up my spine. Because I, too, thought I had seen something tucked away in that corner between the largest of the hog barns and one of the lesser silos. Something vaguely man-shaped that was there one minute and gone the next.

Shades of Quasimodo.

Shades of something.

I shivered. I just hoped it wasn't the shade of Mr. Joel Turner himself. Was that too much to ask?

Chapter 8

It was with great relief that I was finally able to extricate myself from the grief-stricken tension in the office with the excuse that I needed to get back to my car. Leaving the three Turners alone to comfort one another, I darted here and there across the feed mill complex to avoid the emergency crew milling about the scene. I was heading toward the road and my car, knowing that Liss would have been far too polite to ditch me no matter how long I'd been absent, when a dark *something* caught my eye.

Despite the beginnings of a headache starting at the base of my skull, I found my feet veering off on a completely different path toward the far end of the pig barn.

The smell of the hogs, as I drew near the long, narrow building, was even more atrocious. New building or no new building, it didn't take long for the stench of pigs to permeate the concrete, the steel, the insulation, the beams. Everything.

The smell was one thing, but the sounds were downright

ghastly. I couldn't say that I'd been this close to a hog holding barn in over twenty years, but the sound that the animals made was something that a person could never quite
forget. It was a cross between a scream and a guttural
squeal, made somehow worse by the knowledge that they
were in a holding barn on their way to slaughter. I wondered, sometimes, whether they could sense it, their im-
pending demise. Did they know?

The shadow was too tall for a hog that had gotten
loose, far too stealthy. There it was again, darting into the
cove created by two grain silos.

I fished in my pants pocket for my key ring and the
handy little LED flashlight I kept clipped to it. *Damn.* I'd
left the keys in the car with Liss, and there was nothing
there but dryer lint left along the pocket seams.

As surreptitious as a person could be when in the middle
of what amounted to a big paved lot without a single bit of
cover in sight other than the fact that they were one of
twenty people moving around the area, I made a zigzagging beeline for the pig barn, flattening my back against its
newly painted surface once there. I know I probably looked
ridiculous, had anyone been paying attention—but sometimes a girl had to sacrifice dignity and an aversion for
trouble when there was a higher purpose involved. Namely,
to figure out whether Spook the Shadow was a real, live
person, or the manifestation of something else entirely. Although given a choice between the two, I'm not sure which
was the better alternative at that particular point in time.

I inched my way down the barn in my best Fred "Twin-
kletoes" Flintstone style—back and hands flat to the wall,
tippytoes tootling along—until I was within a few feet of
the end. I'd sharpened my ears to the noises around me,

but I had heard nothing out of the ordinary considering everything else that was going on. Just the grunting and squeals of the pigs, commentary slung back and forth by police and medical personnel, a whisper of a breeze every now and again, the crunching of footsteps across the pavement where gravel had scattered, and the occasional squelch of police radios.

Nothing to make the fine hairs on my arms stand on end. So why were they?

The Shadow knows.

I was creeping myself out. Heh. I really needed to stop doing that.

There was nothing to fear. There were people—big, strong men, in fact—all around me. All I had to do was step around the edge of the barn, stay within sight, and see what it was that was creeping along the fringes, watching the processing of the accident scene. I could, I suppose, call for Tom . . . but was there really any reason to when it was most likely nothing? He already thought I was halfway to the loony bin for my involvement with the N.I.G.H.T.S. in general and Liss in particular . . . not to mention for my current predilection for all things esoteric and mysterious. No reason to confirm his worst fears without just cause.

I took a deep breath, steeled myself, and leapt out to confront . . .

Nothing.

The cove was actually just an alley created by two grain silos, and this particular alley led around and about the maze of other alleys created by still more silos. The security lights and spotlights had eliminated some shadows and created others. Maybe the shadow I had seen was nothing more than a bat or a bird that crossed into one of the beams of bright light.

Or maybe there had been something there. Something that knew I'd been watching and had eluded me in the thrill of the chase.

I wandered a little farther down the "alley," but I didn't see anything else that might have caused the moving shadow. My vote was on a bird—specifically, one of the enormous buzzards that I had seen circling above, silhouetted against the glow of moon and clouds. Though I had to admit, the thought of that kind of creeped me out, too.

Confused by the events of the evening, I headed back toward my car and hoped I could find some way to make amends to Liss for leaving her alone for so long.

I found her standing ever so elegantly beside one of the police cruisers that had arrived after us, and speaking earnestly with a state police officer who appeared to be around fifty years young, a bit gray at the edges, but still in sporting good shape.

"Here she comes now," she said before I'd even had a chance to announce my return. "Maggie, my dear, I'd like you to meet Trooper Gary McKenzie of the Indiana State Police. Trooper McKenzie popped by to lend a hand to the officers already on the scene here. I was just telling him about your Tom, and what a wonderful job he does for Stony Mill. That's Tom over there with poor Mr. Turner, isn't it?"

I held out my hand, and Gary took it, well, like a trooper. "A pleasure. Yes, that's Tom. He's the department's Go-To Guy for anything out of the ordinary here in town, so I guess an accident on this scale qualifies."

"I'd heard about the Special Task Force that Chief

Boggs had created between the police and sheriff's departments," Trooper Gary commented in an almost offhand
manner. "Stony Mill sure has had its share of bad luck this
year."

Luck. Yeah, that was one way of looking at it.

"Well," he said, eyeing Liss the way a hungry man
might eye a really juicy Porterhouse, "I guess I should be
heading over to see what kind of help I can give to the
emergency crew. I'll, uh . . ." He cast an embarrassed
glance my way, but I busied myself pretending to look for
my car keys. He angled himself toward Liss and said, "I'll
be in touch."

I waited until he was gone before I raised my brow at
her. " 'I'll be in touch'?"

She almost looked embarrassed. "It's completely innocent, I assure you. Trooper McKenzie happens to be in
charge of a chapter of Tots on Wheels—you know, the
annual drive for toys. I told him I'd be happy to host a
gathering bin at the store."

Uh-huh. Except it was obvious the trooper had had
more than charity drives in mind. Maybe it was the witch
in her.

I surveyed the emergency crews working ahead of us.
"Do you think we should try that three-point turn after all?
At this rate, we could be here all night."

"I'm game if you are."

She handed me the keys and we headed back to my ag-
ing Bug. I was about to get in the car when I heard it: the
tiniest little wail.

"Did you hear that?" I asked Liss.

She had stopped, too, her head cocked, listening. "Yes,
I did."

I wasn't sure what it was, but it sounded pitiful, and it was calling to me. I knew it, just as surely as I knew that whatever it was needed help. I had to find it.

I found my answer in the shallow drainage ditch across the road, where a steel culvert created an open passage for water beneath the driveway into the feed mill complex. I had been standing by the edge of the road, about ready to give up and dismiss it all as imagination or the wind (not that there was any) whistling through the conveyers, when I heard it again. Closer, this time. Tentative.

Lost.

The sound tore at my heart. I bent down to look in the culvert, getting ready to shine the flashlight inside . . .

And then something black and small leapt up my body by increments and set its claws into my chest.

"Gaaaaaaaah!"

Coherent thought and vocal abilities eluded me. My arms pinwheeled at my side as I double-stepped backward. Unfortunately, I stepped in a hole and lost my balance, ending up immediately on my back, staring at the glow of the feed mill's security lights and the colorful flash of police lights on the misty undersides of the clouds. My brain was now officially knocking against my skull. Whatever had leapt at me remained attached to my shirtfront. Oddly enough, it was nearly but not quite weightless, and . . . it rumbled. I was afraid to look, half certain it was going to be of the rodent persuasion. Did rats rumble?

Liss came running to my rescue. "Are you all right, my dear—oh! Well, if that isn't the cutest little thing!" she said, two thoughts in one breath.

The source of the nonweight, the rumbling, and the claws was all in one compact, fuzzy package: the tiniest little kitten with the biggest pair of saucer eyes I'd ever seen. It was black as pitch, but not quite sleek; there was too much in the way of mud and other intangibles in its fur for that. But the oddest thing about it was that one of its eyes was green, and the other blue, and they glittered in the lights.

Its claws were still making a pincushion of my shirt-front, poking into my tender skin like eighteen tiny little razor tips, but not in malice. As I watched, it closed its eyes, and . . .

"It's purring!" Liss said, chuckling, as she bent down to touch a fingertip to the kitten's head.

"It just scared the bejeebers out of me. Maybe it's purring in self-satisfaction."

"It did come out of nowhere, I'll give you that. Here."

She reached down to scoop the kitten off my chest, then held out her hand. I took it and got to my feet, dusting off the dirt and grass bits that were undoubtedly clinging to me. "Thanks."

The kitten watched my every movement and let out the tiniest *mew* when our gazes met.

"She likes you," Liss said, scratching the kitten under the chin.

"She?"

"Now you're not going to tell me I have to instruct you on the intricacies—"

I laughed and held up my hand to stop her in her verbal tracks. "No, no. I think I have that all figured out, *thankyouverymuch*."

"Oh, do you now." She assessed me closely. "That's good to hear. A girl should have that ability down pat at your age—"

"Hey!" I protested. My birthday—my *thirtieth* birthday—was right around the corner, and I was *not* looking forward to it much. If at all.

The kitten stretched out a paw toward me, gentle, with soft pads like fine leather and no claws in sight. As though she was reaching out to shake hands with me. I tried not to look at her, because I knew my heart was in serious danger. Full-out frontal attack. As though wondering why I wasn't paying attention, she cocked her head, looked at me again, and bleated out another soft *mew*.

"I think she wants you."

Reluctantly—but not really—I held my hands out to take her. The sweetpea tucked herself up into a tight little ball in my curved palms, her toes barely peeking out, then leaned her head back and lifted her chin to look up at me from upside down. She appeared to have the tiniest patch of white under her chin. "Aww . . ."

It just slipped out. I swear.

"What are we going to do with her?" I asked. "We can't leave her here. She'll get run over by a farm truck or eaten by wild dogs or something."

"We'll just have to take her with us," Liss responded immediately and predictably. "She's far too young to be out on her own. And just look at how taken she is with you! Great Goddess. Have you ever seen anything so sweet?"

Hm.

We got in the car and sat for a few minutes with the windows rolled down, discussing Joel's death. "Poor, poor thing," Liss murmured when I told her about Libby. "More trouble."

Maybe Libby's worries hadn't been so off base after all.

We tried to decide whether it would be best to make

another attempt to leave now or wait a few minutes more. The mosquitoes were thicker here with the far-reaching fields on our right than they had been on the feed mill complex with its extensive concrete lot. I had the kitten in my lap, mostly because she refused to sit elsewhere, even when I waved my hands around like a maniac in an attempt to dislodge the mosquitoes that were trying to feast in places I couldn't easily slap or rub or brush. She had fallen almost instantly to sleep and was now purring away like a motorboat on overdrive.

Liss, I noticed with the teensiest bit of envy, wasn't affected by the mosquitoes at all.

"How do you do that?" I asked her when I'd slapped the back of my neck for the fourth time.

"Do what?"

"How is it that the mosquitoes aren't after you? I mean, is it a spell that you cast? Because if it is, I'd really like to know. I think I might be game to try it after tonight."

"Oh, are they bothering you? Perhaps it's the energy work I do, keeping them at bay. Or maybe they don't like the taste of my foreign blood." She laughed, then said, "Far more likely it's the vervain—verbena, that is—and lavender that I use to scent my drawers and closets. Most flying insects don't seem to enjoy the scent of it. You should try it."

I made a mental note to raid Enchantments' stores in the A.M. This was one old-school Craft "remedy" I was more than happy to adopt into my modern-day lifestyle.

"In the meantime, perhaps we should radiate more." At my blank stare, she explained, "Our personal energies. Perhaps we should send out a little power surge. Sometimes that helps to keep the unwanted at bay."

That sounded like yet another handy-dandy witchy tip. I couldn't help wondering what other little helpful tidbits she had hidden up her sleeves. I was about to ask her to explain when I saw Officer Johnson heading in our direction.

He ducked down by my open window. "Looks like you'll be able to head out, ladies. They're getting a path cleared for you now."

Thank goodness.

He looked back over his shoulder, took a message from someone over his radio, and spoke into the mouthpiece clipped to his shoulder. Then he stepped out to the side of the road. "Okay, what you'll want to do is turn into the drive, go into the complex past the office, and just past the second hog barn you'll find a drive that passes through. You'll turn right and follow behind the buildings. You should be able to come out on the other side with no problems. Thanks for being so patient."

I followed his instructions to the letter, creeping through the feed mill complex at five miles per hour. The last thing this town needed was for an emergency aid worker to be run over at an actual emergency. We Stony Millers had enough trouble on our plate as it was. I motioned to Tom as we passed him by, sticking out my pinkie and my thumb and holding it to my head like a phone receiver in the universal sign language for *"Call me!"* until he acknowledged me and nodded. Thank goodness we couldn't see past the crunch of people, vehicles, and equipment. Viewing the hideous result of a tragic and violent accident was not tops on my To Do list.

Finally we were on the move again.

"Well, that was interesting," Liss said with her usual talent for understatement.

"I'll bet Mr. Turner said that very thing as he was plum-meting toward the ground," I said wryly. With the comment came an instant mental pang. Oh, that was bad. Joel Turner might not have been the friendliest of people the one and only time he came ever-so-peripherally into my life, but my Grandma Cora would never have stood for one of us speak-ing ill of the dead. Especially not someone so recently passed. Knock wood. If I had salt, I'd throw some over my shoulder. Except then I'd have to vacuum.

"Speaking of your love life," Liss said conversationally.

I blinked, and my brows shot up. I kept my eyes on the road. "Were we?"

"Feel free to tell me it's none of my business—because Goddess knows that wouldn't be far from the truth at least ninety percent of the time; you know how I love to be in the thick of things—but . . . well, I'll just go right ahead and say it, then, shall I?"

"Sure," I said, a trifle faintly. "Shoot."

"You see, I've noticed something."

"And that is?"

"You don't seem to have much of one. I mean, between your Tom's work schedule, and the store, and even your family, there doesn't seem to be much time for you left."

Tell me about it. "It won't last forever," I said, not voic-ing the selfishness that was my first instinct. "Sometimes we have a hard time getting all of our schedules in sync."

"Sometimes when you want things to work, you make them work," she said, as enigmatic as ever.

I mean, what was that supposed to mean?

"I won't even ask you about Marcus," she continued.

That was good. I didn't know what I could tell her about the most dark and dangerous-to-my-equilibrium member of the N.I.G.H.T.S. that she didn't already know anyway. Because actually, I hadn't seen him in a couple of weeks. Since the last N.I.G.H.T.S. get-together, in fact. And yes, I was avoiding him. I know, I know. Tom and I weren't an exclusive, and in fact, we had even less of an actual *relationship* now than when I had realized that Liss and Marcus weren't an item. We'd never said we'd date each other and each other only . . . and yet I found that, even though modern dating rules made it clear that I would be perfectly legit in accepting a date with another man, getting my mind wrapped around that was a little harder. Call me old-fashioned, but I was raised to honor the boyfriend-girlfriend factor from the get-go; to treat every prospective boyfriend in the way that I would want to be treated as well. For me, the Golden Rules of Dating still applied. Which meant, of course, that any attraction I felt toward Marcus was better left unexplored, unscrutinized, unprobed.

Un-everything. Because that single kiss we'd shared so *un*intentionally might have raged out of control if it had remained *un*checked by reason. And ethics.

"And I can see you won't be offering any information either," she said with the usual pinpoint perception. "I had hoped the two of you . . . well, of course it's none of my business . . . and of course you're still with Tom, so that's that, and I suppose that's for the best." She paused, then said, "At least for now."

I shook my head and uttered a short, nervous laugh that made the kitten raise its head and blink at me. "You're amazing, you know that? I promise, if anything improves in that area of my life, you'll be the first person I tell." Then, because it was easier to remain on the defensive by going on the offensive, without being offensive, I nudged, "So, what about that state trooper, hm? That looked promising."

"Don't be ridiculous, dear. He's young enough to be my younger brother. But if anything develops in that area of my life, you'll be the first person I tell."

"Deal."

Continuing on our belated path toward the store, I explained more about how I'd been shanghaied by the Turners' distress and by their need to distance Libby from what was going on at the scene. "It was really uncomfortable," I admitted to her. "I don't know Libby very well at all, and she . . . was so open with her grief and despair. And then with her brothers-in-law, too . . . trying to hold it all back . . ." I shook my head. "To tell you the truth, toward the end it was getting to me. I have the beginnings of a migraine right now."

"It was just too much for your shields, that's all. Did you remember to strengthen them when you felt them slipping?"

Effective shielding was of key importance to a person with sensitive/intuitive tendencies. A method of reinforcing our personal boundaries—our auras—against the accidental intrusion of the emotions of others. Some people wear their heart on their sleeve as a matter of course. What that means, metaphysically speaking, is that their emotions bleed out of their personal space and into the world around them. What that means to an empath whose protections are failing is that all those sneaky little tendrils of rogue emotion can infiltrate and overwhelm her own energy fields faster than she can ward them off.

All of this I already knew. Liss had been a very patient

teacher. Why hadn't I remembered the rest? "I guess it happened too fast," I said, answering my own question with my musings. "I didn't even think to . . ."

"And that's the source—"

"Of the headache. Of course." The kitten woke up and stretched itself out over my lap, flaring its toes. The purring started up again, louder than ever, but it was . . . nice. Soothing.

Liss reached over and patted my hand. "When you get home, take a wonderfully hot shower and let the water stream down you and rinse away the emotional grunge. Then take some aspirin and go straight to bed. Trust me, it will do wonders for you. And when you wake up in the morning, *voilà*. A whole new you."

It was nearly eleven o'clock when I dropped her off by her car and told her I'd see her in the morning. I waited, wanting to make sure she got off okay. It was only after she'd backed out in front of me, taillights flaring red, and then pulled away with a wave in the rearview, that I realized I still had the kitten in my lap and neither of us had made any suggestions about what to do with her.

I sighed.

"You just suckered me, didn't you?" I said to the fuzzy little creature who was probably shedding black hairs, dirt, and goodness knows what else all over me.

What could I do? I stopped at a quickie mart that I knew carried emergency supplies, including pet food and, more importantly in this particular case, kitty litter. The kitten had been found outside, so all I could do was hope—fervently—that she would know what to do with cat litter. I had had a traumatic experience the last time I had taken in a lost and needy animal. Good bathroom habits are so important in a temporary roomie, don't you think?

"I expect you to be good," I told her, speaking as I would to one of my nieces. "You have to mind your manners. None of this shredding my furniture, or marking your territory in the corners. I'll just keep you in the bathroom tonight, and tomorrow we'll see about finding you a home, 'kay?"

My To Do list was growing by the hour. Return my sister's calls, find home for helpless orphan, consult with the N.I.G.H.T.S. on the best way to banish evil whatchamacallit from my sister's home, banishing the actual . . .

Heeeeeeeeey now. Maybe Mel was the answer to one of my To Do's. Maybe she'd be willing to take in the little fuzzball as a thank-you for getting rid of the weird energy she'd invited into her house.

I pulled up to my apartment on Willow Street with a sigh of relief. It had been a long and eventful day, and I was ready to call it that. Just a few things to take care of first, and then I could haul my headache off to bed. So to speak.

The kitten woke up the moment I switched off Christine's old engine with the usual hiccup-choke-cough of its cylinders. She stood up on all fours and stretched with a great, arching back, all her claws digging into my legs. "*Yeouch*, little one. How sharp are those things?"

I shuffled her around with my bag and the jug of cat litter until I had them all situated securely, and made my way across the yard and down the sunken steps to my apartment. Unfortunately I had forgotten to keep my keys out. *Dumb-de-dumb-dumb.* I ended up tucking the kitten inside my purse at the bottom of the steps while I dug for the keys and then used them on the door. She actually seemed to like her impromptu cubby.

A flip of the switch reassured me that all appeared to be in order within my little apartment. No lights burning where none had been left on, no strange smells or sounds, and most importantly, no funny stuff for me to see out of the corners of my eyes. Perhaps the spirits could sense my weariness and were giving me the night off.

A girl could hope.

I set my bag down on the floor and closed the door, sliding the deadbolt into place with a solid, reassuring switch of metal into casing. The bag of kitty litter was surprisingly heavy, so the first order of business would be to set it down, followed by locating a box to use as a temporary litterbox. I went into the bedroom and began searching under my bed for the box that had held the strappy silver sandals that were my last impulse buy. Aha. There it was, near the head of the bed. I laid myself out on the floor, reaching, stretching with all my might. My fingers bumped the box, pushing it about a centimeter out of reach. Bloody hell. I closed my eyes and gave one final full-body lunge . . . *Success!* My fingertips curved over the rim of the box, and I bent my fingers to draw it toward me, a fraction at a time, carefully so as not to lose it again.

I felt a wet scratching on my nose and opened my eyes. Two eyes stared at me point blank, one blue, one green, while a bubblegum pink tongue slid repeatedly along my nose.

"Well, hello to you, too."

It was the most action I was likely to get for a while, so I supposed I should enjoy it. The kitten sat back on her hindquarters then and, lifting one long, rabbitlike rear foot,

began to vigorously scratch at her ear. She finished off the
energetic ministrations with an equally vigorous and energetic shaking of her head. She looked a little dazed when it
ended. I couldn't say as I blamed her. That was hard enough
to rock anyone's world.

"Hmm," I said aloud while she blinked at me. "First order of business, litterbox. Second order of business might
just be a bath for you, little one. I don't know if it's the dirt
that's making you scratch or something more insidious,
but I'm hoping just dirt."

As though she'd understood what I said and didn't like
the sound of it, she took one last look at me and skedad-
dled out of the way.

"Right, then." I slid the box out the rest of the way, then
got to my feet. Cardboard shoeboxes probably wouldn't
hold up well to anything wet, so I pulled an empty trash
bag from beneath the kitchen sink and stuck the shoebox
inside it, molding it to the box and tying off the excess before pouring an inch or so of cat litter into it. Instant litterbox, kitten-sized.

I went to look for the little furball, but didn't see her.
Then I heard a crashing, skittering, bumping sound beneath my sofa. I lifted the skirt to see a black blur bouncing
back and forth, up, down, and all around the low space. It
was a lot of racket for one small critter, and rather impressive in an alarming sort of way. She must have found a bit
of paper or cloth or something to entertain her, I decided,
shaking my head.

Or it could have been the mouse that zipped out from
under the sofa, passing very near my nose.

I shrieked, and for the second time that evening, I
found myself rearing back in surprise, losing my balance,

and falling on my behind. Immediately I scrabbled away, crab-style, then leaped up on the old sofa itself in a single bound while the kitten burst out like a shot from beneath it and spun around wildly, looking for the mouse. Catching sight of it, she took off like a shot. I watched the crazed procession, rooting the kitten on when it got close, cringing when she caught it in her paws and wrestled around with it. Finally, this little bitty kitten somehow managed to get a stranglehold on the wriggling, squealing mouse. It was the squealing that mobilized me off my perch on the sofa. She was way too small to do any real damage to the mouse. I was going to have to lose my aversion in order to get rid of the beast so that I could actually get some sleep tonight without feeling little scrabbling feet, imagined or otherwise, climbing over my sheets.

The only thing I could think to do was to grab a big pitcher from the kitchen. The kitten growled and wrestled around with the ball of wriggling beastie. I was starting to lose my objectivity, because I was actually beginning to feel sorry for the mouse . . . and yet I couldn't quite decide how to part the two of them. Soon enough, the inexperienced kitten lost its tenuous grip. The mouse ran in one direction, then another, obviously disoriented. I took the opportunity and clapped the pitcher down over it before the kitten could figure out how to recoup her loss.

She looked up at me and blinked reproachfully as if to say, *What are you doing? Couldn't you see I was busy?* And then . . . *All right, if you're so smart. Now what?*

Now what? A fair question. I hadn't thought that far ahead.

The answer I came up with was to slide a piece of cardboard under the lip of the pitcher until it went right under the terrified critter itself. I tried not to panic as I felt the scrabbling of tiny nails on the cardboard as the mouse continued its desperate bid for escape, but just lifted it, pitcher, cardboard, and all, and made my way to the door. The kitty followed me, watching me intently with her bicolored eyes.

"Oh, no you don't," I told her, shooing her back. "I don't think I need a helper with this part."

More reproachful stares. I ignored them and took the mouse outside, into the night. Within minutes I had dispatched it into a bushy copse a couple of blocks away from my apartment and had run back the entire way, just in case it decided to follow me.

It wasn't enough that I had pests of the supernatural kind; now I had to have regular, everyday, twitchy-nosed pests, too? I was never going to get any sleep at this rate.

I let myself back into the apartment, expecting my new black friend to be waiting for me by the door, eager for my return. Nope. She was nowhere in the kitchen or the living room that I could see—and I was *not* looking under the sofa again, no matter what! I headed for the bedroom, and probably should not have been surprised to find her there, curled into a ball on my pillow. Which looked pretty inviting, I had to admit. I thought briefly of the dinner I had missed out on, and the bath that the kitten needed . . . and none of it impressed me enough to nudge me out of the blue funk of weariness that I felt pressing in on me.

I fell into bed in utter exhaustion, without a thought in my head for anything but sleep. *Just for a few minutes,* I told myself. *Long enough to get the cobwebs out of my head.* I found the ball of kitten and stroked her into a purring puddle, absentmindedly smoothing her fur and lulling myself in the process.

I woke up sometime later to a banging noise resounding through my muddled brain, strange, dusty light coming through the windows, a heaviness in my head, and a complete sense of disorientation. It had been too hot for a blanket, and my clothes, which I hadn't managed to remove before I collapsed onto the bed, were now horribly wrinkled and twisted. I tried to sit up, but couldn't seem to get up more than an inch off the pillow. I sighed, thinking it must be that I was still half-asleep. I closed my eyes and breathed deeply, trying to warm up my brain for optimum receptivity to thought processes, then tried the whole procedure again. And again, I couldn't rise more than an inch off the pillow. This time I felt a distinct tugging on my hair. It was like the crown of my head was stuck to the bed with superglue.

What. The. Heck?

Chapter 9

I put my hand up to my forehead. My fingertips connected with something solid, and yet somehow squishy, but that was most definitely not me. It was about that time that I realized that something was pinning my head to the bed.

It was also about that time that I remembered the kitten.

Who seemed to have made a *nest* out of my hair and was curved around the whole of my head like some kind of furry headband.

I was now really wishing I'd taken the time to bathe her.

My hand closed around her body and I lifted her straight up out of my hair, which I could not wait to shampoo, carrying her down to my chest. Her body was like a ragdoll in its relaxed state, hanging straight down by all fours, all feet and tail. When I set her down on my chest, she resituated herself slightly, stretched her paws out, and blinked at me. *"Mew,"* she said softly. I touched her soft footpads and she peered at me, then rolled herself over and sat up on top of me, her whiskers and her sparkling personality both twitching to life. She looked somehow cleaner this morning . . . which, now that I thought of it, probably did not bode well for the state of my own shining mane.

"Good morning to you, too," I said out loud. She responded by running in circles around the bed, her tail up and fully bristled, before she settled for an attack on my bare feet. "Okay, ow, I don't think we're going to be doing that. You have teeth, you see, which you don't seem to realize, and—*ouch!* Claws, too." The little minklike beauty had grabbed on to my whole foot with all four of her own and was now wrestling back and forth like a dervish. "They're the pointy, razorlike things coming out of your toes. Okay, then. What *is* that banging?"

The banging, which I had originally assumed was a remnant of my murky dreamworld, began again with a vengeance. My heart pounding, I leapt out of bed, realizing there was someone at my door at the same moment that my cell phone began ringing. I grabbed it, flipping it open on the run and ignoring the warning for a missed call that would have to wait until later. "Hello?" I said, checking the mirror over the dresser as I passed it by. Oh, God. Total beauty annihilation.

"Are you in there, Sleeping Beauty? I saw your car at the curb. Don't tell me you're actually taking a day off."

It was Steff, best friend extraordinaire. Normally the sound of her voice would have lifted my spirits instantly, but just then, all I could do was groan as I opened my front door, my cell phone still stuck to my ear. Steff's eyes widened when she saw me. I lifted my hand in a weak wave. "Hi."

"Oh. My." Her lips twitched. Her gaze darted around the still dim apartment. "Sleepover?" she asked in a hopeful tone, her gaze darting back and forth over my shoulder. "Got some hot hunka man sequestered away in there?"

"I wish," I grunted, stepping out of the way so she could come in. I did have a sleeping partner, but not one that would fit the bill.

"Should I assume that you threw caution to the wind last night and are nursing the rare hangover?"

Despite the fact that I felt like I had one, minus the fuzzy tongue, I shook my head. "I just woke up. What are you doing home at this hour?"

"What, nine thirty-seven? I got called into work unexpectedly last night, so I have the day off, and I'm wired. Imagine my delight in finding you home, too. So . . . why are you? Home, I mean. Not working today?"

My brain didn't quite feel like functioning, but her nurse's getup seemed to confirm her statement. Still . . . My mouth fell open. "What time did you say it was?"

"Nine . . . thirty . . . seven," she said slowly. "Are you not feeling well?"

Without a word, I raced into the bedroom to check my alarm, but the glowing green dashes corroborated Steff's claim. My cell phone was still in my hand. I lifted it in front of me and pushed the display button. Nine thirty-eight. Even worse.

I had overslept. Dreadfully.

The kitten roused herself from her nap with a yawning stretch, then sat in the middle of the bed, staring at me. Steff came to the bedroom door. "*Sooooo* . . . not supposed to be here right now, I take it?"

"I'm late." So late. And getting later by the minute. *Must. Clear. Head.*

"Who's this?" she asked, nudging forward to the edge of the bed and holding out her hand.

"My hot hunka. I picked her up last night when I was caught by the accident at the feed mill."

"You were there?" she asked, picking up my fuzzy friend and cradling her in her hands. "My, you do get around. I heard about it from the ambulance drivers who brought the body in."

"Yeah, I was there. Purely by chance. They'd stopped a train over the tracks, so we tried to circumvent it, only to get stuck by the emergency crews."

"Poor Mr. Turner," Steff mused. "He didn't stand a chance, falling from that height. The accident was the talk of the hospital last night." She caught me looking at the clock again. "Oh, my goodness. Here I am, chatting away, and you've got to get to work. Why don't you hop in the shower, and I'll take care of your new friend here."

"Deal!" I smiled at her. "Thanks, Steff."

I jumped into the shower as Steff asked, "I'm thinking you need food, little minx. Let's go see what we can find, shall we?" and I couldn't help smiling. Another one bites the dust.

I emerged from the shower less than seven steamy minutes later, threw on a pair of cotton capris and layered on a pair of complementing T's, and pinned back my unruly hair at the nape of my neck with a healthy dose of frizz serum. I was as ready as I could be under the circumstances.

Steff had found the tins of cat food I'd bought last night

and had broken one open for the kitten, complete with a splash of milk. The furball was eating with gusto, one foot inside the dish to prevent its escape. "This is surprisingly entertaining," Steff said as I joined her. "Her belly is bulging at the seams."

She also had a milk mustache. And beard. And her foot was soggy. I would have liked nothing more than to stay and stare at her cuteness all day, but I really had to get to work. "But what am I going to do with you?" I asked her as she sat back from the empty dish and began to wash her foot. I flicked my gaze to Steff hopefully.

She held up her hands. "Don't look at me!" she said with a laugh. "I have to be back to work at three this afternoon and I've got to try to sleep before then."

Hmm. I couldn't exactly leave the little minx here by herself, could I? I could only imagine what kind of trouble she might get in for entertainment purposes. Must think.

I scooped her up and tucked her under my arm. The kitten went amazingly still and looked up at me with such complete trust that my heart just melted. "Oh, that is so not playing fair." I ran my fingertips over the sleek bridge of her nose. She closed her eyes and nudged against me, pushing her head into the curve of my fingers and purring loudly.

"She sure doesn't pull any punches, does she?" Steff agreed.

I knew then that I wouldn't be looking for a home for her. Somehow, in the midst of last night's tragedy, and against all odds, she had found her home, with me.

Brightening up, I said, "Hold on a sec. I need to make a phone call." I grabbed my cell phone and dialed the store. After ten o'clock now. Why hadn't Liss called?

"Enchantments Antiques and Fine Gifts. Felicity Dow, at your service."

Explanations and regret spewed forth instantly at the sound of her voice. "Liss, I am so sorry. I don't know what was wrong with me last night. I apparently didn't set the alarm, and I woke up just a little while ago with a cat in my hair, frantic, and I—"

"Slow down, slow down," Liss said with a chuckle. "No worries, ducks. With all the extra hours and effort you put in, I'm hardly likely to quarrel over a little time here and there. These things happen. The winds of fate are stronger than either of us. Best to accept that and allow ourselves to bend and flex in their wake, don't you think?" Liss at her most Confucian.

"All right. If you say so. Anyway, I'm awake, I've showered so as not to offend, but I seem to have a little problem."

"A furry one?"

"You guessed it." She always knew what I was talking about, too. Our sensitive-to-sensitive connection had always been strong, from the first moment I'd stepped into the store and had been exposed to this strange, new world. "I, um, *think* I've decided to keep her."

"Imagine that." Amusement came through in her voice, loud and clear. She had known that, too. "You're bringing her in with you today, of course. She's too young to leave alone just yet. Besides, I think the store could use a cat for atmosphere, don't you?"

Relief swept through me. Thank goodness for soul connections. "I'll be in shortly."

"Take your time. I'll see you when I see you." And that was one of the things I loved about working for Liss.

Nothing ever fazed her. She didn't just go with the flow. The flow seemed to work *with* her. Always. She had so much positive energy and light in her personality and aura that anyone who came within her sphere was carried along for the ride.

"You know," Steff said as I clicked the button to end the call, "I really like your boss."

"Me, too," I beamed.

"In fact, I wish mine was more like her. Mine's had it in for me since someone let the cat out of the bag about me and Danny," she said with a gloomy grimace. Then she let out an unexpected yawn. "Whoa. I don't know where that came from."

"Looks like your lack of sleep is catching up with you."

"Looks like." She stood up, watching me as I gathered the things the kitten and I would need for what was left of the day.

Grabbing the kitten herself, a can of cat food, a spare dish, and the rest of the cat litter into a department store tote bag, I gave Steff a big hug. "Wish I could stay longer, but you wouldn't be awake for long anyway. Go on and get some sleep."

"Will do, Shamu." She grinned at our childhood rhyming game. I just rolled my eyes.

At the door, keys in hand, something made me pause and ask, "Steff . . . have you ever heard of a Dr. Dorffman?"

"Hm. I don't think so. There are a lot of doctors commuting between hospitals nowadays, though. Why do you ask?"

"No matter. No reason." And really, I didn't have a reason. Not one that I recognized. Only that Joel Turner's doctor's name was stuck in my head, and there was no earthly reason why.

In the car, I set the stuff down on the passenger seat but kept the kitten in my lap, despite the fact that I could already see several short black hairs dusting my thin sweater. She seemed supremely comfortable there. In fact, she wasn't budging. I looked down at her as I put my hands on the wheel and the gear shift, and I couldn't help giving her an adoring smile. Yes, I know, it was the first step down that steep and slippery path toward becoming a bona fide Crazy Cat Lady sometime in the distant future, but . . . how could I resist the pull? I was smitten.

How did this happen?

The trip across town was uneventful, the morning commute traffic having dwindled down to leave mostly soccer moms going to the grocery store or some of Stony Mill's elderly heading to various appointments around town. I had just hit the stoplight in front of the courthouse and was about to turn onto River Street when my cell phone rang. My sister's home number was displayed in the display window.

"Hi, Mel."

"Maggie, where were you? Why didn't you answer my call?"

The missed call . . . it must have been Mel. "Sorry about that. I overslept this morning, and—wait, is anything wrong? Where's Mom?"

"Downstairs with the girls."

"And everything's okay?"

"Yes, it's fine. Everything's quiet right now. Edgy, but quiet. But that's not what I'm calling about. You want to tell me what happened last night?"

She was Libby's friend. Of course it was perfectly natural for Libby to have sought solace by phoning her first thing.

I cleared my throat. "You mean the accident at the feed mill?"

"Libby called me last night, nearly incoherent. After all of the trouble that she and Joel had gone through to get their marriage back on the right track, something like this happens? No wonder she was beside herself."

I thought about this as I pulled into my usual parking spot in the alley behind the store. I tried to remember how Libby had looked when I'd left the Turners to their private grief. She'd seemed calm enough by then, but there was nothing like talking to a friend to break down all the carefully built walls, and before you know it, everything just comes tumbling out.

"She said she had seen you at the feed mill. After the accident."

"Yeah, it was pretty awful. Liss and I happened along at the wrong time, I guess."

"That's it? You didn't have any . . . intuition . . . or vision, or something . . . that led you there?"

"Nope. It was pure coincidence." Well, some people say there is no such thing, but Mel didn't need to know that.

"I knew it. I told Libby there wasn't any funny stuff behind you two showing up there, but I don't think she believed me. She seemed to think it was awfully strange coming upon you there. You know. Especially after what we found out about you and your boss . . . well, can you blame us for wondering?"

Actually, I couldn't. I must be mellowing. "Listen, Mel,

as long as everything's okay for now, I'm going to have to let you go. I need to get in to work."

"Oh. Okay. Should I call you if anything—you know— *odd* happens?"

"Definitely. And hopefully I'll have an answer for your problem today. Until then, hang tight."

Relieved, I pressed the End key before she could think of anything else. As always when I got off the phone with my sister, I felt as though all my energy had drained out through my feet. I didn't know why. Maybe it was just a deficit of my own quirky personality. I sighed deeply and turned to the kitten, who had gotten bored through my lack of attention and gone to sleep on the passenger seat. "Well, little one. If Liss hasn't given up on me entirely, maybe we could go in now, hm?"

I tucked her inside my purse again so that I could carry in her few necessities without making another trip. Her fuzzy head popped out the front end as I walked, sleep forgotten as she watched our progress with bright eyes. It amazed me that I already felt such a bond with this tiny bit of fluff and energy. She'd been in my life only around twelve hours now, and already I felt like a mom.

"There you are!" Liss said as I—*we*—came through the back door. She held out her arms to take the bag. "Here, why don't you give me that and bring the little dear in here. My goodness me, just look at her."

I grinned and held her aloft in both hands. "She is a beauty, isn't she?"

"She's brilliant. Here, I took it upon myself to have the hardware store send a few things over for her, things I thought she'd need while she's here in the store."

The few things, I could have sworn, turned out to be

half the cat supply aisle. Some of them were essentials—a litterbox, litter bags, the most expensive kind of cat food money could buy that wasn't freshly steamed chicken breast—while others, like the Krazy Kitty Kubicle set, probably were not. Though I was sure the kitten would be more than happy to put it to good use. She was already down on the floor, sniffing at all of her newfound booty.

Liss was happily unpacking things and setting them up where she thought they would get the most use. "I have always had an affinity for cats, you know," she remarked. Unnecessarily, I might add. Her feelings toward them were pretty hard to mistake.

I didn't remember seeing one at her house, The Gables, though. "Did you ever—"

"Oh, yes, of course! When I was younger. My mum and grandmum always said a house wasn't a home without a cat or three. White ones we always had. White cats are considered unlucky by some people back home, so there were always a goodly number of them lurking about, searching for food and a warm bed. Geoffrey was allergic, though, so we never had pets in our homes here."

I thought back, trying to remember how long Geoffrey had been gone. A couple of years now? I also couldn't help wondering why she hadn't offered to take the little fuzzball herself . . . although I was very glad now that she hadn't. "Why don't you get one now, to keep you company?" I asked her. "Or a puppy, or something?"

"What, you don't think Cecil is enough company for an old woman?" Liss remarked with a twinkle in her eye.

I'd forgotten about Cecil, an animal spirit Liss considered her family's totem protector, which had followed her all the way from the U.K. I had seen him once in her house, in the shape of a large black dog. "Maybe Cecil would like a little company," I suggested, not dissuaded at all. "Maybe Cecil is lonely, being so far away from his homeland."

She smiled, but I could tell I had gotten her thinking. "Perhaps."

A customer came in then, so I went up front to assist him while Liss entertained herself with our new feline friend.

"Maggie?" I heard her call as I counted out the gentleman's change. Sending him on his way with a wish for a wonderful anniversary, I watched him go and then popped my head between the curtains.

"Yes?"

Liss was seated on the floor, her long legs folded to one side, while she used the new Tickle Teaser to delight the kitten. Torture by feathers seemed to be the ultimate in kitty entertainment, if the rapt attention the kitten was lavishing upon her was clear indication. "What's her name?"

I stopped short. "Her name?"

She looked up at me. "You haven't named her?"

"I . . ." I cleared my throat. "Well, no. Not yet. I didn't even realize I was keeping her until this morning, and I guess I just didn't think that hard yet."

"There's no thinking to be done, ducks. She'll tell you herself."

I frowned slightly. "I don't follow."

"She convinced you she was yours soon enough, didn't she?"

"I guess she did, at that."

The smile Liss gave me was gentle. "Well, then, do you really think she'll not tell you her name?"

I thought about last night, and our interactions, however

brief, this morning. The kitten came over to me and nosed at my fingertips, its bristled pink tongue touching briefly there.

"Minx!" I said suddenly, startling myself, because I knew instantly that it was right. "I've been calling her Little Minx all night and all morning long." I scooped her up and held her aloft. "She looks like a minx, doesn't she. Sweetness and sass, all mixed together in one furry little package. Although . . ." I thought for a moment. "I almost think Minnie fits her better. As in, mini-Minx."

Liss chuckled. "Minnie, it is, then. Minx when we wish to be formal. What do you think, then, Minnie? Does that sound right to you?"

Minnie was too busy trying to squirm out of my hands to bother with a silly thing like names, especially when she had already conveyed hers to her utmost ability. I set her down and watched her dart around the floor.

"One thing's for certain: She'll definitely keep the shadows at bay," Liss commented approvingly.

I lifted my head. "What did you say?"

"She'll keep the shadows at bay. They are attracted to undisturbed centers of energy."

Like basements . . . Hmm. I was seeing a whole new reason to love my new fur-baby. "I didn't know that."

"As are other entities of the in-between world. Cats have long been revered by the ancients as the protectors that they truly are. Even a kitten can be enough of a shielding presence to convince them to manifest themselves elsewhere."

"What about regular human spirits?"

"Some say so. At the very least they're a kind of early warning system. They almost always sense them before we do."

Minnie, it would appear, was just what the doctor ordered. With her by my side, my apartment might actually become almost livable again. No more dark, scrambling shadows skulking about the peripherals. No more ominous closet creatures. We would have peace and world order again! I could kiss her.

Perhaps Stony Mill should consider taking a page from the ancients and become a cat-revering society, and just skip out on all of the spirit-infested antiques.

Just a thought.

I had gotten quite the late start to the day, but that didn't cut down on the number of things populating my growing To Do list. And first thing on my list was:

"I just talked to Mel," I told Liss as I checked the water levels in all of the makers up front. "She already knew about what happened to Joel Turner at the feed mill last night."

"Good news travels fast."

"Especially when you're part of Mel's crowd, which Libby most definitely is. She called her last night to give her the news."

"Speaking of your sister . . . I've asked Marcus to come into the store this afternoon so that we can discuss what the best approach would be; whether we'll need all of the N.I.G.H.T.S., or whether the three of us can handle the banishing of the dark entity."

Wait, what? "The three of us?" I questioned.

"Right, ducks. Well, I assume you'll want to be involved, since it's your sister we'll be helping."

Right. Yeah. That was a good point, actually.

And then I had another thought. Marcus was coming here. It would be the first time I had seen him in weeks.

And before I knew it, my traitorous heart skipped a beat.

I cleared my throat. "I might have to stop in to see Tom before I head over to Mel's this evening," I made myself say. The timing was intentional, but at least the excuse was a valid one. For one thing, I wanted to see what I could find out about the accident scene investigation. I know, I know, I was supposed to be minding my own business . . . but some things are easier said than done. There were a couple of things nagging me about the situation surrounding the Turners and the feed mill, the hanging of the dummy, and shadowy figure I felt sure I had seen there last night. Of course, it all could amount to a load of codswallop, but I would feel better just talking it out with him.

"That's all right, dear. Marcus and I will talk things through, we'll pull together all of the supplies we think we'll need, and then you can call us when things are ready on your end. How does that sound?"

So why was I feeling so uneasy all of a sudden?

Chapter 10

I had been planning to leave before Marcus arrived, but a final spate of browsers crossed that plan off the drawing board. I was just locking down the register and heading toward the front door to put out the CLOSED sign when I saw his motorcycle pull up to the curb. I froze, wondering whether I should turn around and hurry back behind the velvet curtain, avoiding him entirely, or whether I should meet him at the front door with an air of nonchalance and easiness as I never seemed able to master in his presence. Before I could decide, Marcus walked through the door.

Looking as dark and dangerous as ever with his motorcycle helmet dangling loosely from his fingertips and his leather boots scuffing against the plain wood floor, he was a sight to behold. Not to mention the errant waves escaping from the leather thong at the nape of his neck, and the trademark shades that he had hooked through the neck of his plain black T. Despite the heat and humidity, he was wearing a pair of dark jeans . . . although I had to say, I couldn't imagine him in a pair of shorts. Ever. They wouldn't look right with the boots. Boxers, maybe. Although to his credit, he didn't seem to be affected by the weather in the least. How could he look so cool and composed when I felt as bedraggled as a puppy left out in the rain? It wasn't fair. He probably wasn't even human. Maybe he was one of the In-Betweens that Liss had been talking about. A member of the Fae realm, come to tempt and seduce me with his otherworldly ways.

Yeah. Sure. There was no mistaking the kind of blood that ran hot and heavy though Marcus's veins, and it had nothing to do with the Fae. It was pure, Grade A male, and human all the way.

Funny, the sheer number of thoughts that could run through a girl's head in the space of a single breath. Heh.

He stopped when he saw me, and for a moment I thought I had seen his chest lift with a quick intake of breath, too. Then he gave a slight, lift-of-the-chin nod, and said, "Maggie."

Cool, calm, and collected. Good, good. I gave him a sweet but distant smile as I continued my whirlwind accumulation of my things. "Hey there, Marcus. Wow, it's good to see you. I wish I had known you were going to be here tonight, we could have chatted. As it so happens, I am on my way out."

"Yeah?"

"Mm-hmm. Plans and obligations. You know the drill." It was on the tip of my tongue to bring mention of Tom into the conversation, but in the end I couldn't do it. I couldn't use either of them as leverage against the other. I just couldn't.

Marcus nodded gamely. "Too bad. I haven't been around much." *Not that you've noticed.*

I heard the thought attached as clearly as if he'd stated it aloud, and I stuttered to a halt. Had he been expecting me to make the first move? I knew instinctively that I'd read him correctly, but . . . how? I *must* be imagining things. Projecting thoughts upon him. Or maybe I was reading something else. Body language and expression. Was that it?

I turned and looked at him, speculating. "Yes, we've both been busy, it seems." And in my head, I thought, *But perhaps that's for the best.*

For now . . .

His thought response came as instantaneously as my own. I pretended not to have picked up on it, but it was hard when my pulse made a shockingly immediate leap in response.

Down, girl. Down!

What was going on? I wasn't a mind-reader. Was I really picking up on his thoughts telepathically? I couldn't be. It just wasn't possible. An empath I might be, but that was all. Wasn't it?

I really needed to take back control of my life.

And I was about to do just that when Minnie attacked . . .

By soaring from the uppermost shelf, where she had somehow managed to climb unnoticed, in a fearless arc straight to Marcus's shoulders. I giggled, having served as her target myself many times throughout the afternoon— rarely had she let me out of her sight. But Marcus was at a slight disadvantage. Seeing only a black flash in his peripheral vision that then caught and held through the thin material of his T-shirt, he froze. "Um, what is it?" he asked carefully.

Minnie answered the question herself, balancing effortlessly on her tiptoes as she leaned over and chirped a teeny, tiny meow in his ear.

"Marcus, meet Minnie. Minnie, this is Marcus. I'm sure you two will become fabulously acquainted very soon."

"I think we're becoming acquainted already," Marcus said with a nervous laugh as Minnie began to lick his ear. "If this was some other female, I might actually be turned on right about now."

I turned away with flaming cheeks, because it was too close to a dream sequence I'd had a couple of weeks ago that had filled me with guilt—which was really too bad, too, because it had been a hellaciously good dream.

Tom, I reminded myself. Time to go.

Was it wrong of me to want to give Tom a real chance before I allowed myself to lose focus for another guy? Not that that was my intention. To lose focus, I mean.

"Then again," Marcus said, following behind me, "it has been quite a long time."

"Oh?" I asked, trying not to seem interested, and thinking it was probably better that I get out of there ASAP. "Not seeing anyone right now?"

"No. There was this girl," he replied, "but here I am . . . still waiting."

Really. Time. To. Go.

I turned to face him, to tell him good-bye. He had taken Minnie down from his shoulders and he was now holding her on her back, cradled against him in his big hands as he might cradle a newborn child, while he scratched her chin and belly. And from the way she was melting in his grasp, her head lolled back and her oversized hind feet gone limp, you just knew it was good.

"I think she likes me."

Minnie. He was talking about Minnie. "So I see." And then, "Listen, I have to go."

"Right. Yeah." He followed behind me again as I stowed the antique jewelry from the front window in the safe. "So, what's this I hear about the owner of the feed mill? You and Liss been at it again?"

"At what?"

"Fortuitous coincidence. Right place, right time."

"Well, I prefer to think of it as being in the wrong place at the wrong time, but . . . I suppose you could say that."

"I know Noah Turner," Marcus remarked. "He used to come into the bar that the band was playing regularly, over in Saint Edmunds. Drinking to beat the Devil, but he never picked up on any of the women who wanted to go home with him. Talk was he might be gay."

"Gay, really? I didn't get that vibe. I thought he was just . . . oh, I don't know . . . more yuppie than gay. Definitely out of place at the feed mill, though, with his expensive loafers. Miles of personality between him and his brother Frank. So, heavy drinker, huh? What about Joel? Did you know him?"

He shook his head. "Nope. Heard plenty about him today, though."

"Yeah? Like what?"

"Like he was considered a hard-ass by most of the farming community. Tightfisted, greedy, coldhearted sonuvabitch. Word is, the accident couldn't have happened to a nicer fellow."

"Yeah, well, one of those saintly, salt-o'-the-earth farmers strung up an effigy from the conveyer system two days before Joel had his little accident. Left it there for him to find with a warning tacked to its chest. And Turner's wife said they'd been receiving threatening phone calls at home. She said Joel had installed a security system there to keep her safe."

Marcus nodded thoughtfully. "Wouldn't surprise me, actually. Farmers are, by and large, a tough lot. Stoic, you know? It takes a lot to move them, but one way that's guaranteed is by hitting 'em below the belt—the money belt. From what everyone is saying, the big upgrades Turner made out there at the feed mill were being billed to the farmers, lock, stock, and barrel, one load of grain at a time, and there wasn't a one of them who was willing to forgive and forget. Especially with the buyout of all the other feed mills . . ."

"They felt they had no other options," I finished for him, chewing my lip thoughtfully.

He nodded. "The timing of this accident was stellar. Who knows what might have happened otherwise?"

There was that niggling feeling again. I really wished it would go away and leave me alone.

Marcus handed over Minnie. "You were going, remember? Places to go, people to see?"

"Yeah." Our hands brushed, featherlight, as I took the snoozing kitten from him, but I successfully ignored the contact. At least, on the surface. "Thanks."

Liss came through the curtain just then, and I pulled back to a safer distance. "Oh, is the little darling asleep again? I see you've met our new mascot, Marcus. Isn't she a dear?" Before Marcus could respond, she turned to me. "Maggie, I thought you would have been off already."

"I was just going."

I tucked Minnie into the fancy soft-sided carrier that Liss had so thoughtfully purchased—the little furball would really be stylin' in this baby—and grabbed my things before heading out the door. Between the mental nudges from On High that I didn't want, and the physical nudges from Marcus that I really kinda-sorta did, I couldn't help feeling like I was on the run. From myself.

Guilt has always been a terrific motivator. I'd been on the receiving end of it a lot growing up, and it would appear that it was still capable of meting out its special kind of magic on me. I started beating myself up about Marcus the instant the door closed behind me. Chiding, castigating, chastising, up one side of the issue and down the other. And you know what? In this one instance, the guilt was well earned. Why couldn't I make up my mind? I wasn't the type of girl to rattle a man's cage just because I was on the outside, free as a bird to fly from this cage to the next. I never had been. So why now?

A honeybee flits from blossom to blossom, Margaret. It makes sweet honey, but it never finds the perfect flower to assuage its hunger. Better to stick close to the hive.

Consciences. Always a good source of confusion. I mean, wisdom.

A kitten toys with a mouse for hours before ending the play forever.

Well, at least that was slightly more on point. But it wasn't necessary. I was perfectly capable of hauling myself over the coals over my lack of focus.

To that end, I headed immediately for the police department, where I thought I would be able to find Tom . . . assuming he wasn't out on the road somewhere, in which case I would leave him a message to call me when he was free.

I was in luck. His squad car was parked before the low-slung brick building, front and center. I parked in an open space across the street and grabbed Minnie's carrier case from the passenger seat to take with me. I didn't know what the PD's policy on animals was, but she was fully contained, I reasoned, and there was no way I was leaving her in the hot car.

My intention was to head immediately for the dispatch desk to ask for Tom, but I never made it there. I opened the door, stepped inside, and stopped short. Tom was standing in the center of the sparsely furnished lobby, in all his uniformed glory, with two men. One, a smallish young man he had evidently taken into custody. Upon closer inspection, the man wasn't as young as I had first assumed owing to his small stature. His face was lined at the eyes and mouth, and grubby with grizzled whiskers—but not as grubby as his clothes, which were liberally streaked with something that looked like mud but didn't smell anywhere near that clean. He stood by with saucered eyes as witness to the full-fledged discussion going on before him between Tom and Man Number Two.

Frank Turner.

Oddly enough, none of them paid any attention to me.

"Frank, I understand your concern for Eddie here. But there was a report duly filed, and as such we have no choice but to bring him in for questioning. Especially under the circumstances. I know I don't have to spell that out for you, what with the concerns you shared with me last night."

"A report of what?" Frank demanded, and in that moment of stubbornness I could see the Turner family resemblance even more clearly.

"You know very well what. Trespassing on private property. Possible break-in. And with everything else that's going on out there, maybe more."

"That's bullshit, Tom."

A muscle ticked in Tom's jaw, but as a cop he'd dealt with far worse. Besides, restraint was his middle name. "Bullshit, is it? The report came from your quarter."

Frank flinched, but seemed to know what to expect when he asked, "Who?"

"You need to get with your sister-in-law to compare notes."

"Libby."

"Yeah."

All the fight eased from Frank's bulwark shoulders to be replaced with resignation. "I probably shouldn't say this, but I think you'll understand. Libby's under a whole lot of strain right now."

"There have been other reports of Eddie being seen in the vicinity several times after the feed mill was closed. It's not just Mrs. Turner."

Frank looked back and forth between Tom and the worried-looking man standing docilely beside him, waiting for his next order. I didn't know who Eddie was, but his fear and uncertainty were unmistakably compelling.

"Eddie had a reason for being at the feed mill after hours," Frank said at last.

Tom stopped and gazed at him more closely. "And what might that reason have been?"

Frank's jaw clenched and unclenched. Then he blew his breath out in one long exhale. "He had my permission."

A cold wind swept through my mind as worry and suspicion blew into my soul. More niggles. Tom was being awfully serious for someone who'd told me just last night that sometimes an accident was just an accident. It made me think that maybe, just maybe, he'd been saying that to keep me from guessing the truth. Which was sneaky, if you asked me, but a method of protection I might have employed myself, given the right circumstances.

"Your permission."

Frank gave a curt nod. "Yeah."

Tom inhaled deeply, his gaze distant as he turned his head a moment to stare out the plate glass windows, still not registering my presence. "I know you're a Turner, Frank, but I was under the impression that the feed mill was owned solely by your brother Joel. That how you see it?"

"Yeah. Joel bought it from my dad when the cancer hit and Dad needed money. Paid him top dollar for it, too," he said approvingly, as though he wanted us all to know there had been no family squabbles over ownership of the business that carried their name. "That place was Joel's life. He slaved over it, night and day. It was his doing that made the place what it is today. Pure and simple."

Tom took this into consideration. "Did Eddie work for your brother in some capacity?"

"No. He'd helped us out before—shoveling out the holding barns and stuff—but things have been pretty tight lately, what with all the renovations and upgrades, and the mill buyouts, o'course. Joel had to cut back where he could."

"Then you won't mind me asking what reason Eddie could have had for being on the property after hours, with your permission."

Frank stuffed his hands in the front pouch of his overalls, but said nothing.

Tom tried a different tack. "You were older than your brother, weren't you, Frank?"

"What's that got to do with anything?"

"No animosity toward him? No bruised feelings that your dad sold the feed mill to your younger brother rather than you?"

From Frank emerged a wry half-laugh. "Hell, I couldn't have afforded it anyway. My ex-wife saw to that. And the responsibility of all those people . . . it was never my thing. Nah, it was better that Joel had it. I worked for him, and it suited me just fine. In my mind, I got the best of both worlds. I got to work at the place I loved, without all the headaches of ownership. Not that managing the livestock department wasn't important to the feed mill, but . . . well, there it is," he summed up what for him as a man of obviously few words must have amounted to a monologue.

"And what about now that he's gone?" Tom asked him. "Ownership would go to the wife, I'm assuming, unless the will says otherwise. She doesn't look the type to want to run the place herself. Who'll do it with Joel gone?"

Frank looked at Tom as though he had two heads. "You saying what I think you're saying? You think I had something to do with my brother's death?" His eyes flashed, cold steel. "My own brother?"

"I'm not saying anything of the kind," Tom stated evenly. "I'm just offering up things that might need to be thought about."

"Well, that's what it sounded like to me. And I'll tell you what, just so's you know. Family is family, and blood is blood, and there ain't no one who's gonna be accusing me of not standing by my own." The tersely spoken words cut through the thinly veiled accusation that was a part of any investigation, laying his position clearly on the line.

"And Eddie?" Tom asked quietly. "How does he fit into all of this? Come on, Frank. You said you gave him permission. Permission for what?" When Frank didn't answer, Tom pivoted Eddie gently toward the door to the jail intake area and began to punch in the security access code.

"Wait."

Tom's hand hovered over the digital display.

"He had my permission to be there . . . because he needed a place to stay for a little while. The home he was assigned to wouldn't let him in because there was some bungle at state level and no one was paying, so I told him he could stay at the feed mill until they got it all worked out. He doesn't have anyone, you see. Family's all gone. There's a spare storage room in the barn where the bulk of the payloaders and other equipment's kept, up on the mezzanine. I just . . . put him up there with an air mattress, even though he spends most of the time with the hogs in the holding pen. And I've been making sure he was getting enough to eat. I knew Joel wouldn'ta minded."

Suddenly I understood why Frank had been doing all the talking while Eddie stood by looking scared and uncertain. Eddie was . . . *special*. And just as suddenly, I was seeing rough-edged Frank in a whole new light. Sometimes angels come in the most unusual packages.

Tom got Eddie's attention. "Is that true? You've been staying at the feed mill, nights?"

Eddie's saucered eyes focused, unblinking and scared, on Tom's face before flickering in Frank's direction and then back again. He nodded.

"You're sure?" Tom persisted.

Eddie opened his mouth, closed it, then opened it again. "I take care of the cats. I like cats. You like cats?" He darted a glance in Frank's direction again with a lift of his brows as though to ask, *Is that all right? Did I do good?*

Frank nodded his approval. The set of his mouth was grim, but his voice was gentle-gruff. "We like cats, Eddie." He lifted his gaze to Tom. "Eddie's a bit of a Pied Piper with animals. Hogs. Cows. They all follow him around like he was Jesus. But I guess he likes cats best. We get loads of cats out at the feed mill during the night. Joel never minded 'em, because they kept the rats and mice at bay."

R-rats? Ehhhh . . . Still, that would explain the presence of Minnie in the steel culvert.

Tom seemed to have made up his mind. He turned away from the intake door and turned the two men toward the office. "I'd like to talk to you both more, if that's all right with you?"

Frank assessed him carefully. Satisfied with what he saw in Tom's face, he gave him a brief nod. "Come on, Eddie. The police officer would like to ask us a few more questions. That okay with you?"

"You'll be there?" Eddie asked.

"Yeah. Right there with you."

"Okay. Say, you got any chocolate? I got a real hankering for some chocolate. My ma always used to make chocolate cookies. Real good ones. You got any cookies?"

Tom guided them through the office door the dispatcher had buzzed open for them. "First door on the right. You'll find chairs right there." To Frank, he muttered under his breath, "You'll also find a couple of candy bars in the upper-right-hand drawer."

Frank gave him the first real smile I'd seen since I walked through the door. "Thanks." He clapped Tom on the shoulder.

Tom didn't follow them. Instead he let the office door relock itself before he turned to me where I was still standing frozen in the front entry.

I held up a hand and waved. "Hey, stranger."

"Hey, yourself."

"Sorry—I didn't mean to barge in on all of that."

"It's okay. I knew you were there."

Knew it, and was okay with it, his eyes seemed to say. I relaxed a little bit.

"What's in the cooler? Dinner?"

My gaze followed the path his had taken, toward my right hand. I laughed. "Um, not dinner. I have a new friend." I lifted the soft-sided carrier so that he could peep in at Minnie, who was sleeping soundly away.

Tom raised his brows. "First the dog, and now this. You have a real thing for animals, don't you."

"She needed rescuing," I said simply.

"Ah. So you have a thing for rescuing those in need, hm?"

I heard the undertone in his voice change to one of seduction, and I grinned. "Kind of."

"After the other night, I've been thinking I could use a little rescuing," he suggested. He glanced over his shoulder at the dispatcher, but she had her eyes focused intently on the multiple data screens in front of her and was speaking into her headset while her fingers danced across the keyboard. He leaned closer to me, his breath moving my hair, and whispered, "And I'm most definitely someone in need."

"Well," I whispered back, mere centimeters from his ear, "that's going to present a problem, considering that you have two people waiting for you in there, and I have three people waiting for me at Mel's. Remember? My ailing sister?"

It wasn't a new problem for us, by any means. In fact, it was probably our biggest holdup in the larger scheme of things, relationshipwise. This was early days for us. Time for getting-to-know-you. Time to put each other first, to delight in each other's company, completely and utterly. It really wasn't supposed to be this hard to get together. At least, I didn't think it was.

Tom sighed and backed off. "Spoilsport."

"I'm sorry. You know I would like nothing better . . . but duty calls for both of us."

"And you're a taskmaster, too."

I held up the cat carrier again. "Say good night, Minnie."

"And now you have me talking to your cat, too. Will it never end? Good night, Minnie."

"Be sure to let me know how things go with Frank and Eddie, 'kay?"

"Don't know that I can share much, but . . . Hey, why did you come in just now? Did you need something?"

"I just wanted to see you. And"—because I had decided honesty was the best policy in dealing with a man who placed such a high premium on the rules—"I was wondering whether anything had changed with regards to Joel Turner's death. Whether it was still being investigated as an accident or not."

Tom looked back over his shoulder, but the dispatcher was still involved with her call. "There's been nothing definitive either way. Some things aren't really adding up for us, so until the medical examiner's decision is filed, we're taking it all in, as much as possible."

His conversation with Frank and Eddie had provided that much information. "What things aren't adding up?" I asked him.

He gave me his look, that special look that told me I was pushing too far.

"Well, you don't have to tell me," I said, the height of innocence, "but I do have connections to the Turner family through my sister, and . . . well . . . maybe I can help. Sometimes people give out more information to their friends and peers than they think."

He seemed to consider this. "Might have nothing to do with the Turners at all, when all is said and done," he reminded me, "but . . . yeah. Okay."

"You'll call me?"

"Yeah. Later."

Well, at least there was *something* to be looking forward to. And at least I knew he was at least willing to, maybe, possibly, be a little bit open to whoever or whatever might come forward in relation to Joel's death. Which was a very good thing, given the niggling little nudges I'd been receiving all day every time I thought about the accident. Spirit nudges. An accident that was no accident? That was what I was most afraid of. And I couldn't get one particular, meaningless detail out of my head and had no explanation as to why.

"Tom . . ."

He paused at the locked door. "Yeah?"

"This is probably nothing, and I don't even know why I'm telling you, except . . . well. I don't know. I went into the feed mill office with the Turners the night Joel was found, and I accidentally happened to see Joel's desk calendar. And . . . well . . . like I said, it's probably meaningless, but . . . Joel Turner had two appointments with the same doctor this month. Dr. Dorffman. It was on his desk calendar. Maybe you should ask the Turners about them? If he had a serious medical problem, maybe it wasn't an accident. Maybe it was . . . well . . . a suicide. You never know."

His brows quirked together, but his face remained otherwise impassive. "Okay. Sure, yeah. Thanks for the tip."

Chapter 11

Minnie and I made our way to Mel's house once I left the PD. Well, I did. Minnie just snoozed and yawned and stretched her way there. I didn't know how Mel would feel about me bringing Minnie along, but beggars cannot be choosers. Besides, after what Liss had told me about the effects cats can have on the darker spirits out there, perhaps Mel should think about adopting one herself.

Mom was in the kitchen, waiting for me. "There you are!" she said. "I thought maybe I was on my own tonight after all."

"Sorry," I told her, setting the carrier down on a chair. "I needed to stop in to see Tom before I came over."

Instantly her annoyance left her. "Oh. Oh, well, that's fine, dear. Whatever you need to do is fine with me, of course. You know that."

Yeah, I knew that. If it meant I had a boyfriend (i.e. potential husband material) that she approved of, I could get away with murder. So to speak. Mom's goals for us kids had turned out to be fairly simple. Raise us to be good Catholics, who would marry other good Catholics and then very quickly have children who would of course be raised to be—you guessed it—good Catholics. Elevating the family's status in Stony Mill society was a secondary plan that followed neatly in line with the first. It wasn't a bad plan; just slightly suffocating. My older brother, Marshall, had escaped her watchful eye by making a bid for freedom and autonomy in New York City, which had the unfortunate side effect of focusing Mom even more intently on my life. Especially since Mel had married her college sweetheart the weekend after graduation and immediately set off on fulfilling the details of my mother's master plan down to the minute. I, on the other hand, had disappointed Mom at every turn by leaving school without a degree, by breaking up with a fiancé owing to technical difficulties, and even by avoiding the Church she loved so well because my heart just wasn't in it. I think she had almost given up on me entirely when I started seeing Tom. In her mind, I think we were already well on the way to the altar and Babyland. And what she didn't know . . . would keep me out of the doghouse.

There really was something to be said for a breakdown in communication.

"What have you got there?" Mom asked.

I showed her Minnie.

"Oh, how sweet. But did you have to choose black, dear? I mean, I suppose that is just superstition, but sometimes I think it's better not to tempt fate."

I had never really taken notice of my mother's superstitions before. Or maybe I had viewed them as an offshoot of her religious convictions. "I didn't choose her. She chose me."

Mom gave me a sidelong glance. "Don't be silly, Margaret. She's a cat. Beings without souls do not choose. They simply act based on the instincts God gave them."

There would be no arguing with her, so I didn't even try. How could I explain that even in the space of a single day, Minnie had shown a very special affinity to me? That she had followed me around the store, preferring to be in my sphere over all others, and that she would watch me, her jewel-toned eyes bright and happy whenever I looked in her direction? That she seemed to be trying to communicate?

"Where are the girls?" I asked instead as I took Minnie out of the carrier. Immediately she scrambled up my arms and took up her perch on my shoulders.

"Well, I never . . ." Mom's eyes were focused on the kitten. "Oh, the girls? They just left. They have a double dance class tonight. Margo Craig offered to take them with her daughter. With everything going on right now with your sister, Margo thought it best that their lives were disrupted as little as possible."

I nodded. "That was . . . nice." When it came to Margo, that was a supremely difficult admission for me to make, but the truth is the truth.

"Mm. Anyway, they won't be home until eight-thirty." Mom gathered up her bulging purse, an equally bulging tote bag, and her latest reading material, Agatha Christie's *Sleeping Murder*. My mom was a big aficionado of Dame Agatha. She must have read each of the books at least five times, but she still found enjoyment in the simple truths Christie put forth: That nothing was as it might seem, and yet everything made perfect sense. That the only truth was the one that facts supported. That people always have reasons, right or wrong, for the things that they do. And that no matter how much people lied, or tried to hide, the truth, eventually it would come out in the most mysterious of ways.

Come to think of it, no wonder she liked them. Considering the events of the last eight months, maybe I should reread some of them myself. I could use a bit of reassurance that good would prevail.

"Mel is waiting for you upstairs," Mom was saying. "She's been itching to see you all afternoon. I think the exile of her condition is getting to her. She's been worrying constantly about noises, and she's been just a bit overprotective of her things. This morning she yelled at Greg for moving a water bottle, because she knew she'd put it on the bedside table and when she turned to get it, it wasn't there."

"Yes, well, too much solitude is never good for a person." No way I was going to tell Mom what had happened and what we were planning to do about it. Some things are better left unsaid. "I'll just go on up."

Mom nearly beamed at me. "You do that. Thank you, dear. You've been such a big help this week."

Was that approval I heard in her voice? Verifiable approval? Real, honest-to-goodness approval? Would wonders never cease.

"Tell Dad and Grandpa G hello for me," I said as I hurried her out the door, eager to get a move on with everything that was going to have to be done.

Minnie had draped her body across my shoulder like some kind of small, furry parrot, which was surprisingly comfortable and actually quite handy as it left both of my hands free to do other things. Mom had already tidied the entire downstairs in the girls' absence, and the kitchen was spotless. I scouted around, making sure all was in order before heading up the stairs to Mel.

The intercom buzzed at me. "Maggie, is that you?" There was the slightest edge of nervousness to Mel's voice.

I walked over to the control panel and pushed the Talk button. "Yes, it's me. I'm just finishing things up down here, and I was thinking about throwing a load of laundry in for you—"

"No, don't go down in the basement," she said, urgency coming through loud and clear. "Just come upstairs. I've been having the most horrible feelings all day. Like hot flashes, but that's not it at all. More like . . . like a panic attack. And can I just say, I have been stuck in my bedroom all day *with this thing*, whatever it is, breathing at me. Mom thinks I've gone crazy. At least you know the truth."

"Whoa, whoa, whoa. Back up a moment. Feelings, you said?"

"Yes. Haven't you been listening to me, Maggie? It's not just my fear speaking. I've been *stuck here* with these god-awful *feelings* and with the *breathing thing* that is in *my bedroom*. Do you understand? *Capisce? Savvy?*"

"I've got it, I've got it." Feelings. Mel had never had feelings before. I know that probably sounds odd, but it was true. She wasn't the type. She had always been one of the most self-involved, self-absorbed people I knew, completely convinced that she was the undisputed center of her universe and that the rest of us were there to make her look good and feel good about herself. Feelings would have been in direct conflict with her goals of looking and feeling the best about herself that she could. Feelings about anything else would have made her vulnerable. Like all the rest of us.

There was, of course, one exception to her no-feelings rule. Well, two. Three, if you counted the little one in her belly. When it came to her children, Mel was fierce.

"Liss is ready to come over to do the house clearing," I told her. At least I hoped she was. I knew she and Marcus were to have been discussing a plan. I just hoped their efforts had been fruitful.

"Tonight?"

"Yes. As long as that's okay with you."

"Well . . . yeah. Of course, tonight would be great. I mean, well, I don't *think* Greg is going to be back early. He never is lately. And the girls *are* out at a double dance class with Margo, so . . . yeah, I guess that's okay."

She's hesitating. The thought came to me out of the blue. But why the hesitation? This was what she had wanted. Maybe it was just cold feet. Uncertainty over the unknown. Yes, that was probably it. She'd seen the same horror movies I'd seen throughout our teenage years. They were good about spreading fear and uncertainty through an audience looking for a cheap thrill. Maybe she was afraid the situation would get out of hand. She didn't know Liss like I did, and even I was a little nervous about watching the banishing of an unknown entity.

"All right, then. I'll give Liss a call and let her know that it's okay to come on over. Don't worry about a thing," I told her. "We'll take care of everything. And I'll be up in a minute."

Keeping one hand on Minnie to prevent her from

toppling when I bent over, I retrieved my cell phone from
the bag I'd left in the kitchen and connected with Liss's.

"Hello, ducks," came Liss's warm voice over the airwaves. "Right on schedule. Is everything good to go?"

"Good to go," I confirmed, giving her a thumbs-up that
she couldn't see. "Er, is everything set on that end?"

"Absolutely. We've gathered everything we think we'll
need to get the job done. Although . . . the spirit isn't entirely human in my estimation, so the results are a bit . . .
uncertain. We may need to do this more than once."

Not entirely human. Oy. I hoped Mel learned her les-
son from this. No more dabbling!

To Liss, I said, "Is there anything you'll need me to do
before you get here?"

"Look out the window, ducks. We've just arrived."

"How . . ." I was about to ask the question that always
popped into my head whenever her psychic sense kicked
into high gear, as evidenced by her amazing ability to
read my thoughts and act on them . . . and then I decided
it was a moot point. Instead, I walked to the kitchen door,
opened it, and waved at the black Lexus parked in the
drive. "Never mind. Come on in."

Liss came first, with Marcus on her heels. He was carrying a medium-sized gift bag, promisingly chockablock, by
the satin ribbon handles. A bit incongruous, as images go,
but hey, I'd take him. Er, I mean, *it*.

Liss gave my shoulder a reassuring pat as she passed
by, taking an extra moment to scratch Minnie behind the
ears. Marcus paused in the doorway and cast an amused
glance down at me. "If the cat was a dead fox, you'd look
just like my Great-Aunt Lucinda."

I reached up and hugged Minnie to me, covering her far

ear with my hand. "Don't listen to him, Minnie. He didn't mean to compare you to a dead fox. It just slipped out."

I was relieved when he continued on into the kitchen. The doorway was just a little too small for the both of us to stand comfortably within.

"Shall we go on up?" Liss asked.

I nodded. "Mel's waiting for us. The girls are out of the house for now, and Greg—her husband," I explained to Marcus, "isn't expected home anytime soon. But I'd still feel better if we hurried. Just to be on the safe side."

"Right-o, ducks. Coming, Marcus?"

"Right behind you."

I led the way up the stairs. As it had that first night, the very air seemed to swell and grow thick the farther we climbed.

"I feel it, too," Marcus muttered behind me, demonstrating that he, too, was no slacker in the intuitive abilities department.

"It knows we're here," said Liss.

She might have been announcing the weather, for all the concern she injected into the words. I, on the other hand, could feel my nervousness ramping up. *Deep breaths, Maggie,* I told myself. *You're in good hands here. And so is Mel.*

Melanie was sitting up in bed, waiting for us. Her eyes were as big as I'd ever seen them. "It's here, isn't it?" she asked me as I came through the door. "It is. I can feel it."

I sat down on the bed beside her. As though she sensed a person in need, Minnie immediately leapt from my shoulders, down onto Mel's lap. Settling herself into a compact shape with her feet tucked beneath her body, she began to purr. The sound was somehow reassuringly normal in the cold strangeness of the room.

Mel looked down at the kitten, confusion puckering her brow. "What—"

"Cats are a wonderful protective presence," I explained to her, echoing what Liss had told me. "This is Minnie."

"Oh. Okay." Without further protest, she tucked her hands into Minnie's soft fur. Minnie closed her eyes, but her ears were moving constantly, quirking and cocking in all directions as though tracking the movement of something that was in the room with us. I turned and looked, but I didn't see anything. It didn't matter. *It* was there.

As though It had been waiting for us.

Chapter 12

Marcus walked into the room slowly, but with a calm sense of strength that emanated from his stance, the lift of his head, his very pores. Liss headed straight for the table in front of the window and began unloading the things from the gift bag Marcus had toted in.

"It's strongest here," Marcus said quietly to Liss.

She nodded. "Sage, for purification. Lavender, for protection. Candles, for the quarters. An elements infusion, for anointing the doors and windows. Salt to consecrate the space. Herbal packets, to tuck away as blessings. And patchouli incense."

I had been listening to her run down her laundry list of supplies, trying to make sense of them through all that I'd learned thus far. "Patchouli incense . . . for power?" I asked hesitantly.

"Well, that . . . and because it smells lovely." And she laughed. "Sometimes, the key to summoning the Light back into a place that darkness has chosen to invade can be quite simple. As simple as filling the room with pleas-antries and our own energies. Things that make us happy and that are filled with good thoughts. With a bit of luck, that's how it will be today."

That sounded a bit more basic than I was expecting, so it would be interesting to see what went down.

The last thing she placed on the table was a glass that she had filled with water from the tap in Melanie's bath-room.

Mel had been eyeing Marcus up and down with open curiosity, so while Liss finished up, I played hostess with the mostess. "Mel, have you met Marcus? Marcus Quinn, this is my sister, Mel."

"Melanie Craven," she clarified with a distant nod, fold-ing her hands primly in her lap, overtop the purring kitten. She was playing her favorite queen bee role again, right down to the fussy bedjacket and prissy attitude. "I take it you're one of the Ghostbusters, Mr. Quinn?"

"At your service."

"Ah. Well, you definitely look the part."

I groaned, because Mel's complete lack of tact had raised its ugly head yet again, and it was so uncalled-for . . . but Marcus just gave her a lazy smile. "I'll take that as a compliment."

"Don't mind my sister, Marcus," I apologized, sending her a warning glare. "Pregnancy sometimes scrambles a woman's brains."

"I'm perfectly capable of excusing myself, Maggie."

As we'd all noticed. *Just another pregnancy pass moment*, I reminded myself, gritting my teeth.

Liss saved the moment, as usual. "Are we ready, then?"

So soon? I felt a quiver pass through my body. Fear of the unknown is such a powerful thing.

Marcus caught Liss's eye. "What do you think. Sky-clad?"

Naked? My breath caught in the back of my throat, and I choke-coughed. Holy sheep. I'd not yet witnessed a sky-clad ritual, but I'd heard of them. Not that the thought of Marcus in a clothing-challenged state hadn't at least crossed my mind (or was that *double-crossed*? *Hmm . . .*), but I wasn't certain that I was ready for it. At least, not with an audience.

"Or not." Marcus laughed. He hadn't missed a thing. "Sorry, Maggie. Just a little witchy humor."

"Witchy?" Mel hadn't missed a thing either. She looked at Liss and Marcus, and then back at me. "Wait. You . . . you don't mean . . ."

"Oh, didn't Maggie tell you?" Liss asked, innocently enough.

I cleared my throat before Mel could get on a roll. "Well, that's not important right now. What's important is getting to work to get rid of this thing that Mel invited into her home."

Miracle of all miracles, Mel closed her mouth. Apparently, she agreed with me.

Marcus clapped his hands together. "Good, then let's get this show on the road."

"Maggie, you sit there on the bed with Melanie. What I want you two to do is quite simple," Liss told us. "You will be in your own protective circle, to ensure Mel's safety. I want you to hold each other's hands and focus all of your thoughts and intentions and energies into the positive.

Whatever it takes, you do it. Imagine it pouring in from above, surrounding you, filling you. *Feel* it. And when I call for you to, I want you to consciously push it out and up from you, sending it to the skies and clear out into the universe. And then, my dears, I want you to listen for me to give you any further instruction. Does that make sense to you?"

We both nodded, our eyes wide and solemn. Mel, I thought, was probably just too boggled to disagree, but I knew enough to be able to guide her through the motions if needed. "Do we need to turn off the lights?" I asked, unable to keep the tremor from my voice.

Liss shook her head. "This is not a séance. What we want is to fill the room with as much light and lightness of being as we can. Right, then. Marcus?"

He appeared beside her, the container of salt in his hand. At Liss's command, he drew a circle around the bed, continuing it along the wall behind the headboard. Beside me I saw Mel's mouth open in protest. I squeezed her hand fiercely and whispered, "I will vacuum!" She shut her mouth again.

"All right, you two," Liss said. "Begin to fill your circle with light. Just as I described."

When she was satisfied with the progression of our efforts, she took the salt from Marcus and set it down with everything else on her makeshift altar, then took his hands and looked deep into his eyes.

"Together we do this, without fear, our hearts beating perfectly as one," she intoned, her voice quiet but clear.

"Together we do this," came Marcus's strong reply, "our strength in our binding of ourselves to one another. In Magick and in Light, we are two halves of a perfect whole."

As I watched, he leaned forward then and kissed Liss

lightly but lingeringly on her soft mouth. And a pang of emotion struck me, against my will. My breath caught in my throat again for the second time in ten minutes. Thank goodness no one heard me.

I couldn't look away. Next to me, Mel stirred, and I felt a sudden jolt of her fear. Her hands gripped mine tighter. I scarcely registered it, even as her wedding rings bit into me, because by then I had realized that cold, cold air was pouring into the room—the Otherkind was gaining strength again. Circling us all, testing us, as though It had decided that whatever Liss and Marcus planned to do might be apart from Its liking.

Circling us as though considering Its next move.

I redoubled my efforts, projecting with every ounce of my being. Liss and Marcus were completely involved with their actions as they calmly and without urgency continued with the ritual.

Marcus took the salt and, using the window as a starting point, drew a large, room-sized circle on the floor, falling just shy of the bed. "Widdershins we cast our circle round," Marcus intoned as he went around the room in the counter-clockwise direction of banishings, "as we mark the boundaries of this space between the world of spirit and the world of the living. Lady of the Silver Moon, Goddess of Ten Thousand Names, protect us within this circle. Keep safe all who gather here in your name, and in the name of the God, your consort and partner in life, in death, in Light, and Shadow, in chaos, and in balance. In your name we ask for shelter within the bower of your embrace."

Liss placed the white candles at equal quarter-points around their circle. She touched them with a match, each in turn, and continued the chant. "By the earth that is Her body, by the air that is Her breath, by the fire of Her bright spirit, and by the living waters of Her womb, our circle is cast. None shall come to harm here, by any forces, on any level."

The flames leaped high, higher than was normal, twisting and darting about with the energies testing the circle.

Liss and Marcus turned toward each other and locked gazes as they finalized the circle. "As we will it, so shall it be done. As we will it, so mote it be."

The air in the room had grown heavier still. My skin was tingling, every hair on my arms and the back of my neck standing at attention.

They were holding hands again, facing each other. Marcus closed his eyes, but Liss's gaze never wavered from his face. His head fell back on his shoulders, his shining dark hair reaching to just between his shoulder blades. His breathing slowed, his chest rising and falling deeply with each effort. I watched them both, fascinated, and more than a little scared. What was he doing? He looked as though he was reaching out, searching . . .

"We were wrong . . ." he said at last, each word coming with difficulty. "It is . . . *was* . . . human. At some point in time. He was strong. Tyrannical. He . . . killed many. Many warriors. He was a soldier. No regrets. It was his job to do so. And yet . . . what the priests tell us . . . what will be waiting? He has never crossed over. 'Tis better to stay here in the shadows, aye, 'tis."

Was I the only one who noticed the difference in his speech? That definitely wasn't normal for Marcus. His face, too, looked slightly different. Harder. More angular through the cheekbone. As I watched, he turned and gazed at me through eyes that weren't quite his own, and yet weren't quite not. Tears burned suddenly at the back of my eyes, but I closed my throat against them, cutting them off from the fear that would make them flow.

Strength and light. That was what he needed from me. That was what I would give him. I closed my eyes so that I couldn't see him, and I focused my attention inward to that spark of self that dwelled deep within me. With my mind's eye I stared at it, and as I stared, it began to expand. Just a little bit at first, but it was enough to encourage me. I breathed deeply, letting my lungs fill with the breath of life, and it made the spark flare even taller, the light stronger, more confident. And as it grew, I felt my spine grow stronger, my shoulders square. I let the light build within me until it felt as though it burst free of me, expanding ever outward, brilliant and white.

"We'll not go forth," Marcus said in a voice that sounded like his and yet not. "Here we'll stay, forever."

"Why here?" Liss pressed. "Why this place?"

"Why would I not? The door opened. 'Twas a simple matter to walk through."

Liss inhaled deeply, standing taller with each passing moment. She squeezed Marcus's hands lightly. "It's time, Marcus."

The words acted like a trigger. As we watched, Marcus's shoulders shivered. He straightened them . . . shook his head . . . the shivering stopped, and with that simple movement, he came back into himself by increments, until every last bit of the aggressive spirit had retreated from his physical space. It was still here in the room with us, trapped within the circle of their making, but barred from regaining the entry it sought. It reacted in the way of a petulant child, pushing a glass jar off the slick top of

Mel's vanity. The jar bounced onto the thickly carpeted floor and rolled away.

Liss had seen enough. As Marcus came more and more back to himself, she asked, "Are you okay?"

He nodded, letting his head fall forward and breathing deeply. He nodded again.

Liss took the sage smudge stick in hand and lit one end of it, blowing lightly on it until aromatic smoke wafted steadily from the burning embers at the tip. I love the smell of sage normally—and it goes great with chicken and noodles—but I decided I didn't much love it when it was spewing smoke forth into the charged atmosphere in the room. On the other hand, if it helped matters, what was a little lung damage between friends?

Liss began to walk around the circle, counterclockwise, carrying the smudge stick before her and fanning the smoke outward with her right hand.

"Great Mother Goddess and Father God. You who are One and All combined, both Feminine and Masculine, perfectly balanced, and yet You are neither. I call upon the true energies of Universal Balance. I call upon the energies of my ancestors. I call upon the living energies of the earth, the seas, the skies, the primal fire of creation. I call to all beings of the Light. Bless this circle as we clear this house of all negative energy and seal it from accepting negativity anew. I call also all beings who help lost souls, that you may come for the dark spirit who has sunk his claws into the fabric of space and time within this home and is refusing to let go. I call upon your love and your protection as you reach out to help guide this confused soul over. He believes himself to be of the darkness, and he acts accordingly—threatening, intimidating. Shine your light upon him now. Show him that which awaits him so that he will not fear. Bless this place with love and protection and healing light."

The coldness in the room was utterly, absolutely without remorse. I could feel it swirling about, from corner to corner, testing, touching us all. I reeled back when I felt its icy presence testing the boundaries of my circle, raising hackles up my neck and down my spine. Mel huddled behind me like a child, her face tucked against my shoulder and her hands clutching at me. All thoughts of holding my hands appeared to have been forgotten in her fear. I grabbed hold of the only one I could reach and held on to her for dear life, projecting light, projecting love.

Marcus stepped forward to add his energies to Liss's efforts. His eyes had cleared of all vestiges of foreign energy, thank goodness. He stood tall in the center of the circle, his back and neck unbowed, his strength in his bold stance and absolute lack of submission. Whereas Liss's approach to the banishment had been a gentle bidding to oust the entity to where it belonged, Marcus faced it down like a man.

"Earth Mother and Father God of the skies above. Heed us now as we rid this home and these good people of this troublesome spirit. As I will it, any and all lower energy beings must leave this place and return to their own space and time. Only beings of the Light will be welcome here. This is a place of love, of light. Darkness cannot reside here. By Air, by Fire, by Water, by Earth, and by the genuine spark of Spirit, I claim this place for the Light. The Light calls to you, too. The spirits of your ancestors are there, waiting to welcome you home. Go now. Let their energies circle around you. Go with them now."

"Focus, Mel," I whispered to her. "They need our help. Focus on light and goodness and all good things, and really feel it." I felt her nod against my shoulder.

Liss came before Marcus and took his hands again, and again they stared into each other's eyes and began to chant. "Where darkness came to this house and land, we reject it out of hand. Take this spirit from our sight. Help it cross, make it take flight."

Over and over and over they said it, until the energy that swirled around the room was no longer discernible as light or dark in a distinctive way. It was just sheer power. It buzzed in my ears and made my head feel light as a feather, and yet heavy with pressure from within, too. A circular pattern was being traced in my palms, the spiral of the life force inherent in all. To me it meant spirit was present, and energy was at work. It was strong, and headier than anything I'd ever felt. I felt myself flowing with it, spiraling, too. And in my mind's eye I saw a blue-white glow encircling us.

From somewhere very far away, I heard Liss's voice: "Now, girls. Release the energy you are holding. Push it out and away from you, up to the sky, to the very stars!"

I exhaled hard with the effort. Behind me, I heard Melanie instinctively do the same.

"Wonderful. Brilliant! Well done."

I opened my eyes and looked around, feeling a little dazed and still light-headed. Things looked the same, but the air did feel different suddenly. Better somehow. "Is it gone?"

"Can't you tell?" Liss answered with a smile. She pressed her hands to the small of her back and sighed. "I'm out of practice. Completely wrung out."

Marcus reached out and smoothed his hand down her cheek, across her brow. "You are *not* out of practice."

"And I'm not getting any younger. It's been a while since I've attempted a true banishing. I'd almost let myself forget how much it takes out of you."

"Have you done . . . many of this sort of thing?" Mel squeaked, finding her voice at last.

"No, actually. Ironic, isn't it, given my ghoulish little pastime. Most of the time, though, the spirits we deal with are simply lost or misguided souls that need our compassion, not fear. Sometimes it is the innate fear of the individual that is coloring their experience of a passive spirit or even a positive spirit. Not every spirit who wanders through a person's world sphere is in need of banishing. Sometimes they want only to let you know they are there. And sometimes they are there to watch over you. Like what most people refer to as Guardian Angels." She smiled. "Now. Let's finish up with this one, hmm?"

From the table she took the powdered herbs she'd brought and began to sprinkle them around the room. Beside me, Mel squirmed uncomfortably. Probably thinking about her carpet again. I laughed at the incongruity of it all.

"What's so funny?" Mel hissed at me.

I shrugged, but I was feeling so good that even Mel's bristling couldn't touch me. "I was just thinking that if Mom knew what we were doing, it would be that slumber party séance all over again."

Mel giggled, in spite of herself. "Oh my gosh. I had forgotten that. Whose idea was that anyway? I had to say so many Rosaries, I didn't think I'd ever get those words out of my head. She was so upset!"

And some things never change. Mom would not be amused. She'd be more likely to haul us both off to church for a long confession and a heartfelt blessing. You know, to deflect any evil that might have attached itself to us.

The last step involved what Liss had called her Elements Infusion, a small, stoppered bottle of what looked like some sort of tea, but was actually a brew of magickal herbs, one for each of the elements: pine for air, fennel for fire, the water base of the brew for the water element, oats for earth, and finally, a pinch of sage for wisdom and purity. With this infusion, she anointed all the windows and doors to the room, blessing the home and all who entered there.

The glass of water Liss handed to Melanie. "Not to drink, my dear," she told her. "We'll leave this out until morning to gather any remaining vestiges of negativity, and when you wake, I want you to flush it down the toilet while you say a prayer. Whatever prayer you wish, to whatever god you honor. Does that make sense?"

Melanie agreed readily enough, though she was looking at the glass as though it held sewage. And in a way, perhaps that analogy was closer than we would have liked. In fact, when I looked at the glass, I thought I saw a swirl of energy sinking into its clear depths. Not good. "Yes, flush it," I said firmly. "First thing."

"This Ouija board you used," Liss said. "Where is it?"

Mel pointed to the closed door. "I hid it. In the closet."

Liss opened the closet door and, following Mel's instructions, located the Ouija board. She said a prayer over it that was meant to close the portal that Mel and her friends had unwittingly opened, anointing it with her special brew.

"I don't recommend using these," she told Mel. "You've probably already guessed that."

"Yes," Mel said, actually blushing. "Don't worry, I have no intentions of using it again. In fact, as soon as I'm allowed to get around and about, I'm going to burn it."

"Would you like me to take care of the board for you?" Liss's offer seemed innocent on the surface, but intuition told me that she wanted to get the Ouija board out of Mel's hands, and I knew instantly why. Dealings with the spirit world are best left to those who know exactly what they're doing. Fewer opportunities for costly mistakes that way.

Relief shone instantly on Mel's face. "You'd do that?"

"Of course," Liss said, passing the board to Marcus for safekeeping. The whole thing was accomplished without fuss or fanfare. Very smooth. "You have enough to worry about here. You don't need to be worrying about something like this as well. Marcus, could you hand me one of those small packets of herbs from the table?"

Marcus placed one in her hand, and she tucked it in an out-of-the-way place within the closet itself.

"Basil, dill, and marjoram," she said when she saw Mel watching her. "To bless and protect this space, and to welcome in positive energy. I have more that we'll tuck away here and there about your room. Now, are there any other rooms that have been giving you trouble?"

Mel exchanged a glance with me. "Well, the girls *might* have been experiencing something out of the ordinary in their room. Maggie has heard them talking to someone— or some*thing*—invisible. She'll back me up on this."

Liss nodded in understanding, but she and I had already checked out the girls' room the last time she had been there, and I knew we were of like minds on this key point. She sat down on the edge of the bed and took Mel's hand in hers.

"There is more than one kind of spirit that a person can experience, my dear," she explained. "The dark entities get the most press, and they can be fearsome. What most people don't realize, though, is that evidence indicates that the majority of true hauntings are actually by benign spirits who mean no real harm. And some are positive and protective influences. Most people think of them as Guardian Angels or Spirit Guides, if they think of them at all." She paused, waiting to let the information sink in. "This is the case, I believe, with the beings your daughters are experiencing. Children are wonderfully open and trusting. They accept what they see, what they hear, without question. An adult experiencing the same might pass off the communication as flight of fancy, or being overtired. A waking dream. We're told these things don't exist, so we disregard such experiences, rejecting them outright. The truth is far simpler, and yet far more complex, than we will ever understand, because we're not meant to."

"So . . . the girls are communicating with protective spirits?" Mel asked, struggling to keep up.

Liss nodded. "I truly believe so. But I'll say a few words in their room as well before I leave, shall I?"

Mel grabbed her hand and squeezed it. "Thank you. For everything you've done here."

"You're welcome, my dear."

The girls' room went quickly. As promised, Liss anointed the walls and spoke to the attending spirits, but there was nothing dark or sinister lurking there, so she and Marcus packed up the rest of their supplies and prepared to leave.

"Things should settle down from here on out," Liss told Mel. "But if you do have any more trouble, just give me a ring down at the store."

Minnie was beginning to stir, so I took her from Mel's lap—a little reluctantly on Mel's part, I noticed—and followed Liss and Marcus downstairs to show them out.

"Do you really think it's gone?" I asked Liss.

"I really do. Didn't you feel the change in the room? Now, of course there's no guarantee, but we'll keep our fingers crossed."

Cross your fingers, throw salt over your shoulder, knock on wood . . . simple folk remedies for unfortunate situations. Silly superstitions . . . but were they based in truth from a past long forgotten? I didn't know, but it wouldn't hurt to just do it and let the Universe do its job if it was of a mind to. Don't you think?

Liss reached out to pet Minnie's sleek head. "You watch out for your mummy now, you hear, little one?" Minnie tilted her head back to gaze up at me as Liss withdrew her hand. Honestly, I was starting to think she might actually understand everything that was going on.

I opened the kitchen door for them since they had their hands full, only to find Margo standing on the other side with the girls. "Oh. Hi."

"Auntie Maggie! Auntie Maggie! We're learning ballet! Wanna see me do a peer-er-rette?" Jenna squawked. She spun around so fast that she fell over, her flouncy tutu flying up with her feet to reveal her ruffled tights.

"Oooh, pretty kitty!" she said, noticing Minnie for the first time.

"Kitty!" Courtney squealed in echo. She held her hands up and made the universal Gimme gesture with her fingers.

"You can see Minnie in a bit, girls. Why don't you run up and show your mommy what you learned at class tonight first?"

They scampered off like a pair of rabbits toward the stairs, their chatter wafting behind them.

Margo stood on the threshold, shifting her weight from foot to foot as she tried to see past me. "Goodness. I didn't realize that Melanie had company."

Of course she didn't. Because the big Lexus in the driveway was no indication whatsoever. She needn't have bothered with the lie. The curiosity burning in her eyes was a dead giveaway. Besides, she was doing her best impression of the Leaning Tower of Pisa to see over my shoulder to where Liss and Marcus stood waiting, bags in hand.

"Actually they were just on their way out the door." I gave her a bright, if unhelpful, smile and made room for Liss and Marcus to pass.

Like the intuitives they both were, Liss and Marcus seemed to instantly grasp the benefits of avoidance. They made polite noises of acknowledgment to Margo, all the while saying their good-byes in as few words as possible before leaving entirely. Margo peered after them, frowning. "Hmph. Not the friendliest people, are they."

She brushed past me without another word and headed

for the stairs herself. Minnie reached out a hooked paw, but I managed to catch her before she snagged her quarry.

With Margo upstairs, that was the last place I wanted to be. I loitered in the kitchen, pouring Minnie a small dish of milk and warming it in the microwave.

Until I realized that I had left Mel and Margo alone to do what they did best.

"Oh. Holy. Jesus."

I tucked Minnie into her carrier with her dish and flew up the stairs, hoping to avert the situation I had a feeling had been unfolding as I oh-so-trustingly microwaved.

"Witches!" Margo's voice, rife with a mixture of shock, disbelief, and excitement, all wrapped up into one quivering package. She had sucked her breath in through her teeth so hard that even I heard it from where I had stumbled to a halt in the hallway.

I was too late.

I bit my lower lip, waffling. What should I do? Barge in and break it up? Try to come up with a cover story? Deny everything? Denial always had its advantages. I could pretend it was all in Mel's head. Or at least, her belly. Those hormones can really get you. She had been cooped up, after all. That was enough to turn any sane pregnant mommy into a raving whackadoodle, wasn't it?

"You've *got* to be joking. Aren't you?"

The joke card was a possibility. Of *course* Mel was joking. Hehe. There be no witches here! Nope, nope, nope.

"No jokes, Margo. I watched the whole thing myself. It was most definitely a witch's ritual to rid the house of ghosts. You should have heard the chanting! It was like a scene right out of the movies. No broomsticks, though.

And no magic wands." If I hadn't been so annoyed with her, I might have laughed, because she almost sounded disappointed by the lack of the usual suspects of witchy accoutrements. And then, maybe because she had remembered that Liss had actually been nice enough to help her out of a scary situation she had brought on herself, she said, "Oddly enough, it did seem to work, though. It feels much better in here right now. Don't you think?"

Magnanimous of her.

"But still," Mel continued. "Yeah. Witches. Right here in Stony Mill. Can you believe it? I could hardly believe it myself. And my sister has known about it this whole time. It was weird enough when I thought it was just ghosts, but this is so much bigger than that."

I cringed at the tone of excitement in her voice. I couldn't break in on this. What would I say? I needed time to think.

"But what are they doing here?" Margo this time. "I thought that kind of thing was limited to the cities. Like New York and L.A. You know, where people are more—"

Open-minded? I filled in.

"—apt to give . . . alternative lifestyles a try. Not that there's anything wrong with that. I mean, I'm as forgiving as the next person," Margo asserted, puffing herself up as usual. "But . . . well . . . you know what I mean."

Small towns were filled with forgiving people like Margo. Of course, forgiveness and acceptance were two very separate concepts. And unfortunately, tolerance wasn't always a part of the deal. Repentance . . . their way . . . now that was another story entirely. Everyone loves a sinner who is willing to get down on his knees and cry Uncle. Especially if his story is a particularly good one.

I kept a low profile until Margo left fifteen minutes later, feeling fortunate that I wouldn't have to suffer her presence for longer than that. In the last few days, I'd seen her more often than in the whole twelve years since graduation. I must say, I preferred things the way they'd been before she became Mel's cohort and confidante. Why couldn't Mel have shown better taste in friends? Had she conveniently forgotten all the stress Margo, as Resident Mean Girl, had put me through in high school?

I made my way to Mel's room and stood in the doorway, my hand on the brass lever, until she looked up.

"What?" she asked, all sweetness and light.

"You weren't supposed to tell her all of that."

"All of what?"

"About Liss, and Marcus, and . . . you just weren't supposed to say anything."

She waved away my irritation. "Oh, don't be such a worrywart. Margo won't tell anyone. If there's anything Margo knows how to do, it's keep a secret."

Somehow, I didn't see that. At all. "And did you *ask* her to keep it a secret?" I grated out.

"Well . . . no, but . . . I really don't think you have anything to worry about, Mags. I really don't think she'll tell. Why would she? She wouldn't want to be associated with that kind of thing by default, you know. She has her reputation to consider."

And Liss didn't? And while we were at it, what about my reputation?

It was a pointless argument. Mel was never going to get that her need to gossip often left others at the wrong end of the double-sided barrel. And I was always destined by virtue of family ties to be caught in the crossfire. And the end result, my friends, is rarely pretty.

"So. Mags. Tell me. What's with all this witchy stuff anyway?" Mel pinned me with one of her famous dig-deep-and-dig-hard stares. "You aren't *really* involved in anything like that, are you? It's just your friends, right?"

I avoided her gaze while I thought about her loaded question. Was I involved? To a certain extent, yes, it was fair to say I was—if involvement meant being accepting of their spirituality, respectful of their experience and knowledge in matters heretofore unbelievable to me, and newly open to the possibilities within myself that I had found so very empowering. Was I a witch? I didn't even entirely understand what that meant in the modern sense of the word, despite all my reading, and I was long past beginning to suspect that the issue was far more complex than the have-spells-will-hex image most people associated with the word. But did I seem to have a natural flair for certain things that fell into the metaphysical scheme of things? You bet your booties I did . . . and how cool was that?

On the other hand, how much of this did I feel comfortable revealing to Mel, aka Have Gossip, Will Spill? You guessed it.

So I did what any intelligent, worldly, self-preserving girl would do. I changed the focus back on her. "Whatever gave you *that* idea? I mean . . . jeez, Mel."

"Hey, I'm just checking. You never know." She laughed then. "It's a good thing you're not. Mom would have a cow."

Yeah, and unfortunately the deflect-and-duck method didn't work as well on mothers. More's the pity.

"Then it's a good thing Mom doesn't know any of this. And let's keep it that way."

She held her hands up in a stopgap motion. "Hey, hey. Would I talk?"

I think we all knew the answer to that question.

Chapter 13

The added duties of caring for Mel and the girls after putting in a full day of work were already starting to wear on me, I had to admit as I found myself yawning all the way into the store the next morning. Minnie was in her carrier on the seat next to me, bright eyed and bushy tailed—literally—as she watched me turn the wheel. Liss was right about one thing, though—it seemed to me that the atmosphere in the apartment had taken on a more relaxed feeling with Minnie there. Or was it only that I was so taken with watching her play with bits of paper and found treasures like the fringe on a dish towel that I didn't have time to notice any of the more unusual happenings? I didn't know, and I didn't care. Whatever worked was just fine by me.

Christine seemed to like her, too. Halfway across town, the old radio suddenly tuned in and began to blare "Stray Cat Strut."

"You're too young for strutting," I told Minnie. "Wait until you have a little bit of life under your paws."

Just another day.

The store was quiet as we entered. Liss wasn't in, but it was early yet, so I let Minnie out to have her way with things while I set about preparing the store for customers. A knock on the glass at the front door startled me. I glanced up to see Tom standing just outside. He waved at me through the window.

Smiling happily to myself, I hurried to open the door. Minnie made a race of it, circling around my feet to show that she was much faster than me. I picked her up out of the way as I pulled the door open. "Tom!"

"Thought I would pop in before I headed home for some much-needed sleep," he said, grinning tiredly at me and stretching out a finger to Minnie's black nose. She grabbed it with both paws, claws gently out, and started to nibble on it, her bicolor eyes wide and bright.

I noted the weariness that had settled into the faint squint lines around Tom's eyes. "You haven't been home yet?"

He shook his head. "Too much going on last night. I don't know what has gotten into people lately, but it's been crazy, that's for sure. There's talk of adding people to the department, just to try to keep things under control. I'm not sure that I've ever seen it like this. If I were a superstitious bastard, I'd credit it to the full moon. Except it isn't full moon."

I had my own theories on this, but I'd been chalking them up to general nervousness about the weird undercurrents I'd been experiencing myself. I really didn't think he'd want to hear them.

He looked me in the eye, his expression softening. "I didn't get a chance to call you last night. Sorry."

I shook my head. "No need. It wouldn't have done any good anyway. I was at Mel's until ten thirty, waiting for Greg to get home."

"We haven't been very good at getting together lately, have we. Things keep getting in the way."

"Life is full of complications, even when you don't want it to be."

He nodded, then put out a hand and hooked me around the neck, pulling me to him. I set Minnie down on the counter and leaned into him, enjoying the moment of warmth. Not heat, just nice, warm, comfortable, comforting. That was Tom. But the weariness he'd walked in with hadn't left him, and the kiss ended all too soon. He leaned a hip against the counter, watching me as I made him a hot cup of coffee.

"Anything new on Joel Turner?"

"I looked up that doctor you mentioned."

So he *had* heeded my recommendation. "And?"

"The phone book is a handy thing. Dorffman's a psychotherapist out of Fort Wayne."

"A psychotherapist?" That wasn't what I had expected to hear. Though I'm not certain what I was supposed to expect. The nudges I sometimes received weren't exactly specific; they just called attention to detail I might otherwise miss. Unfortunately my nudges also didn't always pan out, which made it all seem a bit too random to put much faith in. Still, though I didn't have anything more than first impressions to go on, Joel Turner hadn't seemed the sort of man who'd be open to therapy and introspection. To me he'd seemed wholly a man's man, an alpha male, tough and impenetrable. "What was he seeing a psychotherapist about?"

"I don't know. I plan to give the good doctor a call, but his office doesn't open until noon and I need some shut-eye anyway. Four hours should do it."

"Four—Tom, that's just crazy. You can't do your job on no sleep."

"Someone has to do it. Besides, you're one to talk, Miss Overtime."

I could have argued, but what would be the point? Of course, half of the overtime I put in was because Liss and I had gotten to talking about things that made Tom nervous. Ahem.

"What about the medical examiner's preliminary report?" I asked. "Anything in on that yet?"

He leaned in close until he was nose to nose with me. His gray eyes sparkled in the muted lights from the coffee bar. "That would be official information, darlin'."

I raised a brow at him. "Hmph. As if the psychotherapist info wasn't?"

"Weeeell, here's how I see it. Since you made the suggestion, I figured I wasn't giving out anything that you couldn't have found out yourself by looking in the phone book or on the Internet."

True, that. Actually, I'm not sure why I didn't think of looking it up myself. Too much on my mind, I guess.

"Well . . . I have a strong hunch that there was more to Joel Turner's death than meets the eye, and I'm also thinking that the M.E. is going to corroborate that. I can't help it!" I said when he gave me that long-suffering, sideways-through-the-lashes glance. "I can't help the way my mind works."

"If I thought you could, I would have reminded you of your promise to me to keep your nose clean. I guess

I'll just have to stand by with the hanky." He winked at me.

A thought struck me. "You know, I keep thinking about that dummy at the feed mill the other day. The timing of it was too coincidental for words. If the M.E.'s report comes back as not accidental or inconclusive, wouldn't it be nice to have a head start on the investigation as a whole?"

"You're just not going to give up, are you."

"I'm not very good at giving up."

"Lucky for me."

"Well, do you?" I persisted.

He looked up at the ceiling rather than at me. "As a matter of fact," he said finally, "I have been working on that angle. Just in case."

"I knew it! I knew you weren't satisfied with the timing of things."

He shrugged, not looking at me. "You aren't the only one who gets hunches. Cops are known for that, you know." A small smile played around his mouth. "Even those who don't believe in them."

This was even better than I'd hoped. Proud of him, I asked, "Is this the same Tom I've been kissing for the last few months, or are you too tired to think straight?"

"Maybe a bit of both." He edged a little closer to me and put his hands on my hips, gazing down at me. "I've been thinking I'd, uh, like to do more than kiss you one of these days. I think it's about time, don't you?"

I opened my mouth, and . . .

And it was at that very moment that Liss chose to come breezing into the store. Wouldn't you know it? Even Liss was conspiring against us.

"Oh, hello, you two. Don't mind me. Maggie, you're

here early, aren't you?" She bent down and scooped up
Minnie, who was staring up at her with eager eyes. "And
good morning to you, too, little one. I don't suppose you're
hungry for a treat, are you?"

Tom had backed away the moment Liss had walked in.
"I'd better be going."

"Oh, don't let me chase you away. I'll just get out of
your way—"

"No, really, ma'am, I'd better be going anyway. I'll
see you later."

I walked him out. "You are going to let me know what
you find out about the psychotherapist, aren't you?"

"Hmm . . ."

"Considering what you were just talking about, you'd
think you might be a bit more accommodating . . ."

"Is that bribery of a public servant I hear?" He laughed,
and reached out to brush the hair away from my cheek.
"We'll see how things work out, okay?"

The first customers of the day arrived, brushing past
us. I smiled a little self-consciously. They seemed to be
watching us out of the corners of their eyes, so I took an
awkward step backward and waved to him. "Well . . . bye.
Talk to you later."

When he'd gone, I turned toward the two middle-
aged ladies who had come in. I didn't recognize them as
regulars, so I broke out in formal Enchantments dis-
course and lexicon. "Good morning, ladies. First time
here?"

Both looked at me as though the language I had spoken wasn't plain English. *Oooookay* . . . Still smiling
pleasantly, I backed away. "Well, if there is anything
that you are looking for in particular, I'm sure I could

help you find it. Please give me a shout if you require any assistance, all right?"

But they didn't. And they were only the first. Throughout the morning, customer after customer filed into the store, stayed for a while, looked at all the merchandise, and then departed, often without saying much of anything. Liss gave up on the whole process by ten o'clock and told me she was going upstairs to the Loft to meditate, and to let me know if she was needed for anything. I kept myself busy by playing with Minnie using the new feather teaser that Liss had brought in that morning as a surprise. It wasn't until Marion Tabor, the local librarian and aunt to Marcus, walked in around lunchtime with Marcus on her heels that I saw a familiar face. Well, make that two.

The two seated themselves at the coffee bar that had gone empty all morning and waited for me to come to them. I set Minnie down on her favorite shelf, where she could loom over the proceedings like a queen surveying her subjects, before heading over.

"At last!" I said, keeping my voice pitched low so that the other customers couldn't hear me. "A friendly face. This has been the strangest morning. None of our regular customers have popped in. Dozens of others have . . . but no one has bought a thing, or even wanted help finding something."

Marion and Marcus exchanged a glance. "Yes, well, there might actually be a reason for that," Marion said in a tone that was perhaps a bit gentler than her usual matter-of-fact ways.

I didn't need intuition to tell me that something was going on, that the two of them knew something they didn't really want to tell me, but knew they were going to have to. It was written all over their faces and in every nuance of their body language. "What is it? You know something you're not saying. Spill it."

Marcus leaned back, resting his arm along the top of the bar stool next to him. The effect was long, lean, lanky, and somehow luscious. I kept my eyes up, up, up.

"Your little sister is the one who spilled."

Yeah, I knew that. She'd spilled to Margo, who . . .

Sweet Mother Mary.

Had the two of them spilled to the entire town?

My mouth open, I lifted my gaze to take in the store and the "customers" milling about. And I started clocking the number of similar customers of varying ages we'd had that morning whom I hadn't recognized.

"Oh. Oh, they couldn't have."

Marion nodded sympathetically. "I'm afraid so."

"All of these people?"

Marion rounded on them. "I'm afraid it could very possibly be."

Oy.

"I'm sorry, Mags," Marcus said, looking at me. "Liss and I should have known better. We're not exactly in the broom closet, but we're not looking for publicity either. In a normal situation, we would have done the clearing while everyone else was gone. No specifics, no witnesses, no personal background needed."

"But Mel was bedridden, and so that wasn't even an option," I finished for him. I nodded. I understood. It couldn't be helped. But Mel's gossipy nature could. As usual, she didn't think of the consequences others might have to suffer so that she could play Queen of the Subdivision Sandbox. Then again, she did live in Buckingham West, so maybe that was par for the course.

Oh, the irony.

"What are we going to do?" I asked weakly. Suddenly the unknown quality of our new "customers" took on a sinister hue. At any moment, any one of them might morph from dowdy, middle-aged lunch lizard, wiling away the last few minutes before heading back to their own version of Hell on Earth, to religious zealot bent on exacting divine retribution for presumed evils on an unsuspecting populace. That woman in the turquoise capris that clung to her broadening hips? She could have a gun in that oversized handbag, no question about it. That elderly man with the droopy handlebar mustache? Jim Jones's Harley-riding great-uncle. The tall, distinguished-looking gentleman with the sleek head of white hair and the blazing blue eyes?

The gentleman saw me looking at him and veered in my direction. "Good afternoon," he said, just a bit stiff in his manner. "I am looking for the owner of this establishment."

I smiled pleasantly, trying to place him. He looked a little familiar, unlike so many of the others today. "Actually, she's unavailable at the moment. Can I help you?"

"And"—he looked down his nose at me—"you are?"

Oh, boy. As stiff and unyielding as one of Grandma Cora's old girdles. "Her assistant."

"Assistant, assistant, yes, I see. You do have a name, I presume?"

I saw Marcus pull a face, his eyebrows rising high in his forehead. I dared not look at him; we had a connection in our way of thinking sometimes that was a little too close for comfort. Instead, I kept my expression as neutral as possible. "Maggie O'Neill. May I ask what the nature of your—"

"My concern, young lady," the older man said very plainly, "is about your employer, and her activities in this town."

Had I thought his eyes were blazing? My mistake. They were as frigid within as an ice cube touching hot, bare skin. "My employer—"

"Don't worry, Miss . . . O'Neill, did you say? I'm not holding you accountable for your employer today. Only God can do that." This wasn't getting any better. "I simply wish for you to give her something for me. On behalf of my congregation."

He reached inside his suit jacket, which must have been sweltering on this summer day, and withdrew a small, pleather-bound volume, sliding it across the scarred, antique countertop. "The New Testament," I said, barely glancing at it.

"I think she could stand to put it to good use," he said, his eyes raking me as though to determine what, if anything, I was hiding. "It has some very important information in it for her. If she could just take a gander at it, read through it carefully, I'd be more than happy to schedule a meeting with her to discuss her spiritual health. More than happy."

"I see." And I did. Boy, did I ever.

"The Good Book," he said as though instructing the congregation he seemed to hold in such high esteem, "has all the answers she'll ever need. It will tell her how to think, how to act, how to feel, what to avoid. She'll never suffer the abyss of her evil ways again."

Evil ways? Marcus was really rolling his eyes now. In fact, he looked as though he might be considering a confrontation that would be better off avoided at this point in time. "Yes, well, thank you, I will definitely give that to my employer. I'm sure she'll know just what to do with it. If you'd like to leave your name, there's a pad of paper and a pencil just there—"

He whipped a business card out of his inner breast pocket and slid it under the front cover of the pleather-bound volume. "I'll keep in touch."

"You do that."

He turned on his heel and caught sight, as if for the first time, of Marcus and Marion listening in. His gaze traveled the length and breadth of Marcus's person before pulling a piece of paper out of his pocket, consulting it, and then replacing it with care. Then he transferred his attention to Marion, whose nostrils were flaring with suppressed fury. "Why, it's Miss Tabor, isn't it. What a surprise to find you here. The library isn't keeping you busy enough these days? *Tsk tsk.*" He let his gaze drift down her plus-sized curves, not in appreciation, but in wary distaste. When he got to her shoes, his eyebrows shot up like a rocket. "Zebra print, Miss Tabor?"

Marion opened her mouth, but I saw Marcus's warning frown and almost imperceptible shake of the head. She snapped it shut again.

Having said his piece, the man walked with highly disciplined precision from the storefront without a backward glance.

"Who was that masked man?" I mused, shaking my head.

"That," Marcus said in sour tones, "was the Reverend Baxter Martin. Didn't you recognize him?"

The very reverent Reverend. How could I forget? The Reverend Baxter Martin had first come to my notice during the aftermath of Isabella Harding's death, so sinister and mysterious in his zealous beliefs that he made a perfect suspicious person. A suspect, if you will. He was still zealous, I could see. Still rather on the sinister side. Still looking for Devils in all the wrong places.

"I guess he heard the rumors."

"I don't think there are many who haven't by now."

I was starting to feel faint.

"That man," I said, shaking my head. "What church is he with, again? I got the feeling that he is ready to cast stones at Liss for her evil ways, didn't you?"

"First Evangelical Church of Light," Marcus supplied. "And I think you've got him pegged. He doesn't exactly look like the forgive-and-forget type, does he? Good thing he didn't recognize me."

"I'm not so sure," I told him. "Did you see the way he looked at you? What was on that piece of paper he was looking at; that's what I want to know."

"The man's an idiot," Marion barked. "Who does he think he is, coming in here to act all high-and-mighty?"

"A man of God, I guess. Doing what he's supposed to do. Passing the Word along to those he feels need it most." The small book lay on the counter, face up, its gilt lettering all spangly and fresh. I wondered what Liss was going to say when she saw it. "Maybe we should just leave it there on the counter to make all the curiosity seekers feel better."

"Let's hope it's that easy," Marion said. A little ominously, I thought. "And let us hope your mother is far, far away from the phone today."

Oh God. I'd forgotten about Mom.

Good thing Tom was sleeping. Maybe he'd miss all of this particular hullabaloo. Goodness knows, he was skittish enough about my woo-woo interests as it was.

Who knew Marion was such a backdoor prophet? Of course, prophecy run amok was rarely pleasant. And when the phone rang moments after Marion and Marcus took their leave, I just knew . . .

"Enchantments Antiques and Fine Gifts. How can I help you?"

"You can help me by quitting that place and getting a real job again, far and away from the ungodly situation you've somehow gotten yourself into."

"Mom. *Hiiiiiiiiii.*" Extra syllables on the greeting almost always upped the cuteness factor, which in turn diminished the irritation factor, with any luck, on the part of the person on the other end.

"Don't *hi* me, Margaret Mary-Catherine O'Neill. You can't talk yourself out of this one. Not this time. I've heard what your boss has been getting up to. As has the entire town by now, I might add."

"Whatever you've heard, I'm sure it's an exaggeration."

"Oh, so you're telling me that your boss, that Dow woman, isn't a witch, that she hasn't been consorting with the dead, and that she doesn't communicate with the Devil in the process."

"Which part of that did you want me to answer?"

"Don't get smart with me, Margaret."

"Mom. What would you have me do? Felicity Dow is the best boss I've ever had. She's a wonderful person. A wonderful woman. Very warm, very caring, very compassionate. She wouldn't hurt a fly. In fact, when I asked her to help with Melanie's little problem, she wanted to help. To *help*, Mom. To help someone she doesn't know, because it was someone I care about. Does that sound like the work of a woman who's been—what did you call it?—consorting?"

"The Devil's people don't always work on the surface. In fact, if you went to mass with me more often, you would know that."

And there it was, her usual nudge toward living the good life, the pious life. Her version of my life, actually. "I've told you why I don't really see the need to go to mass with you, Mom. Several times."

She ignored that, as she had every time I had ever brought the subject up. "That is neither here nor there. You still should go. At the very least you would know right from wrong now. But maybe that's my fault. Maybe I should have been harder on you to begin with."

I closed my eyes and clenched my teeth. "Mom . . . come on. I don't have time for this today."

"Oh, you have time for your boss and her witchy ways, but you don't have time to listen to your mother when she has your best interests at heart."

"I do have time for my boss. Because she's my boss. I work for her. She pays me. She's paying me for my time now, in fact. Which I am currently spending not working. On the phone. With you."

"Are you trying to tell me that you aren't having anything to do with the other things she's involved in?" Mom pressed. "That you aren't . . . ghost hunting, or whatever you want to call it? And that you aren't involved in any way, shape, or form with her . . . witchcraft?"

I didn't have to defend Liss to anyone. In my mind, her beliefs were her own, and that was the way it should be. Her actions? Above reproach. "Mom, I'm sorry. I have customers to take care of," I lied. "We can talk about this later, if you feel the need to push."

"Push? That you would accuse me like that breaks my heart. All I want is the best for my daughter. I want to know that you're safe, and that your spiritual essence is intact. You don't know the kind of evil that's out there, Maggie. I do. You need to trust me, it's nothing you want to get ensnared in."

"Exactly."

"So we agree that you aren't involved."

I weighed my words carefully. "I'm not involved in anything with Liss that would risk my soul, no." Because Liss was there to protect me, to show me the way safely through the craziness, the sickness that was attacking Stony Mill on so many levels. Because Liss would never let that sickness attack me. I was safer with her by my side, teaching me the Ways of the Wise, her ways, than I was with any other person I knew.

"Good. Then you need to think about looking for another job, Margaret."

"Mom . . ."

"The sooner, the better. You don't want your own reputation to be sullied by your association with . . . the people you have unwittingly allowed into your circle."

Sullied! "Mom, I'm not looking for another job."

There was a pause, and then she said carefully, "I

know you must feel you need to be careful around them, to not anger them . . . but Margaret, Father Tom will stand by you. Father Tom will help us protect you. The Church—"

"Mo-*ther!* I have nothing to fear around my friends. They're my *friends*. To hurt me or anyone else would never enter into even their wildest imaginings. They're good people, and that's that. And furthermore, Father Tom needs to worry more about his own quirks and foibles before narrowing his eyes in censure at anyone else's actions or thoughts." I took a deep breath for composure and clarity, because the conversation had pushed a lot of old buttons I had thought forgotten, but were quite active after all. "I am twenty-nine years old, Mom. Almost thirty. I am a grown woman, and I have always felt like a defensive child around you, no matter what I do. And I just find that really, really sad. You see me as some kind of lost little girl, incapable of directing my own life. When you question my taste in friends, what you're really questioning is my ability to choose for myself. But don't fool yourself into believing that it's all for my own good. What you really don't want is for my actions to embarrass you, because your friends aren't nearly as forgiving or accepting as mine are."

On the other end of the line, Mom had gone coldly, deathly silent. "Well, I can see that my advice isn't going to be listened to. What you do with your life, Margaret, is up to you. As always. I was just hoping to save you from some of the heartache I have experienced. We're more alike than you might think, but I suppose you've never wanted to see that. Don't worry, though. I won't intrude anymore."

She hung up before I had a chance to soften my accusations in the slightest, but it didn't matter. The argument had left a sour taste in my mouth, one part annoyance, one part longing, one part guilt. In self-defense, I decided to work to rid myself of the extra, chaotic energy that had settled in my bones by going into hypercleaning mode. I had frightened more than one "shopper" with my wild feather dusting by the time Liss made her reappearance from the Loft, looking as refreshed and calm as I did not.

"Hull-o. What's this? I thought we had finished all of the dusting this morning."

"We did. Then I talked with my mom—well, argued with my mom is probably a more fair assessment—and needed something to distract me, so dusting it is."

"Do you think it will help?"

"I've worked off the desire to eat an entire chocolate cake on my own, so that's a good thing."

"I see."

"Mm. And did you know," I asked, slapping the feather duster ferociously at a particularly dusty—well, kind of dusty . . . well, at least a little bit dusty—cut-glass vase that hailed from the artisan enclaves of Ireland, "that all of the people who have been popping in for a look-see today haven't actually been customers at all? That they have been—"

"Rubberneckers?" Liss supplied sweetly. "Eager for a glimpse of the Witch of Stony Mill and her evil ways? Yes, I am aware of these things."

I stopped abusing the vase and gaped at her. "And you aren't upset? Doesn't it make you angry that they are only in here because they think you're Voldemort's twin sister, and they want to catch a glimpse of you in your element but in a safe, sideways manner, because they all think to look evil in the eye is to invite it in? Doesn't that make you mad?"

"Should it? Because, really, it says more about them than it does about me, doesn't it."

Chapter 14

I blinked at her. I couldn't help it. All of a sudden, I got it. In a moment of complete and utter clarity that was almost frighteningly simplistic, I understood everything. Why everyone was here today. Why my reaction might have been human, but didn't help matters. Why Liss's calm poise set her miles and away above the rest of us poor mortals wallowing in the mire beneath her feet.

Liss smiled at me, and shook her head. "Maggie. My dear. The views of others reflect not at all upon you unless you allow them to. Their views are colored by their own life experiences: their fears, their loves, their hatreds, their needs, their insecurities. Nothing you can say will ever change their minds. Only they can do that. What better way to show them the error of their ways than to demonstrate to them that the Light that they revere is in every path to spirituality? To lead and instruct by being the best that we can be, always? And that darkness can be found in anyone, in any faith, and that it is not so much to be feared so long as it is in balance with the Light within. Balance is the key. Tolerance is the way."

I would have answered her, telling her how brilliant she was, but the brass bells on the front door jingled yet again. I let my breath out and braced myself for yet another intrusive presence interloping on store property for the sake of looking evil in the eye. But it was only Libby Turner, looking harried and distressed and oddly disheveled, which I chalked up to the heat and the loss of her husband. Any woman was entitled to look not quite her best when the rest of her life was in a shambles. Heck, some of us didn't even have that excuse to fall back on.

She walked with purpose up the main aisle of the shop, and stopped in front of Liss and me at our usual positions behind the counter.

"So," she said, giving Liss the eye, "you're the witch?"

Liss drew herself up to her full height, resplendent in her summery chic linens, silvery streaked auburn waves, and half-moon glasses, and in the most pleasant voice possible, said, "Well, I am the shopkeeper."

Libby looked confused and pushed her fingers back through her hair, which, on second thought, must have been the reason the glossy brunette strands had been so out of place. "But . . . well, I thought . . ." She glanced at me, then back at Liss. "But Mel said . . ."

Mel said. Of course she did. I sighed.

"And I am also a witch," Liss said evenly. "But I don't let that stop me from having a good time."

"No. No, I don't suppose that would be at issue," Libby said, her smooth brow furrowing. "Um . . . could I just get right to the point?" she asked, glancing at me again as though seeking support.

"I think that would be wonderful," Liss encouraged. "Go right ahead, dear."

"Well . . . the thing is . . . Mel told me all about what you did at her house the other night—"

Of course she did.

"—and I was wondering if you could possibly come out to the feed mill and to my home and do the same kind of thing."

"Have you been having trouble with spirit energies, my dear?" Liss asked.

"Yes. Well, no, not exactly. Not yet."

"I'm afraid I don't understand, dear."

Libby took a deep breath. "I want to make sure we keep it that way."

"Oh. Oh, I see."

I frowned. "You're worried that Joel is going to come back from the other side? That he'll appear to you and frighten you, perhaps?"

"It does work as preventive maintenance, doesn't it?"

"There are things that can be done," I answered. "Liss, of course, is the expert in that."

"Oh, I don't know," Liss said with a modest smile. "You're getting quite the education yourself of late."

Not that I was trying.

"What kinds of things? Do you mean rituals and things like you did at Mel's house?"

Liss answered this time. "That, and there are protective wards that can be used that would probably do the trick. A general blessing of the site, welcoming the Light and banishing the darkness. Straightforward, really."

"Will the wards and things help to keep out unwanted persons from here in town, too?"

Liss considered her carefully. "That can be part of the process, yes."

"Great. Wonderful. When can you be there?"

I blinked. "What, you mean today?"

"Well, yes. Of course. The sooner, the better, wouldn't you say?"

"Um . . ." I looked at Liss. "Well, yes, sure. I guess. I—"

"I'll pay you, of course," Libby said, taking my hesitation as a bargaining chip. "Whatever you like, within reason."

"No, that's not it—"

"What would it take? One hundred dollars? A thousand? I don't know what this sort of thing goes for. Am I even in the ballpark?"

"Libby, we wouldn't charge you for the service. If we can help you, then that's wonderful and we're glad for it," Liss reassured her. "But . . . are you *sure* this is what you want? That you won't regret it later on?"

Libby shook her head, her mouth set. "No. I won't change my mind. This is the way it has to be. I can't always be looking over my shoulder, wondering whether Joel is there around me, watching out for me. That's no way to live. And Joel wouldn't want that either, to be tied here by earthly obligations and a needless sense of responsibility. He needs to be able to move on, and I . . . if I can't be blissfully ignorant, at the least I . . . don't want to be wondering. I mean, who knows what the future holds. In the event that I should someday remarry"—she frowned and rubbed her palm wearily over her forehead—"I don't want to think that we'll always be watched. That's just a bit too— *intense*—for me. And Joel deserves better."

"My dear," Liss said, "I would be happy to help you.

Perhaps this weekend. But I'm afraid all of my evenings until then are booked solid."

Libby turned immediately in my direction. "Maggie, then. You can help me, can't you, Maggie? Please say yes. This is . . . important to me."

I raised my brows in question at Liss. She nodded.

"All right. I can try," I told her. "I'll come out before I head to Mel's for the evening. But you do realize I'm not the expert in these things. At all. I'll do what I can, but if anything goes wrong, we'll have to get someone else in to help us."

"I understand. Thank you! Thank you, thank you, thank you," Libby said, grabbing both of my hands in hers and giving them a squeeze. "You have no idea what this means to me. What time do you think you can come by tonight?"

Feeling a little overwhelmed by the swiftly changing events of the day and boggling at my own role in the bigger scheme of things, I made arrangements to meet her at the feed mill after I left work. When Libby had left the store, I looked at my witchy boss with wide eyes.

"How do I get myself into these things?" I asked her.

"Well, in this case, I think it's safe to say your sister got you into it," Liss said with a laugh.

"That's right. It's Mel's fault."

"Why don't we see if we can find you some company?" Liss suggested.

Marcus was simply the best choice outside of Liss for the more complicated magick-related activities like banishings and protective measures. Evie and Tara were away at camp, so that wasn't even an option. The rest of the N.I.G.H.T.S. were involved more in the investigative aspects of the group's activities, but while they all had what

Liss liked to call abilities, straight-up magick was not their primary focus.

Liss made the call. As it turned out, Marcus was tied up, but would be able to meet me at the feed mill later. That was going to have to be good enough. Liss took the time in the afternoon to write down the instructions for me, including detailed diagrams of any symbols to be used as wards and how to employ them. My time with Liss over the last months had been well spent—I was comfortable enough with her instructions in hand to feel that I could adequately pull off what needed to be done. Amazing what a little time can accomplish. I knew that belief and personal energies were the largest part of the equation, and without an actual entity involved to distract me from my focus, I should be able to do this.

And that was how I came to be driving up to the feed mill for the second time in a few days. Funny, sometimes, how life works.

Liss had offered to keep Minnie for me, but I couldn't help remembering her words about how a cat can serve as a protective presence. I would keep her in her carrier for safety's sake, of course, but I kind of liked the idea of her being there with me as I set out to do what Libby wanted done. I looked over at her where she was sitting so calmly within the carrier. She blinked her eyes at me and let out a peaceful *mew*. I patted the top of the carrier. "This won't take long, swee'pea, and then we'll go visit with the girls and you can play with them, okay?"

Another *mew* followed, just to let me know she understood. At least, that's what I interpreted it to mean. *Hey, it works. Just go with it.*

The sun was heading on its downward slope on the

horizon as I pulled up to the feed mill. It was later than I
thought, I realized, noting the long shadows stretching
from the feet of the various silos across the complex. I
checked the time on the old digital clock still tenaciously
Velcroed to the dash. Six fifty-one. How did it get to be so
late? It seemed to me that when last I'd looked at the clock,
it was three thirty, or thereabouts. I hadn't even eaten dinner, and yet there I was, expected in two places this evening. Someday I would have a life of my own. Maybe then
I'd get a chance to breathe.

I pulled Christine through the concrete complex,
where there was some activity, but not much. The sign at
the road had stated closing time was seven o'clock, which
would explain the scattering of trucks whose drivers were
shutting their doors and tightening down ties in prepara-
tion for the next leg of their trip. I was a little surprised to
see the feed mill open, actually, but I guess for farming,
the mail, and show business, life goes on.

I skirted a pair of feed mill employees, recognizable
by their chaff-dusted jeans and T-shirts and dusty Wellies
suitable for cleaning out silos and barns, who were heading toward the employee parking at the town end of the
complex, and came to a halt in front of the feed mill office
building. There were three other vehicles parked there; I
parked between Libby's little sporty number and a pickup
that was slightly dusty, inside and out, but appeared to be
fairly up-to-date with bells and whistles. The third vehicle I recognized as belonging to the youngest brother,
Noah, a big F350 that loomed head and shoulders above
the others.

I straightened my clothes and flipped down the visor to
the makeshift mirror I had Velcroed there years ago. A girl

was up a creek without a visor mirror, I had always thought. Quickly I ran my hands over my hair, and touched up the color on my lips. There, that was as good as could be expected when the temps were in the nineties and so were the humidity levels. Powder for shine was out of the question, since it would have just slid off my face within minutes outside anyway.

Personal grooming taken care of, I grabbed Minnie's carrier and took her with me as I made my way to the office door. I paused. Should I knock? Just walk in? In the end, I decided a combination of both would suffice. Slipping the carrier's handle over my arm, I reached for the doorknob with one hand and knocked with the other.

"Hello?" I called. "Anyone there?"

No answer. Not a sound. Nothing.

I pushed the door inward a little farther and stuck my head in. "Anyone home? It's me, Maggie. Libby? Hellooo?"

The lights were on. No one appeared to be home.

Hm.

I stood on the doorstep a moment, fidgeting and trying to decide what I should do. Should I go in and wait on the sofa? That didn't seem to be quite kosher. I mean, sure, it was an office, but it was obviously not an office that was used to people wandering in off the street—expected or not.

There were still a few—very few—people loitering here and there around the various buildings. Maybe I'd wander around a little and see if I could find someone who knew where I would find Libby. With the carrier over my arm and feeling a little like a modern-day Dorothy with her Toto, I set off to locate my missing erstwhile friend. Seeing a man disappear into a big storage barn across the way, I headed in that direction first.

I heard raised voices before I arrived at the threshold. I held back and edged to one side, not wanting to interrupt anything personal in nature.

"I want him gone, Frank. I don't want him here. I don't want anyone here, lurking around after hours. I can't believe you brought him back here, in spite of my wishes . . ."

"But Libby, he really doesn't have anywhere else to go. Just a little while longer, that's all I'm askin'."

"What are we, the Salvation Army? Surely there are better places for people like him."

"The home won't take him until the state gets the paperwork resolved. His family's gone." There was a pause, and then, "Joel didn't have a problem with it."

I heard Libby's sharp intake of breath. "Don't you *dare* throw that card at me. I'm doing the best I can do, Frank. And that's all I can do. Don't you dare try to make me feel guiltier than I already do. Don't you dare."

"Libby, I'm sure he didn't mean it that way . . ." Noah's voice this time, trying to inject reason.

"Oh, didn't he? I'm not so sure, Noah. Ever since . . . ever since Joel . . . died"—her voice broke—"he's been acting funny. Like he's the owner of this place, like he wants to run everything. The will hasn't even been read yet, dammit. And all I want is for Joel to be here. I don't have the heart to fight like this."

"Libby, I'm not trying to pick a fight with you," Frank said. "But little girl, what harm does it do to let ol' Eddie here sleep in the loft?"

"He's just not going to, Frank. Take him home with you if you feel you must, but he can't be here when the insurance adjustors come for the reassessment, and you know they're bad sometimes about letting us know when they'll be dropping in. God only knows what's going to happen to our rates after they hear about Joel's accident. Yet another thing that will have to be taken into account in our rates. Old Cullins'll love that, won't he? God, I'm going to have to invest in extra security at the house, too."

"I don't know, Libby," Frank said, an uncertain note playing beneath his voice's usual gruff overtones. "Bart Cullins . . . well, the Turners have known him for forever. Since I was a boy, at least. He may be a hard-nosed old sonuvabitch, and that's the truth, but I just can't picture him hauling his hairy ass up that ladder."

"Joel thought it was him," Libby said stubbornly. "It had to be someone, didn't it? And now, with the police asking so many more questions that none of us has answers to . . . it would be nice to be able to give them some real leads to go on. I mean, Frank," she said, her voice softening with concern, "they even asked me whether I thought you might have had something to gain from Joel's death. Well, of *course* I told them that was ridiculous, that the two of you had always been on good terms despite your father's favoritism—"

"Stop it, Libby." Noah's voice cut through the tension and frostiness that were like a weighted blanket in the atmosphere. "This isn't the time, nor is it the place."

"Funny thing about that ladder," Frank shot back, apparently not taking Noah's hint. "I hadn't seen Joel up on a ladder in a long time. Not since . . . well, not since what happened when you two were first married. Seems kinda strange that he would have chosen that night to go up on one. Especially *that* one. That silo's the tallest in the complex. And then to not use the safety measures he insisted upon? It just doesn't make sense. It seems to me the police should be investigating that."

"Maybe he was in a hurry. Maybe he saw someone messing around up there and decided to catch him in the act," Noah offered up, obviously deciding that a little unbiased mediation was just what they needed to get them back on even footing.

"Maybe it was '*ol' Eddie*,'" was Libby's tart suggestion. "He's as good an answer as any. Besides, did Joel ever tell you, flat out, that he was afraid of heights?"

"Well . . . no."

"Exactly. Because I'm sure we all know, there were a lot of *menial* things Joel wouldn't lift a finger to do. He didn't have to. He had *underlings* to do it for him." Her inference did not go unnoticed by Frank, who was bristling.

Maybe Noah's interference wasn't quite strong enough.

Maggie O'Neill, suspected glutton for punishment, to the rescue.

I stepped forward and to the side, appearing in the pole barn's open doorway with a wave and a bright smile. "There you are, Libby! I knew I would find you here somewhere."

Libby started, her hand flying to her breastbone. "Oh! Maggie. I wasn't expecting you quite yet. When you said you'd be late . . ."

I let my smile grow in brilliance. "You know what they say about how time flies . . ."

Libby exchanged a glance with Noah. "Evidently."

"I brought the things we'll need to do the energy clearing back at my car," I told her. "I'm parked in front of the office."

"Wait," Frank cut in with a frown. "What's this?"

A sudden sheepish expression crossed Libby's face; it was a far cry from her confrontational stubbornness of moments before. "Never mind. Maggie's just here to help me with something."

"She said an energy clearing," Frank said. "What is that exactly? Libby?" he prompted when she wasn't responding.

Libby heaved an exasperated sigh. "All right, fine. She works at that shop uptown, the one that the witch owns, and she's going to be clearing all the negative energies from this place. With all the threats and the animosity, and now Joel, well, I just think this place could use a turnaround in its luck, and I'm willing to do anything to change it. Even if it means using a witch's tricks to do it."

Frank's face squinched up at the revelation. "A—wait— a what?" He looked at me as though I'd suddenly grown horns and cloven hooves. "A witch's tricks? What the hell you about, Libby girl?"

"Aw, hell, Frank. Let her alone," Noah said, scuffing the toe of his boot against the cement flooring. "If a little bit of voodoo mumbo jumbo makes her happy, what's the difference, huh?"

"I just want to understand the reasoning behind it," Frank persisted, his eyes never leaving Libby's face. "I think we have a right to understand, don't you? So, we're just going to be making the bad luck turn to good with these . . . tricks, is that it?"

Libby cleared her throat. "Well, that. It does have the added bonus of preventing hauntings . . . now don't look at me like that! With the way Joel died, I just thought it would be good preventive maintenance. Like sealing the concrete and keeping the fan motors oiled and checking the electrical from time to time."

Frank's eyes nearly bugged out of his head. He opened his mouth to speak. A girl didn't need to be a sensitive to know that it was not going to be pretty, and it was probably not even going to be polite.

"Hauntings. You mean Joel."

"I just thought it would be a good idea—"

"You want to keep Joel's spirit away from the place that he loved best in all the world," Frank said, his voice getting flatter by the minute.

Having apparently come to the decision that her pushier tactics weren't working, Libby tried a softer mode of persuasion. She stepped forward and placed her hand on Frank's labor-hardened forearm. "Frank. You know I want Joel back here with us as much as anyone does. But I couldn't stand it to know that his soul is wandering, lost and alone, rather than moving on to better places. He deserves better than that, I think."

"She's right, bro," Noah said softly, clapping a hand to Frank's shoulder. "I'm not convinced there is such a thing, but if his spirit is hanging around for whatever reason, he needs to be moving on to be with Mom and Pop and all the rest of the Turners in the sky. That's what I think."

I could see the thoughts churning behind Frank's eyes, the need to argue the point mixed with strong emotion. After a few tense moments, he clamped his jaw, muttered, "I'm gonna go find Eddie," and stalked off, his well-worn work boots giving off little puffs of dust and chaff with every stomp.

Libby turned toward me and smiled, but it was a sham,

and we both knew it. She let her breath come out of her. Her shoulders drooped. "I didn't handle that well," she admitted.

"You're tired," Noah told her, putting his arm around her. "It's to be expected, with everything else that's gone on."

She closed her eyes and leaned on him, just a little. "Thanks, Noah. I don't know what I'd do without you right now." Opening her eyes again, she lifted her chin at me as though daring me to react out of turn. "You might as well know, Maggie. I have a feeling the need for negativity filters is going to be running pretty high for the next few months. Frank is expecting to take over the business, but . . . well, I've already consulted with Noah, and I've asked him to do it. We both know that Frank has hands-on experience, but he doesn't have the business sense that's really needed to run a business of this size. With his math and accounting background, Noah is quite a bit more worldly in that way. There will be objections," she said, lifting herself away from Noah's shoulder and squaring her own; a warrior princess from long ago, dark hair flying behind her in the wind, face and body fierce with pride and the determination to institute her will. "But it's for the best. Frank will come around."

I frowned, looking over my shoulder to where Frank's broadly muscled figure was disappearing into the long hog barn across the way. "You really think he'll object?"

She sighed. "You heard him just now. He's very confrontational at the moment, very angry, very caught up in the particulars of Joel's death . . . but he's missing the main point. Joel is gone. He's never coming back. I think that's where we have to start right now. There will be plenty of time for grieving, but right now, we have to make things right with the business. I'm not going to let all of these people"—she swept her hand wide to indicate the employees who had already gone home—"down while the business crumbles around our ears. We have to make things right by them."

"And make sure that his death is fully investigated," I pointed out without thinking. At her sudden stare, I coughed self-consciously. "I, um, heard that they weren't sure."

"I really don't want to talk about that," Libby said, turning away.

Ooh. I grimaced. *Way to go, Maggie.* Offend and insult the widow of someone whose abrupt death might or might not prove to have been accidental.

To make amends, I attempted to change the subject. "Well, why don't we get started on the clearing, then? We can get that over and done with, so that you can feel comfortable here and not worry anymore."

She nodded.

She walked back to the car with me, and even held Minnie's carrier while I wrestled the big bag of goodies from the backseat.

I looked at her. "Did you want to walk around with me as I do this?"

She lifted a dark brow. "Um, no thanks. I'll just wait in the office in the AC while you do your thing."

AC. Sigh. "All right. Why don't you show me where you want me to start, where to focus?"

"In the area by Big Ben—the big silo—of course," she said, indicating with a tip of her head. "And the slaughterhouse. And the big storage barn we were just in. And—oh, just everywhere, please." She glanced at the bag I still held. "I hope you brought enough of whatever it is that you use."

I thought of all that Liss had packed up for me, and nodded. "I brought enough."

She walked me around the complex, pointing out each building as we passed and describing its function or place within the feed mill structure. As we approached the biggest silo—Big Ben, Libby had called it—it occurred to me suddenly what a ghastly mission we were on, and how terrible it must be for Libby to have to face coming to the feed mill when her dead husband, who had passed from this world into the next so suddenly, hadn't even been buried yet.

I reached out and stopped her forward march toward the silo area with a touch on the arm. "Why don't you go back. There's no need for you to show me—"

"Where Joel died?" she asked baldly. "It is what it is, you know. No amount of wailing or crying or tearing my hair out is going to bring him back."

"That's very strong and courageous of you."

She waved her hand to dismiss the comment. "It's practical of me. There is too much to do to collapse now. I need to keep moving ahead, because as we all know, life goes on. In a different way, maybe, than it did before, but it won't cease until it's my turn to go."

We had stopped thirty feet away from the accident scene. Without the forward motion to propel her onward, Libby seemed more than happy to delay the rest of the tour. To give her a mental and emotional time-out, I kept up with the small talk. "If you don't mind my asking," I began tentatively, "how long were the two of you together?"

"Seven good years," Libby said, a pensive gleam in her eye that might have been the beginning of tears. "Oh, we had our differences—every couple out there will tell you the same. He was a good man, though, very support- ive. He gave me everything I wanted. Sometimes even before I asked for it. Sometimes," she said, frowning slightly, "I think he knew me even better than I know my- self. I'd catch him looking at me, and I could always tell what he was thinking, even when I didn't want to know. I think he was the same way."

"Some people have that gift," I murmured, "that syn- chronicity of thought and time and feeling."

"Love."

"Yeah. Love."

"He really was a good man. Getting older, sure. He didn't like that much. Time and time again he'd tell me that one day I would leave him for a younger model, someone who could keep up with me in the bedroom. I always told him I would never, ever divorce him like that. I'm not sure he believed me, though."

I nodded sympathetically, even though discussing some- one else's sex life, someone I barely knew, left me with a prickly, heebie-jeebie feeling. But obviously she needed to talk to someone. If this was helping her to process through the difficult emotions she must be feeling right now, then I was happy to help. It wasn't anything new, really. Through- out my life, I had found myself being momentarily be- friended at odd times by people who needed to talk, to work through something, to get something off their chest. Sud- denly, in the middle of an otherwise innocuous conversa- tion, they would slip into confidence mode, with them later seeming almost as surprised by their own admissions as

I was. It was almost as though I was wearing a flashing sign that said GET YOUR EMOTIONAL RELIEF HERE. I understood now that this was an experience often shared by those sensitives with empathic abilities, but I never had gotten used to it . . . especially when the confidees tended to forget the conversation had ever taken place after the fact. Weird, I know, but true.

"How did the two of you meet?" I asked, curious.

"Honestly?" She laughed self-consciously. "We hooked up over the Internet. Oh, it wasn't like one of those dating sites or anything like that. Actually," she said, glancing at me, "I went to college with Noah, if you can believe that. We even knew each other a little bit, Noah and I. Hung out with the same people. Casual, you know. One day Joel came down to the campus to visit and hung out at the dorm with us all. Bought everyone beer and pizza and talked about football with the jocks and dancing with the girls and . . . I don't know. He just had this air about him that made me want to sit up and listen."

"Confidence," I suggested.

She nodded, thoughtful. "That sounds about right. And he had just lost his dad, and I guess that sadness spoke to me, too. Well, he'd given all of us his business card and told us to look him up if we ever needed anything. I sent him an e-mail a few weeks later, just to thank him for showing everyone a good time, you know, and for being so cool. He e-mailed back . . . and . . . I don't know. We got married the Saturday after graduation."

"Wow. That's quite amazing, really."

"I've always thought so."

I was about to suggest—gently—that we begin. It was getting later by the minute, and Minnie was becoming rascally inside the carrier, reaching her paws through the corded venting and curling them around to try to reach Libby's hand. Instead I was distracted from my mission by the arrival of a low-riding, tricked-out motorcycle purring into the complex. The rider cast a wave in our general direction as he rolled on by, his bike soon joining the other, larger vehicles in front of the office. He parked her, swung one long leg over the seat, and disembarked with the kind of grace most men didn't have . . . and most women dreamed of.

Chapter 15

Beside me, Libby stood up a little straighter. I knew the feeling. Marcus had that kind of effect.

He slipped the helmet from his dark head and set it on his seat. Within moments he'd crossed the cement lot and joined us. "Sorry I'm late, Maggie-girl. I got here as fast as I could. Figured you might be able to use some help."

I told myself the rush of pleasure I was feeling was mostly—*mostly*—due to gratitude for his thoughtfulness . . . but deep down, I knew the truth. I just didn't want to think about it. Dating one man was hard enough. Keeping track of two would be out of the question. No, it was easier to let the quasi-kinda-sorta relationship I had with Tom run its course. See whether there was a future for us. Explore the possibilities. Casually throwing them away for something that might or might not be better, something that might or might not have a future, something that . . . well, you get the picture. There were too many uncertainties in life, in my humble opinion. How was a girl supposed to decide with any kind of confidence?

"Libby, do you know Marcus? Marcus Quinn, this is Libby Turner."

He offered her his hand. "I heard about what happened to your husband, Mrs. Turner. I'm very sorry."

She accepted his condolences with a quiet nod. "So you're here to help Maggie with the clearing. Are you well versed in such things?" she asked, peering askance at him.

"As much as anyone can be. These things aren't exactly a science."

He could say that again. In fact, science postulated that such things were an improbability, if not an impossibility. What you can't measurably see, hear, touch, smell, or taste must not exist. Once upon a time I'd believed that, too. That was the way of madness . . . or at the very least, an overwhelming fear of an unknown that wasn't supposed to exist. You can see where that gets you.

"Well, then. I'm glad Maggie has backup. I'll let you two get to it. The AC beckons," she said, smoothing a hand over the sheath of dark hair that was now showing the tiniest bits of frowziness around the edges. She looked . . . charmingly disheveled. I, on the other hand, could feel my wavy hair bristling free of the clips and clamps holding it under control. Stupid humidity anyway. It was like breathing through a damp towel.

She handed the cat carrier over to me. To placate Minnie, I laced my fingertips through the corded vents and wiggled them around like worms on a fishing line. She pounced, and like magic, after a few playful nibbles, she settled herself down again and sat quietly surveying surroundings that must once have been her playground. Thank goodness for small favors. I couldn't risk taking her out and losing her in one of the many outbuildings or, even worse, the fields beyond.

I showed Marcus the notes Liss had written for me, as well as the supplies she had packed. Before we could even get started, however, voices behind us drew our attention away from the task at hand.

Libby had been sidetracked from her return to the office yet again. Catching a glimpse of Frank exiting the hog barn, his hand gentle on Eddie's back, she'd made a beeline straight toward them. Her voice, strong and officious, rang out across the complex.

"Oh good, you found him. You'll be taking him away, then?"

Eddie was staring at her, mouth gaping amid several days' worth of graying stubble on his chin and cheeks. Even from where I stood, I could see great smears of dirt on his clothes and face. Since he'd just emerged from the hog barn, I had a pretty good idea of what it was and where it had come from. No wonder he had smelled so . . . interesting . . . the other day at the PD.

I was still kind of glad we were downwind; it made eavesdropping easier.

Frank's response was much more modulated in pitch, which made eavesdropping harder. But Libby, bless her, made up the difference.

"No, no, no. For the last time, for the love of God, no. I'm not going to reconsider, Frank. I mean, just look at him. He can't stay here. He's been . . . oh . . . sleeping with the pigs, for God's sake!"

Eddie' stooped down and began rocking up and down and back and forth on his haunches. He stretched out a hand in our direction and beckoned with all his fingers, the way a child might ask for a bottle. "Heeeeeere, kitty, kitty, kitty, kitty . . ."

He'd seen Minnie? Wow, he had good eyes. I looked down at my little girl. She was standing up in the carrier again, her eyes and ears perked at full mast.

Off to our left came the low crunch of gravel against concrete as a vehicle pulled into the complex from the county road beyond. Libby didn't seem to notice.

"He has to go, Frank. I'm sorry, but he has to go."

"I like kitties," Eddie said to anyone who would listen. Or maybe it was just for his own benefit; he didn't seem to be looking for input from anyone else. "Kitty, kitty, pretty kitty. Kitties here, kitties there, little kitties everywhere." He giggled to himself.

Libby's back was to us, but even so I could sense the disgust she held for the unfortunate man who was more of a child. She was young, though, and unmoved by Eddie's lot in life. Perhaps a little too self-involved, but then, most of the women who ran in Mel's circles were. A side effect, perhaps, of the affluent lifestyle she'd forged for herself as the wife of a small business owner—a "notable" in Stony Mill society. Something my mom had always wanted for me. But being a person of a certain social status didn't guarantee happiness. I might not be the wise woman that Liss was, but I had been around the block enough to understand the truth in that little Nugget o' Wisdom. Just look at Libby right now, as prickly as a porcupine over someone who couldn't help what he was any more than he could help what he wasn't, and look at the way Joel's life had ended. Accident or no accident.

Frank said something else that was too quiet to register

on our radar. Marcus was watching the proceedings with
curiosity, though perhaps a little less intently as he hadn't
been here earlier to witness Libby's previous snit. The
car that had just entered the place idled slowly forward.
Distracted, I turned my head to see who had chosen this
particular moment to interrupt, and nearly lost my lunch
as I saw Tom leaning down to eye me over the passenger
seat of his cruiser with the window down as he passed
us by.

"I'm sorry, but that's the way it has to be. Maybe one
of the homeless shelters in Fort Wayne has space if you
don't have a place ready-made."

Now Frank's defensive stance was back, his shoulders
tense and hunched, as tight as a linebacker.

"He is homeless by definition. He doesn't have a
home. He doesn't have a place to stay. He has no way to
pay for a place. Home. Less. I don't care what the state
says. I'm sure all of that will get straightened out just fine
eventually."

Tom pulled his cruiser up behind the Turners and poor,
hapless Eddie, and slowly got out. He nodded at them.
"Ma'am. Turner. Afternoon." He glanced out at the sky,
where the sun was sinking fast on the western horizon.
"Well, I suppose it's evening, isn't it. I was hoping to catch
you all here before you went home."

Frank nodded back. Libby spoke first. "Officer . . .
Fielding, is it?"

"Yes, ma'am."

"How can we help you today, Officer Fielding?"

Grateful that the breezes were working in our favor, I
pretended to be absorbed in Liss's witchy bag of tricks
while I focused all my attention on sharpening my hearing

to the utmost degree, on catching every word they were saying. Yes, it was still eavesdropping, which ethically speaking was, well, wrong . . . but I was beyond feeling shame for it. The way things had been in Stony Mill, it behooved a girl to stay on her toes, by whatever means necessary.

"It's special investigator in this case, ma'am. I'm the officer in charge of investigating your husband's unfortunate death. Just a formality. I thought you all should be the first to know that a preliminary decision has come in from the Medical Examiner's Office with regard to your husband's death, Mrs. Turner. It won't be made final until all of the test results are back from the State Crime Lab."

"And that preliminary decision is?" Frank prompted.

Tom hesitated a moment, letting the tension of the moment build. "At the moment, the findings are . . . inconclusive." He paused. "But . . . there are some things that have cropped up that are troubling me. We're really struggling to come up with an explanation for them. I was hoping one of you might be able to offer us some help."

"Things?" Libby's voice sounded brittle and harsh, which matched the set of her slender shoulders. "What things?"

"Would anyone have any explanation as to how some of the blood that was found on Joel's clothes and body might not have belonged to Joel himself?" he asked. The gentle tone of his voice belied the serious nature of the question.

Frank spoke up: "Well, we do have a slaughterhouse for the hogs here on-site as part of the services we provide. I'm in charge of that department, actually. I suppose he could have gone in there at some point during the day, though I don't remember it, and I certainly don't remember seeing any blood on him. I'm not always the most observant of old dogs, though."

Tom took the flip-style notebook out of his breast pocket and jotted down a few things. "I'd like to take a look at that area before I leave here today."

"Sure," Libby said. She reached into her pocket and took out her cell phone. "I'll just text Noah and have him bring the keys."

"Thank you, ma'am," Tom said. "That's very accommodating of you." He paused again. I had noticed before that he did this quite often while investigating, allowing the moments of silence to work for him to inspire confidence and loosen tongues. "You know, curious enough . . . there were also a few small spots of what we believe to be Mr. Turner's blood on the concrete outside of the projected impact area of his fall."

I grimaced as an image of the impact of two hundred twenty-five pounds of male muck and muscle arose unbidden in my mind. The damage to a body from a height of six to eight stories must be fairly graphic. I'd read somewhere that falling from a seven-story building would equate to being in a car accident while traveling at a rate of around fifty miles per hour—except, in a collision, one is protected at least in part by the outer shell of the car. What that meant to the soft tissues and fragile bones of the human body was unimaginable. At least, *I* didn't relish imagining it. I pushed the thought right out of my head, hoping against hope that the spirit of Joel Turner wasn't the one inserting it there.

White light of protection . . . I closed my eyes and surrounded myself with it, summoning my guides nearer to keep me safe.

By the time I opened my eyes, Noah had joined the group and handed the keys over to Libby.

Frank had put his hands on his hips. "Wait. What do you mean, there were spots of his blood outside of the area of impact? How far outside?"

"I'm afraid I can't say, Frank. Sorry."

Frank exchanged a pained glance with Noah, who had frozen as the realization of what Frank had just said came crashing down on him. Frank's shoulders lifted and fell. "Could it . . . could it have been—" His voice cut off suddenly. He cast a sidelong glance at his sister-in-law and said, "Libby, maybe it would be better for you not to hear this, girl."

Libby stood her ground, lifting her chin stubbornly. "He was my husband, Frank. I have a right to hear it, too. I'm not some fragile flower, you know. I can take it. I may be small, but I'm strong-willed . . . and I can be hard as nails when I need to be, and you know it."

He nodded, but from the way he shifted his weight back and forth from foot to foot, it was obvious he was uncomfortable with her decision. "Could it have been blood spatter?" he asked Tom. "From the impact itself?"

Noah was looking decidedly green at the gills. He ran his fingers back through his neatly styled hair, then stuffed his hands into the back pockets of his khakis.

"If it was, I'm damned if I can see a way how." Tom turned, apologetically, toward Libby. "I'd like your permission, Mrs. Turner, to take a few more measurements while I'm here. Maybe poke around a bit. See if there's anything else I might be able to turn up. I have a feeling we're missing something. I'm sure you'd like to know what that is as much as I would, if not more."

Libby nodded immediately, her neutral expression shuttering any pain she might be experiencing over the revelation. "Of course. Look around as much as you like. Whatever it takes to get to the bottom of my husband's death. That's all that matters." She hesitated, her brow furrowed and troubled. "You're *quite* sure that his death was not an accident after all?"

Tom also hesitated, then shook his head. "I can't say for sure, ma'am, not one way or the other. Not without the M.E.'s verdict. But I don't mind telling you that I'm baffled over a couple of these points. I'd feel better if I could make it all fit together in one neat little package."

She nodded. "Take your time, then. I have somewhere else I need to be tonight—arrangements to be made for Joel, you know—but . . . if you could give me a call when you're ready to leave, I can have someone stop by to lock up the place?"

"Of course."

"Thanks." Tom paused again, and I braced myself, recognizing his technique. "One other thing, Mrs. Turner. What was your husband seeing a doctor for?"

"A doctor?"

"Mm. One Dr."—Tom consulted another page in his flipbook—"Hiram Dorffman, three-two-two-seven Lincoln Boulevard, Fort Wayne."

Libby cocked her head to one side, looking puzzled. "I'm afraid I don't know a Dr. Dorffman."

"He's a psychotherapist—a hypnotherapist, actually—specializing in phobia resolution," Tom said. "I have a call in to his office, but I thought I'd ask . . ."

Libby pulled her chin in and scoffed as though that was the most ridiculous suggestion in the world. "Joel was one of the strongest-willed men I knew. He didn't have any phobias to speak of. None that I can name off the top of my head."

"Ah. Any other reason he might have elected therapy?"

"I really think it's a mistake. My husband wasn't the type to go for such nonsense. He wasn't a touchy-feely kind of guy, except with me. And he certainly wasn't the type to believe in hypnotism. If he was, in fact, seeing Dr.—Dorffman, I think you said—it must have been for help in quitting smoking. He'd been trying to quit for years, with little success. Maybe he would have been willing to try hypnotism for that, considering everything else had failed."

Frank cleared his throat and opened his mouth. "Well—"

"Pigs. In. Blankets!"

The outburst was so out of the blue and startling, everyone turned immediately around to see where it had come from. There could be only one answer, and he was sitting cross-legged on the ground, gathering loose limestone bits from the concrete into a small pile.

"I don't like pigs in blankets, no, I don't, no, I don't," Eddie muttered to himself.

Libby frowned at Frank, who was staring at his feet and avoiding her gaze entirely. "*Frank.* Perhaps you would like to take Eddie away somewhere."

Eddie looked up suddenly. "Not the blood house, no, no, no. Eddie won't go."

"Frank! For heaven's sake. There's no way we can have an intelligent conversation with him here. Just take him away while we finish up with the officer."

To appease Libby, Frank bent over and placed a gentling hand on Eddie's shoulder. "Come on, Eddie. Let's go find the cats, eh? I'll bet you can root out old Tom." He looked up and caught Tom's eye. "Big old cat, part Siamese, I reckon. More like a gray ghost, for as much as he comes out during the day. No relation to you. Heh. Well, come on, Ed. I thought I saw a shadow, over by the office."

When they'd wandered off a little ways, Libby said, "Eddie loves the animals, you see. The slaughterhouse, on the other hand . . . well, it offends his simple sensibilities. He knows what happens there. By the way, I've"—she cleared her throat delicately—"I've changed my mind about letting him stay on here after all, per Frank's wishes. At least for a few days. Frank was right, you know—Eddie really doesn't have anywhere else to go, and it wouldn't be Christian to turn him out onto the streets in his unstable condition."

Well, that was a switch. Hadn't she just been reading Frank the riot act before Tom got there? Mercurial didn't even cover it. I wondered what had changed her mind, when Eddie's need and Frank's wishes hadn't seemed important enough factors before. And what about the insurance assessors she had been so concerned about?

"Decent of you," Tom was saying. "If he becomes a problem, I'm sure there are several church-affiliated organizations that might be able to help you out. I could have someone dig up a few numbers for you, if you like."

She gave him a grateful smile. "Thank you, that would be very helpful. Wouldn't it, Noah?"

Noah nodded, ever the dutiful brother-in-law. I was beginning to recognize that Libby was right when she said she could be one tough cookie. If there had been any question about who would be running the show here, I think the answer had been found.

"What about the situation with Bart Cullins?" Libby posed the question to Tom almost as an afterthought. "If the examiner's report comes back with a decision of homicide, it seems to me that he might be our best bet as a suspect. I mean, considering the harassment of me at my home, and the hanging of the dummy, and all of the break-ins here at the feed mill."

"You know for a fact that Cullins was responsible for the hanging of the effigy and all the rest?" Tom asked.

"Well, no . . . not a fact as such . . . but he did have harsh words with my husband several times over the May price increases, and told Joel he could take a flying leap. Noah was there. He can tell you."

Noah just nodded again.

"We've spoken with Mr. Cullins before, but he denied any involvement with the dummy, and his statement about where he was that night checked out. I'll talk to him again." Tom thumbed backward in time through his flipbook, and read his notes. "There was a note tacked to the front of the dummy. Hm, it did say something about 'how the mighty would fall,'" he mused with a frown. "Mrs. Turner, I'd really like to see that dummy again. We didn't take it as evidence that night because your husband had decided not to file an official complaint. We left it here with him. I don't suppose you would know where it is now?"

"I'm afraid I do. Burned to bits. Joel burned it the very next day. In full sight of anyone who might come by the feed mill that day. My husband was a harsh man,

Officer Fielding. He didn't think much of the threats Cullins had been bandying about. Burning it was his way of telling Cullins where to stick his threats. It was also a way to dissuade anyone else who might have similar ideas."

"Unfortunate. Ah, well. These things happen."

"Not very often, I would hope," Libby said wryly.

"Point taken. Listen, why don't you let me get on with looking around a bit more, and I'll let you get on with your evening."

"And just to confirm, you *will* call me just as soon as you're done, so that I can have someone come by and lock up?"

"Not a problem, ma'am. You have a good evening."

Libby led Noah away by the arm to the office, and stood speaking quietly with him just inside the door before grabbing her purse and keys. She flagged me down and beckoned me over.

"Hi, Maggie. Hey, listen, tonight is not really going to work out after all. It seems that the police want to do a little more poking around, and I don't want them to think . . . I mean, you have to admit, the clearing probably would seem a little loopy to some . . . and . . . well . . . I think it would be better if you and your friend kind of made other arrangements." She huffed out her breath in a sigh. "I'm not saying this very well, am I?"

I smiled, even though she had suggested it was up to Marcus and me to accommodate her. "It's okay. Actually, I know Officer Fielding, and he's fully aware of this sort of thing," I said, holding up a faintly smoldering bundle of sage that I had just lit.

"He is?" Libby frowned. "I mean, are you sure?"

I nodded.

"Well . . . just how long do you think it's going to take? Good Lord, that stuff stinks," she said, wrinkling her nose and waving her hand rapidly in front of her face.

I raised my brows. How fast did she want it? And did she want it fast, or did she want it done right? "I suppose we can make it quick," I said, doubting it, but after all, it was just Tom we were talking about.

"Ten minutes?"

She didn't just want it quick, she wanted a miracle. But I knew it would be pointless to let her in on that little secret. "Sure." Or not.

Libby beamed. "Good. Perfect, in fact. Thanks, Maggie. I appreciate this more than you could possibly know."

She made a show of waving good-bye to Noah, who was watching from the office window, and sped off in her little green sportster.

"What did she want?" Marcus asked, appearing at my shoulder.

"For us to get our butts in gear and get this done for her in ten minutes' time."

"You've got to be joking."

" 'Fraid not. That was the extent of it. It was either agree to that, or come back at another time. And I don't know about you, but I don't think I much like Libby Turner," I said, frowning as I realized how much that was true. I really, really didn't like her. Almost as much as I didn't like Margo, but in a completely different, almost childish way. The thought-emotion was bubbling up inside me, as though radiating inward from my fingers, my toes, my skin, and settling all in one pouting, petty mass in my belly.

"Nice car, though," Marcus said. "Expensive as all get-out. Made my heart skip a beat or two, let me tell ya."

Leave it to a guy to focus on the ride more than the rider. Then again, maybe Libby just wasn't to his taste.

A few minutes later, Noah left the office with a folder full of papers in one hand, and headed for his F350. His other hand was holding his cell phone to his ear. "All right. Leaving now. Thanks, Frank. Yeah, she wants you to stay the night here with Eddie, just to make sure nothing happens. She would hate for him to hurt himself accidentally. All right. Later, bro." He got into his big pickup and sped from the complex.

Behind us we both heard the crunch of heel on gravel on cement and turned at the same time to find Tom approaching us.

"So," he said, his eyes shuttering his thoughts from me. I got the feeling they were hiding a lot.

I gave him a casual wave, trying to act as normal as possible. But inside, my stomach was still a mass of roiling emotion over Libby, and I didn't even really know why. I'd never reacted to her so strongly before.

"What are the two of you doing here, if I might ask?" And underlying his words, I heard, *Together again, I see . . .*

"Libby asked me to come out and do a little bit of positive energy work here for her," I told him. "She said the place has been a little off for a while, with all the bad feelings and bad blood that have been bandied about, and then with Joel's death occurring here, too . . . she just wanted to be safe, rather than sorry."

Tom took this information in, his thumbs tucked behind his utility belt, fingers overlapping its heavy leather surface, tap-tap-tapping inward in rapid procession. At last he said, "And what is *he* doing here?"

Ah. And therein lies the true rub. Again.

I felt my already overloaded emotional state flare with annoyance. "I asked him to come. Oh, for heaven's sake, Tom. He's here to help me. I'm not exactly an adept with all of these things, you know. Liss couldn't come. I needed help. His help."

His face remained as still, his expression as impenetrable, as before.

"And don't you have better things to be worried about?" I snapped, tossing my head toward the feed mill's surrounding buildings. "A pesky possible homicide to be investigating? Any number of elements that don't add up?"

"I guess you overheard quite a bit of that just now."

"Every last word," I said, happy to be able to. "You've got your work cut out for you."

"And you," he said. "This place does have a weirdness to it. But you didn't hear me say that." And with that he started to walk away.

With an apologetic glance at Marcus, I ran after Tom. I caught up with him over by the cars. "Hey. Hey!" When he rounded back on me, his expression was carefully neutral, but I could sense that he was as irritated with me as I was with him. "What was all that about?"

"What do you want from me, Maggie? I mean, really, what do you want?"

The question took me by surprise. I foundered a moment, trying to find an answer that would be true, but one I would not regret. "I want—"

"Seriously, what? I've been asking myself that for a little while now. Every time we start to get close, something happens. Either my job gets in the way, or yours does, or you pull away from me when I have any kind of reservations at all about the kind of work you're doing or the people you spend time with—"

"Like Liss, *aka my boss*. And like Marcus," I filled in for him, still fuming.

His tone was as short as my temper. "Yeah. Quinn. Marcus Quinn."

"I don't see why you don't like him."

"Don't see—every time I turn around, he's sniffing around you, filling in any time you have available, usually when I have to work, as if *that's* not suspicious . . ."

My eyebrows rose toward a sky that was growing darker by the minute. "Any time I have available! Like there's been much of *that* lately, and you know it as well as I do! Between work and my family and everything—"

"But that's the point, isn't it? Neither one of us has any time. Neither one of us makes any time. And neither one of us wants to admit that."

"What are you saying?"

"I don't know, Maggie. Maybe it was just to say it. Maybe it was to get it out there in front of us, so that if we do decide this could be something, we can work on it before it becomes a real problem. I've already had one committed relationship that went wrong somehow. I don't want or need another."

All the fight went out of me. Wearily, I said, "And I want any relationship I'm in to be based on trust and respect and admiration. We're both old enough to know that life isn't just about one other person. I can't give up my friends, Marcus included, or my family, just because you're feeling like my time should be yours and yours alone. And"—because this had become a deal breaker for me—"I need for whoever I'm with to respect *this* part of me," I said, touching my fingertips to my heart and then my forehead. "This sensing part of me. The part of me that knows what people are feeling and thinking sometimes. It's not something that I can will away, Tom. It just *is*, and I don't think I'd wish it away even if I could, now that I know what it is. I wouldn't know how to live any other way. Would you willingly give up something that helped you deal with the world?"

He had gone very quiet. "No. No, I guess I wouldn't." He raised his gaze to mine. "Something to think about, eh?" he said quietly.

I didn't want to think about it anymore. I wanted to curl up in a ball with Minnie and invite Steff over for a real down-and-dirty chat for the first time in forever. This morning hardly qualified, and there was something about man trouble that made a girl need all her best girlfriends around her.

Man trouble. I guess that's what this was, all right. Funny how it could hit you out of nowhere. Unfortunately, Steff was as busy as I was between work and her hot doctor boyfriend, Dr. Danny, and who could blame her?

"I'd better get back to work," Tom said. "Maybe I'll see you later."

It wasn't the most promising send-off I'd ever had.

Chapter 16

I wandered back to Marcus to get going on the energy clearing, but my heart definitely wasn't in it.

"You okay?" Marcus asked after a while, looking at me closely.

I nodded, but didn't have enough energy to say anything. My attention kept being drawn away, toward where Tom was staring at the ground near the jumbo silo as he walked slowly in a zigzagging line away from it, squatting from time to time.

"You sure?"

What was he doing? Maybe taking a closer look at those spots of blood he was talking about. He seemed to be using a roll of yellow tape to mark the places he was looking at.

"Maggie."

"Hm?"

Marcus closed his hands around mine, which I had been holding suspended in front of me, the sage smoldering and smoking away unheeded, while I watched Tom's progress. I dragged my eyes away, only to have them snagged by Marcus's azure blues.

He smiled down at me. "You're a million miles away."

I cast my eyes down. "I know. I'm sorry. I was just thinking about everything, and Tom's over there, and I keep wondering what he's looking at. It's got to be the spots of blood that aren't where they should be, and if *that's* where he was talking about, then I can't believe there was any question that this wasn't an accidental death," I fussed. Something was haunting me, whispering from the edges of my consciousness. I had sensed it there, but I had been so distracted by Tom that I hadn't let it in.

"What are you thinking?"

I shook my head. "I don't know. I just don't know."

"Is it a nagging thought, or is it something more?" he asked, searching my eyes, his hands still soft and gentle around mine.

"I don't know!" I said, feeling so urgent and befuddled and needing to know what was troubling me. "I keep feeling flashes of things, a sense of something, and then it's gone. I know it's important for me to realize it, and I can't quite get it."

He let me be for a moment. He just stayed with me, holding my hands and offering me his support while I thought and tested the strange mental nudges.

After a few moments of this, he said, "Come on," and tugged me toward the low steps leading up to the office door. He'd brought Minnie with us. She was remarkably quiet and calm, staring up at me through the corded vents with her beautiful bicolor eyes as if to say, *What next?*

That was a good question.

Marcus sat me on the step and got down next to me, holding my hand in both of his. "Close your eyes," he said. "Breathe deeply. In, and out. You know what to do. Just do it."

Center, and ground, and investigate from within. The problem as I saw it was, I wasn't a real psychic. Oh, I knew I was a sensitive, and I'd seen a ghost firsthand; felt them more than once. I knew that I experienced emotions from both people and spirits, and residual energy from places. I even occasionally received thoughts at times that were never intended for me to hear. But that wasn't the same thing as being a real psychic. What I was able to do wasn't anywhere near as important or impressive. It was just . . . a different way of experiencing the world. I could never do what Liss did, what Marcus did, and goodness knows I'd never have the power I'd seen in teenagers Evie and Tara.

"This isn't a visit from the spirit realm, Marcus. It's different somehow. And that's the part that I don't understand. All I know is that I really, really, really feel like I don't like Libby. Yes, that's it. She's not nice, not nice, not nice at all."

Marcus cocked his head at me. The odd phrasing hadn't passed by unnoticed. "Are you all right, Maggie?"

No, I wasn't all right. I didn't like Libby. She was a mean, mean girl. She said bad things, and she did bad things. Bad things to pigs in blankets.

Mean, mean, jelly bean, kissed a toad, thinks she's a queen . . .

What was wrong with me? I shook my head to clear it.

All of a sudden, I opened my eyes wide and stared at him. "She said he didn't have any phobias."

"Who did?"

"Libby did. Tom asked her why Joel would have been seeing the doctor out of Fort Wayne. She told him that Joel wasn't that kind of guy, that he didn't have any phobias."

"And?"

"The night when the dummy was hung from the conveyer, Joel said . . ." What did he say? I struggled, trying to remember. "He said that he didn't do ladders. No, that's not right. He didn't so much as say it as . . . as *infer* it. Thinking back now, I really think that's what he meant. But when Frank and Libby were arguing, Frank said that he hadn't seen Joel on a ladder in a long time, and she asked him whether Joel had ever come right out and said that he was afraid of heights, and Frank said no. So did Libby not know? Is that even possible? Why would she say that if she did know?"

Marcus frowned. "Maybe she didn't want it to be true. Maybe she really didn't know. Maybe he hid it from her. Maybe she was doing what she thought was right, trying to preserve his memory."

But Libby was a smart woman. She would have known as well as we did that answering a question posed by a police officer was not the time to be stretching the truth in order to protect someone else, dead or alive. So we were back to . . .

"*Do* you think he had hid it from her?" Marcus suggested.

"Through seven years of marriage? I just can't see that happening, can you? 'Honey, can you clean out the gutters? We have trees growing out of them, and while I like greenery, I think it's going to become a problem.' How long do you think he could stall before she put her foot down, realistically? Good grief, she might be the most un-demanding wife in the world, and I'd give it a year. Tops."

He laughed. "I guess you're right."

"She had to have known, or at least suspected. She had to have. So why would she cover that up?"

We were quiet a moment, each lost in our own thoughts. I looked up at him shyly. "You know, it's funny. I didn't know that you were a spirit medium, until that night at Mel's. It surprised me, to realize how little I do know about you. Do you . . . do you *feel* Joel Turner here?"

A quizzical glance from him in return. "You mean, do I feel his spirit here in an active sense? A haunting?"

I nodded.

Now it was his turn to close the world out in an astral sense, to allow the energies to speak to him. It was something I was only now learning to do, and could only hope one day to be as competent at it as he seemed to be. "I can sense his energy here in a . . . protective sense, but that's all." What he said next surprised me. "There are others here, though. Watchful eyes. Lost, some of them. Wanderers."

"Really?" I glanced all around me. "I haven't felt them."

"There are always spirits, Maggie-sweet. Sometimes they're more background presences, and at other times, they want center stage. Sometimes they're the same ones all the time, and other times different ones pop in at different times for a visit. Some are active and engage with us, and others are more like memories of traumatic times. But there's always something." He paused a moment before adding, "The weird thing about that is that I think the activity is increasing all the time."

His endearment made me smile, but his message did

not. I pushed it away, not ready to think about it too much.

"Tell you what," he said. "We're not getting anything done here tonight. Maybe Libby Turner was right. Maybe we should put this off for another time."

I let my breath out with a sigh. It wasn't what I'd wanted to do, but I could see the sense in it. "You're right. We're just going to have to come back when I can focus. I'm sorry, Marcus. I don't know what's wrong with me."

He squeezed my hand. "Don't worry about it. No one is on all the time, and you don't have to be."

"Should I go remind Tom about what Joel had said that night?" I wondered aloud.

"If you think it's important, then yes. Absolutely." And then, "Would you like me to go with you?"

It was one of the things I loved best about Marcus. He made a great friend, always supportive, always concerned.

Still, I answered, "No, but thank you," because I knew Tom wouldn't like it.

"All right. I'll go pack up our stuff. I'll leave Minnie here with your car, so she'll be out of the way and won't get trampled by my clodhopper feet."

"Good idea. Not that you have clodhopper feet. Unless you like that description, that is." I wiggled my fingers for her. "I'll be right back, sweetpea. You be good."

I headed off to find Tom. He'd disappeared from view, but I thought I knew which building he'd gone into. The door on the big storage barn was open a little, so I stuck my head in. "Tom?" Silence and darkness met my query. "Frank? Anyone in here?"

Nothing.

"*Oooookay.* Not in there, I guess."

Hmm, where else could he be?

I walked around a bit, looking this way and that. Finally I found him poking about around the livestock shuttle, the fenced, narrow gateway that allowed livestock to be loaded without injury, to them or to anyone else, and in a controlled fashion, from a holding pen to a waiting truck for transport. The unprocessed livestock, that is. That would be nonslaughtered to all the tenderfoots out there, although I have to say, unprocessed sounds a whole lot more appealing.

"There you are," I said, trying hard to keep my voice light and my energy neutral. We were already on shaky ground this evening; push any more buttons and it might just end up like a funhouse ride on steroids, and my knees were already feeling like jelly as it was. "I wanted to let you know that we've decided to go. Neither one of us is really in the mood, and we're not getting anything done anyway."

He nodded somberly. "Leaving together, are you?"

I was not going to rise to any bait that was offered. "No, I have to head to Mel's for the evening. At least until her husband, Greg, gets home," I answered quietly. I paused, wondering whether I should go ahead and ask or give him his space, but in the end I decided to live dangerously. "Will you call me later?"

The faint, rugged lines on his face relaxed somewhat. "Yeah." Which made me feel better, until he said, "Just as soon as I get my paperwork done." Because I knew what that meant. If a phone call would be forthcoming, it would be brief and distracted, or else it would come after I'd fallen asleep and would go straight to voice mail.

Welcome to my so-called life.

Not that there was a damned thing I could do about it but suffer unless one of us got our priorities straight.

"Making any headway?" I asked him. "I saw you poking about."

"Oh, you did, did you? Always the curious one." He shook his head at me. "I'm not sure, actually. I just can't see this as accidental. I've taken some more samples of what I'm positive are drops of blood. Small and far between, but still there. I can't blame the guys for missing them, really. They were so far outside the normal range for an accident of that type, it's no wonder. At first glance, it did seem like accidental was the likely way to go. No one was looking for anything more."

"You say drops of blood. You mean, as in a trail?"

"Maybe. They're far enough apart it's hard to tell for sure, but . . . maybe. I just found another over this way. If it turns out to be Joel's . . ."

I felt the cold breath of Truth with a Capital T raising the hairs at the nape of my neck. "It is." I knew it as sure as he was standing there next to me.

He looked at me. "Then I think things are going to change very quickly."

I nodded. "I probably shouldn't say anything . . . I know you're on top of everything, and I know you don't need my help . . ."

"Oh, I don't know about that. That's the way it should be, but you always seem to have a pretty good idea what's going on. Even when you do try to keep your nose clean." He winked to soften the impact of his words, and I knew he was trying to make up for earlier.

"Well . . . it was what Libby had said about Joel, when

you asked her about the doctor. Just before Eddie shouted out and interrupted everyone's train of thought?"

"She said that Joel didn't have any phobias, that he wasn't the kind of man to be afraid of anything, and thought maybe the whole thing was a mistake."

"Right. But do you remember the night that the dummy was found hanging from way up there?"

"Yeah. Of course. What about it?"

"I've been thinking about it, and the more I think about it, the more I think I'm right. Right before he worked the conveyer system to help Jensen get the dummy down, Joel said, 'I don't do . . .', and turned away, almost like he was embarrassed. I think he was about to say that he doesn't do ladders, but he stopped himself. Remember?"

He stared at me, drew his brows together in concentration. "You're right. He did say that. So, either Libby Turner didn't know of her husband's condition, or—"

"Or she's trying to hide her husband's condition. For whatever reason." I nodded as he chewed this over.

"Frank's still here, isn't he?"

"As far as I know."

"I think I should tell you, Frank also shared his concerns with me about Joel being on that ladder in the first place. Working with Joel and being his brother, I guess the evidence of a fear of heights would be pretty hard to hide. Frank was convinced that Joel would never have been on that ladder, and it appears that Joel actually confirmed that for us without a doubt. But . . . did Joel reveal his fear to the world? Or did he hide it? Who knew about it and who didn't?"

"Maybe Dr. Dorffman can answer those questions."

"I've got a call in to Dorffman's office, but I haven't heard back yet. I'll subpoena the records if I have to, but I'm hoping that I won't need to go that far, given the circumstances."

"I think you need to talk to Frank again."

"Agreed. Eddie kind of broke up the party."

Don't like pigs in blankets . . .

"Well, let's go find him. Frank, I mean."

We caught up with Frank by Barn Number 15. He had switched the long storage barn's lights on and was peering inside, his gaze traveling over every inch of the closely packed pallets of fertilizer being held there. He turned when he heard us approaching. "Oh, hello there. Have you seen Eddie?" Frank asked. "I swear I've been looking for him for more'n fifteen minutes. Libby's gonna have my hide if she finds out I wasn't with him every single second of the evening. She wants me to stay here if he's going to be here."

"No, we haven't seen Eddie. Frank, listen. There's something I need to ask you, and I need you to be as truthful with me as you can."

"Shoot."

"Who knew that Joel was afraid of heights?"

Frank looked surprised. He took a deep breath. "Not many, I guess. He didn't make a fuss about it. He never really admitted it even to me, but I could see it. You don't work side by side with your brother and not realize something like that. I've been thinking and thinking about that night, and I can't come up with one single reason why Joel would have been up on that silo. Not one. He had a near miss on a ski trip on his honeymoon that took the daredevil right outta him."

More confirmation, crystal clear: An accident of this nature, for Joel, was impossible. He would never have put himself into such a situation.

"How good do you think he was at hiding it?"

"Pretty good. Joel was proud. Something like that, he viewed as a kind of weakness. He didn't like to be weak."

Suddenly I was seeing Libby's lie in a different light. Maybe it wasn't a lie after all. Maybe she just didn't know. Could that be? I'd wondered before how she could be married to the man and not know . . . but maybe I had been viewing their situation through eyes and opinions too much my own. I'd rather save a penny than hire someone else to do what I could do myself. The Turners would have had the means and the incentive to hire things done. People with money often don't consider home upkeep to be worth their time and effort. Would Libby even notice that Joel stayed off ladders and away from high places if he contracted people for painting, for cleaning, for repairs? Of course, Noah hadn't contradicted her either . . .

"So maybe Libby didn't know. What about your brother?" I blurted out my thoughts without even meaning to. "Noah, I mean. Did he know about Joel's affliction?"

Now it was Frank's turn to frown as he wondered what I was getting at. I didn't even know myself. "I don't know. Like I said, Joel was pretty closedmouthed about it all. And he wasn't exactly the kind of man who let a lot of people in. He didn't have the time. All of his time was reserved for this place. This feed mill was his life, outside of his marriage to Libby, of course."

Of course.

"So what do you think he was doing up there?" Tom asked him.

Frank met him, stare for stare. "I think someone forced the issue. Oh, don't ask me how. Joel was a big man. You both seen him. Weren't many people out there who could have made him do anything he didn't want to do. But you asked what I thought, so I told you."

"Cullins?"

"Ol' Bart? *Sheeeeit*." Frank shook his head. "Now I don't know how Libby got that into her head, but . . . I've known Bart for years. My whole life, really. He knew our dad, way back when I was knee high to a june bug. Now, he might be a hothead, and he might get his balls in a twist from time to time—er, sorry about that," he said, eyeing me with a hint of embarrassment coloring his sun-roughened cheeks. "He's just stubborn enough to boycott the feed mill here, maybe even cart his grain to the next county—which is what it would take, since Joel bought and closed all the others. But do I think he'd ever do anything like this? No way in hell. For one thing, Bart has arthritis. Knuckles the size of walnuts. No way he could manage that ladder any better than Joel."

Which left us pretty much . . . nowhere.

"Is the office still open, Frank? I'd like to take a look at the desk calendar that Maggie saw in there."

"Sure. I can't find Eddie anyway. Looks like I'm going to have to do a complete search and lockdown, building by building." He sighed.

We walked back to the office, where Marcus was waiting for us. He kept his cool around Tom, his expression held admirably neutral, I thought, despite his professed dislike.

"You haven't seen Eddie, have you?" Frank asked Marcus.

Marcus thought about it a moment. "You know, I think I did see him, but he was going so fast, I couldn't even tell you for sure."

"That's Eddie for ya," Frank said with a rueful chuckle. "He's a slippery one. He's probably off chasing after that big tomcat he loves so much."

Marcus looked at me. "Are you ready, then, Mags?"

I shook my head. "In a second. We're going to take a look at something in the office. You can—you can go on ahead, if you want to, Marcus."

Marcus's gaze touched on Tom, then flicked away. "I'll wait for you."

I thought I could hear Tom grinding his teeth next to me, but I decided it would be best to pretend I didn't.

Inside the blissfully cool office, Frank flicked on the overhead fluorescents. Once they had blinked into commission, I walked straight over to the desk I knew to be Joel's.

The desk calendar was gone.

I frowned. "It was right here," I said, tapping on the desktop in front of the lamp. "A notebook-style calendar, flipped open to the month. It was pushed up out of the way beneath the desk lamp that night. I knocked papers off the desk . . ."

Frank frowned, too, remembering. "It should still be there, then. We haven't touched anything here. No one really had the heart to . . . we were just trying to keep things as normal as possible. We should have closed the feed mill down for a few days. That would have made more sense now, I guess."

He started lifting things off the desk, shuffling things, digging through drawers, but the notebook calendar was nowhere to be found. "I guess Libby or Noah could have moved it, but I don't know why they would," he said. The frown was still there on his face, but now it seemed to be filled with worry more than irritation. "Everything else seems to be here."

The dummy was burned, the desk calendar was missing. And none of this made any sense. Why was it we kept running into roadblocks no matter which way we turned?

Finally, Tom stood back and put his hands on his hips. "Well, that's that, I guess." He took out his ever-present flipbook. "I'll make a note to ask Mrs. Turner about it tomorrow."

Frank nodded, but I could tell he was still troubled. We all walked slowly from the office and gathered in front of it. Marcus had his back to us, leaning up against his bike and facing the rising moon with his face lifted. I didn't even know if he'd noticed us.

"Thanks, Frank, for showing me the office, even though it didn't net us what we wanted. I think I'm done for now. I'll call your sister-in-law and let her know."

"Me, too," I said. "I've got to get over to my sister's house. They'll be wondering what's keeping me."

I went to Christine's passenger side and unlocked it so that I could load in the supplies I'd brought with me that Marcus had so thoughtfully packed up. Marcus came up quietly from behind and without a word began handing me things so that I could situate them in Christine's teeny-tiny backseat. A few steps away, I could hear Tom making his call to Libby, chatting briefly, signing off. At last I had everything just so, and I pushed the passenger seat back into position. After setting my purse there, I dusted off my hands. "Thanks, Marcus," I said, smiling up at him.

His eyes glowed down at me, an unearthly blue in the security lights. They seemed to catch the light and send it shooting back out. The effect was mesmerizing. "Anytime, sweetness," he said softly. "Anytime."

My stomach tightened as I realized I was still staring an embarrassingly long moment later. Clearing my throat nervously, I ducked my head down and turned away. It really was time to go.

"Okay, Minnie. Your turn," I said out loud, turning back toward the steps at the front of the office, where Marcus had set her carrier not ten minutes before. Realization struck me, bing, bang, boom.

The carrier was nowhere to be seen.

Chapter 17

"Minnie? Minnie!" I looked around, whirling in one direction after another, frantically, desperately. "She was right there!" *In her carrier.* "Where could she have gone? Marcus?" I wheeled around to him, my eyes wide. When Marcus's eyes showed only confusion, I turned to Tom. "Did you see her?"

He stepped forward and put his hands on my shoulders. *"Don't. Panic,"* he said, as clearly and distinctly as he could in order to get my attention. "She can't just have stuck her feet through the carrier and walked away." And then, doubtfully, "Can she? I mean . . . well?" After seeing my face, he salvaged the moment by quickly backtracking. "Of course she can't have. Which means . . ."

"Someone took her?" My voice rose a notch with each word.

Recognizing a woman poised on the slippery edge of fur-mommy hysteria, Tom wisely backed up a step.

"Eddie."

Frank's calm voice broke through the icy wall of panic that was building higher by the moment.

"It had to have been Eddie," he continued practically. "There was no one else around that could have taken her. Besides," he said, "Eddie loves animals of all kinds. I guess he thinks of himself as their protector or something. He'll have no intention of hurting her, ma'am. He wouldn't ever. I'll bet he just took her off believing he was keeping her safe."

Safe from what? But I didn't have the analytical where-withal just then to ask a rational question like that, and at that moment, I didn't care. I just wanted Minnie back with me.

Marcus and Tom both started talking at the same time.

"Why don't we—"

"Let's just—"

Marcus bowed out, indicating Tom should speak.

"Listen, if we all band together and start looking now, we should be able to make short work of finding him. Are we all agreed that if we find Eddie, we find Minnie?"

Everyone nodded.

"Frank, do you have a master set of keys?"

"Yeah."

"Good. I propose we start at one end of the complex and move forward, one building at a time. We all search the building with one person remaining at the door. Any additional doors should be locked immediately, before searching. Once we've eliminated that building, we lock the door and move on to the next."

Marcus nodded. "Sounds like a plan."

"You in, Frank?"

"Of course. Gotta find Eddie anyway. I'm glad for the extra hands."

We searched the office first. It was the closest building to us and seemed the easiest to eliminate since we'd just vacated it. Next was a low-lying storage barn that served more as a garage for the various types of mobile equipment used around the place. Lots of hiding places, but none of them very good. We switched the lights off, locked the door, and moved on.

By the fifth building, I was beginning to realize just how large the complex was. Huge. Each building long and deep, with enough hidey-holes to house any number of things. The men searched high and low, leaving me in charge of the door. It was an arrangement I didn't much like, because I felt sure if Minnie sensed my presence, she'd let out a chirrup or something, but I knew they were just trying to be sensible and protective and, well, men about the whole thing.

The sixth building proved to be the first of two hog holding barns—the first being reserved for those hogs meant for slaughter in the slaughterhouse next door, and the second serving as piggy motel for those who would be transported elsewhere. By now we all knew the drill by heart. Frank went around the building and secured the additional doors, and then we all filed inside after he'd switched on the overhead lights; they would begin the search while I stood in front of the closed door. This barn was slightly different, though. The first thing to hit us was the wall of stink, horrific and overwhelming. It had been evident outside—boy, had it ever—but inside the closed space of the barn, without the wide open air to dissipate it, the smell was a hundred times worse. My throat tightened as I felt my gag reflex start up with a vengeance. I could tell that the guys weren't handling it much better, all except for Frank, who didn't seem to notice anything out of the ordinary. Somehow we all managed to hold our breath long enough that light-headedness kicked in, which somehow made the odor less awful . . . or maybe it was just that our olfactory senses had been burned away like sulfur on a matchstick. Whatever, I, for one, was grateful.

Regretfully, reluctantly, I closed the door behind me.

The hogs were held in two long pens on either side of a long and narrow straw-strewn aisle. Well, I thought it was straw. At least, it might have been. This morning. Now it was more like . . . pulverized manure splinters blended with pulverized manure dust. Now that I think of it, the aisle probably hadn't been strewn with straw; the manure splinters and dust probably drifted out of the pens them-selves, pushed aside by the . . . I looked over the sides of the pens . . . holy shit, the hundreds of cloven feet and massive bodies populating the pens. And the noise . . . the moment we had approached the door, the squeals had be-gun in earnest. More like the trumpeting of elephants than squealing pigs, I had thought. Kind of creepy, actually.

"He wouldn't be in here, would he?" I asked.

"I don't know why not," Frank said. "Actually, this was my best bet. Spread out, men."

Tentatively, gingerly, the men eased themselves over the wood-sided pens and into the midst of the big, fleshy, snouty beasties. I waited, rat-a-tatting my fingertips against my thighs and feeling more anxious by the minute.

I don't know what it was that first clued me in to the uneasiness and apprehension that was coiling itself into a knot in my belly, and I don't know exactly how much time had passed while the feelings amped up until I couldn't mistake them for anything else. Ten minutes? Maybe more? This building was taking longer (wouldn't you know it?) as the men had to wend their way carefully between and around and over the immovable meaty bodies.

Meaty . . . ooh, probably not the most PC choice of word, considering their next stop along the way.

It was right around the time that thought strummed along my conscience that the lights went out.

Every last one of them.

The cacophony of sound stopped for a full five breathless seconds. Then it began again in earnest, the sound rushing in to fill the void.

"What the hell—"

"Maggie, was that you?"

"It wasn't her," Frank said. "The security lights outside are off, too. See, no light coming in through the window slats?"

He was right. The entire place must be dark.

"Maggie, just stay there!" That was Marcus.

"Wait, I've got a flashlight. Sonuvabi—" Tom swore as he tripped over a hog. A metallic clatter followed. "Correction. *Had* a flashlight."

I dug in my pocket for my car keys, and switched on the tiny LED flashlight that had saved my butt many a time. The glow wasn't much, but it was enough to illuminate a foot or two in front of me with a faint blush of light. "Hold on, guys. Let me find the switch."

"Good girl."

It was there, to my left, a great, big switch in an

industrial-strength steel panel. I flipped it down, then up again. Nothing. "It's not working."

"Musta been a breaker," Frank muttered. "And fine timin', too. You just stay there and keep holding that light, and I'll make my way over there."

The hogs were getting restless, some muttering, some shuffling and bumping up against each other . . . and up against Tom and Marcus, who were muttering to themselves with each collision.

"Yeah, you want to hurry up there, Frank? I don't fancy being mashed out here."

"Likewise," Marcus muttered.

"Hold yer horses, boys. You can't rush these things."

Finally I caught sight of Frank's burly upper body as he hauled himself over the fence with a grunt. He held out his hand for my light. I was reluctant to give it up, but if it got the electricity back on, then the sacrifice was worth it.

"Breaker's outside," he said. "You all just stay where you are and I'll be right—"

The anticipated word "back" was lost in a clumsy shuffle of shoulder meeting the cold metal surface of the door.

"What is it?" I asked, my nervousness growing. I heard the doorknob turn back and forth, back and forth, and then a few more thumps of shoulder against metal.

"You aren't going to believe this," I heard Frank mutter, "but . . . I think we're locked in. From the outside."

"What?"

"For the love of—"

"How?" I asked him. But the minute the question left my lips, the only possible answer presented itself. "Eddie?"

Frank sighed heavily. "Well . . . I don't know how . . . but I also don't know of any other explanation."

Eddie. Sweet-natured, quiet, simple-minded Eddie. Why would he lock us in here? It didn't make sense.

Slowly, painfully, I heard Tom and Marcus make their way back toward us. Once they had made it over the fence, they each took their turn at the door as though hoping against hope theirs would be the manpower to break through to freedom.

Futile hopes, unfortunately. The door remained intact, the locks unbudged.

"Damn," Tom muttered. "Any ideas, or do you want me to call for backup now?"

"No . . . wait, can't you?" Frank pleaded. "Just until I think this thing through. If Libby hears about this, Eddie'll be out on the streets for sure."

"Then we'd better come up with something in a hurry. We can't stay in here forever."

I felt Marcus's hand rub my shoulder. "Don't worry, Maggie," he whispered into my ear. I nodded, grateful for the reassurance.

"Did you ever find your flashlight?" I asked Tom.

"No. I felt around for it, but it must have rolled away beneath their feet."

Frank aimed the faint LED light toward the corner. "There's a ladder against the wall over there. The only way out is up."

"You trying to speak nonsense on purpose, Frank, or did you fall and hit your head out there in the pig pit?" Tom asked, trying for levity.

Which might have worked, except the hogs were starting to scream now, unearthly shrieks that chilled to the bone.

But not as much as the sudden, acrid scent that was tainting the air.

"Fire?" I whispered. Then louder, "Oh, my God, fire! Where is it? Is it here?"

"I don't think it matters anymore if Libby finds out about Eddie, Frank," Tom said ruefully. He grabbed his shoulder mike and began detail the situation to Dispatch.

In the meantime, I felt hands grab my shoulders and shove me toward the ladder. "Climb," came Marcus's voice, urgent, in my ear. "As fast as you can. Go!"

I felt-climbed my way up the slippery round rungs to a loft above, crawling on hands and knees once I'd arrived, to get out of the way for the others to follow without falling over something I couldn't see. It was blacker than pitch up there, a soft marshmallow void of darkness. I hoped it wasn't about to get crispy.

The others were right behind me. I moved farther out of the way, warily. Who knew if the floor was solid, or if there were spaces where a person could fall through to the pig pit below? "Where are we going?" I called out to Frank. I could taste the smoke in the air now, and I was choking on fear—my own and everyone else's combined—but I was trying not to think about it all too much.

"Pretend you're walking down the aisle below. Trace a line straight across the building," Frank said, wheezing just a little bit. "Here."

I heard the jingle of keys, felt a touch at my ankle. I reached back and felt them being pressed into my hand. The LED was still glowing away, thank the Virgin.

Mother Mary, watch over and guide us, keep us safe . . .

I started to crawl, just as fast as I could, closing my eyes to keep from focusing so hard on the blackness beyond the faint circle of light that I forgot to aim. It seemed to take forever, but I knew it had been only a minute or two. I didn't know how far I had traveled when I heard a tiny mewl to my right. My eyes flew open.

I stopped and turned in that direction, staring into the void. "Minnie?" I whispered.

I felt something bump my ankle. "Better keep going, Mags," Marcus urged.

"I thought I heard Minnie," I said, hesitating.

As though sensing I wouldn't be able to move forward without knowing for sure, he said, "Give me the light."

I passed it to him.

"Where?"

"Just over to the right. On a line even with me."

Marcus moved immediately, purposely, crawling on all fours toward the wall.

"What's going on, why are we stopping?" Tom's voice as he came upon me.

"Better keep going," Frank said behind him. "Quick as we can."

"Just a second," I said urgently. "Just—"

I heard Marcus exclaim in surprise. "Did you find her?" I asked, scarcely daring to hope.

"More than just Minnie," came Marcus's enigmatic reply. "Come on out. It's not safe here, we have to get out. Come on, Eddie."

Eddie?

"But . . . but if Eddie is in here with us . . ." I said, stumbling over the words.

Who locked the door?

Somehow Marcus managed to coax Eddie along with him. The two of them—correction, make that three with Minnie, still in her carrier, poor thing—joined us as we filed along the path with Marcus now in the lead, pushing Minnie ahead of him along the floor.

"Everyone, stay together! And stay low."

It seemed to take forever, but at least we reached the wall at the far end of the building. Beyond the walls, we could hear the sirens of the emergency crew approaching. But would they reach us in time? The air around us had a thick, palpable quality from the smoke and the terror of the animals below. I drew the neck of my shirt up over my mouth. It didn't help much. I could only hope Minnie was still okay. She hadn't made a peep since that single, tiny mew.

Tom made contact with his radio again to identify our location. The trouble was, we were at the far end of a very large building, pressed against the wall. "Stand by, Dispatch," he said, before asking Frank, "Now what?"

"Let me through. Just along the wall, a few feet to the left—*got it*." I heard a rattling, rumbling sound, as if an old garage door were being opened manually . . . but smaller in scale.

"A door?" Marcus asked.

"A trap door. Let's hope no one has thought this far ahead. This loft is connected to the loft in the slaughter-house next door," Frank said. "We need to go on through and get down the ladder. The building's not as big, so crawl as fast as you can. Once down the ladder, there's a door right beside it."

"No, no, no, Eddie won't go!"

"Eddie," Frank coaxed, "we have to. We can't stay here."

"Eddie don't like the bloodhouse! Not safe there, not safe, not safe."

"Come on, Eddie. It'll be all right. Come on now."

I was feeling that strangeness again, that weird feeling of being me but . . . not. The fear, the anger, the . . . hatred. "Libby's a mean, mean girl," I whispered to myself. "Mean, mean, jelly bean, kissed a toad, thinks she's a queen."

"Maggie?" I heard Marcus whisper.

It was Eddie, I realized. Eddie, whose thoughts had been invading my mind. Eddie, whose mind was locked away behind the trappings of his mental affliction. I shuffled around until I found him, cowering there beside Frank. "It's okay, Eddie," I told him. "Mrs. Turner's not in the bloodhouse. The animals aren't there either. You don't need to be afraid."

"Pigs in blankets," he whimpered.

"No. No pigs in blankets. In fact, we need to get ourselves out of here, so that we can be sure the pigs are safe, too. Can you help us? Can you help us do that?"

"*She's* not there?"

"No, Eddie. She's not there. But we need to get through and get out, okay?"

He sighed, the tension in his body relaxing with the expulsion of his breath. " 'Kay. We can go get the pigs out now. They'll be safe now. Safe from her."

I didn't know what he meant, I was just glad we could all move along the path toward safety without fear of anyone falling behind trying to help Eddie. One by one we squeezed through the trap door. The last one through was Marcus, and I heard him slide it back into place.

The air wasn't any better here. The strong scent of the hogs might have burned itself permanently into the lining of my nose, but it was infinitely better than the sickly sweet smell of blood and death that seemed to be a physical part of this place. My head whirled dizzily at the onslaught of energy, none of it pleasant.

"Let's go fast, please?" I begged.

Now that Eddie was okay with the plan, we sped through faster than I had thought possible. Frank found the ladder on the opposite wall. While the rest of us half climbed, half slipped clumsily down it, Tom brought up the rear while keeping up a steady chatter over the radio. After crawling so far, it felt strange to stand upright, but we all managed.

"You've got Minnie?" I asked Marcus worriedly.

"Right here."

The door at the bottom of the ladder we found to be locked from outside as well, but we could already hear voices shouting at us to stand back, then the clank of a metal axe striking the door. The room was spinning around me, a red haze of energy and blood and fear.

"Pigs in blankets," Eddie was whimpering again, rocking back and forth with his arms folded tightly, protectively, over his chest. "Pigs in blankets." I went to him while they bashed at the door and put my arm around his narrow shoulders. Narrow as a boy's. That's what he was, a child locked away in a man's body.

And as I comforted him, I noticed something hanging from a peg on the wall beside the door. Eddie seemed to be staring straight at it, too, shrinking away from it, shrinking in on himself.

Finally the door slammed inward with a rush of air that blissfully did not resonate with hog or blood, and for once I didn't even care about the humidity. Gloved hands reached for us, pulling us all to safety, one by one. My left hand brushed the hanging thing as I passed through the demolished doorway. Rough fabric registered briefly. Canvas, maybe. A tarp of some sort?

Pigs in blankets.

They led us to safety, to where the medical team had set up to await us, and I was so happy that tonight, at least, their services were needed. We'd all made it out, unsinged, unscathed. Dirty, oh yes. Smoky. But safe. So was Minnie, who had risen up on all fours the moment I'd unzipped her soft-sided carrier, wide-eyed and bright and rested from a very long sleep. I was so relieved, I couldn't stop kissing her. Then Eddie came and started to whisper to her, working his animal magick, his special gift from the universe. She played with his fingers for a while, then tucked herself up against my chest and began to purr. My girl.

Even the hogs were safe. Terrorized, oh yes. Smoked before their time. But safe. For now. I couldn't help hoping that some kind soul would change their status from "meant for slaughter" to "meant for transport." The poor things had been through enough as it was.

Tom refused to sit with the rest of us, preferring instead to prowl about from one cop to the next to gather every ounce of information that he could. He would never change; I knew that. His job was such a huge part of his life that it had become a part of him. But when you stripped that away, did you still have a whole man? Was there even an answer to that question?

My head hurt even thinking about it.

I had expected to see the glow of flames licking the buildings, but I was surprised to see nothing of the sort. Some brilliant soul had found the breaker box, and the complex was bathed with white light awash with the red-blue flashes from the emergency vehicles, but while there was smoke hanging like a low cloud above the roofline, whatever fire had threatened us had already been put out. I crossed myself and said a quick prayer of thanks to Mother Mary, following it up with a whisper of gratitude to the Goddess and all the powers that ran the universe as we knew it. Whoever wanted to claim responsibility for our safety could have at it. I was just grateful for their watchful eye.

There was a flurry of activity all around me, but I couldn't bring myself to get involved too deeply. It had been a long day, an even longer evening, and I was weary to the bone. And I didn't know if it was because Eddie was still sitting so close to me or not, but I still had his thoughts and emotions running through my head and body from time to time.

Mean girl. Bad things.

Bad things with pigs in blankets.

I let the thoughts swim 'round and 'round as I leaned my head back and watched the scene about me unfold through half-closed eyes. Marcus came to sit next to me and handed me a damp cloth. I smoothed it over my face to wipe away the grime. It left behind a sense of coolness that was surprisingly revitalizing. I was thankful for that, too. Even if the cloth was slightly rough. Still, not as rough as that canvas . . .

Pigs in blankets.

The thought reverberated through my head, relentless, insistent. Meaningful.

A canvas blanket?

Not a blanket. A canvas tarp, heavy duty, with metal grommets, meant to withstand a heavy load. Everyone had at least one of them around, they were ever so useful, they could even stand up to . . .

I tilted my head back, leaning it against Marcus's shoulder as I gazed up at the vast system of conveyers over our heads. We were situated quite near where Joel Turner had been found. Another near tragedy at Turner Field and Grain Systems. Bad things with pigs in blankets.

"It was Joel," I whispered in awe and in amazement as the realization clicked into place. "Not a pig at all."

That's why there had been a widespread trail of blood droplets. That's why Eddie had said that pigs in blankets don't move. Somehow, Joel Turner must have been incapacitated elsewhere—and my guess was that it was in the slaughterhouse. A place where blood was always present, even when it is rinsed away by careful hands. It would explain the presence of animal blood found on Joel's clothing, wouldn't it? And anything that might have been missed was easily explained away. And then he was— what? Wrapped in a tarp, dragged over the ground, and then lifted aloft with the pulley doing the job? Raised to the highest of the high, and then released, without remorse, to fall to the cement below? The tarp would have been easy to dispose of, with no one the wiser. A regrettable accident at Turner Field and Grain Systems. So tragic. Poor Joel.

Who would have thought his wife would have done something like that?

Mean, mean, jelly bean, kissed a toad, thinks she's a queen . . .

"It was Libby and Noah," I said, mostly to myself. And then wearily, lazily, I lifted my gaze to find Tom standing at my feet, staring at me.

"How do you *do* that?" he demanded, half-exasperated, half-admiring.

"Do what?"

"Put everything together like that without knowing all the details?"

I smiled up at him. "I have my connections."

Libby and Noah hadn't expected a police witness to their exploits that night. They hadn't expected a police escort from the property either, especially not in the back of two squad cars. But life has a way of surprising a person in even the most well-planned moments. Going with the flow, sometimes that was the only answer. Too bad for Libby and Noah, going with the flow was going to mean a very long trip up the river.

Tom had no way of knowing when he called in our situation that the perpetrators were still on-site. He might have had his suspicions by then, but at the time his only concern was to get us all out alive. Had he not been there with a direct link to Dispatch and fire crews, would Libby and Noah have had the time to ensure the fires would do the job intended? Locked away deep within the extensive building complex as we had been, without a cell phone among us (from now on, I would have it on my body at all times!), they would have had a hard time finding us, assuming they would have deduced by our cars that there were still people present on-site. Would it have been too late?

I really didn't think they knew that Tom, Marcus, and I were in the building with Frank and Eddie. At least, I hoped they didn't . . . but that didn't make them any less of a threat to our health. Petite, lovely, dark-haired Libby was willing to take not only the life of her husband, but the lives of at least two others, without regret, without any sense of humanity or compassion or remorse. And for what? That was the part I didn't understand.

Tom explained it all to me quietly later. Oh, the two had denied any wrongdoing at first, but when it was made clear to Noah that Libby planned to use him as her scapegoat, he spoke readily enough. He told Tom how he and Libby had been lovers all along. How they had met in college and had a passionate affair that ended badly when she turned him aside for his older, steady, and suddenly quite wealthy older brother, a brother he'd always been jealous of. He spoke of how Joel had returned from their honeymoon changed from something that had happened on the wonderland ski trip holiday, something that had scared him to death. He told how Libby had confessed to him one heated night that she'd made a mistake. That she'd known it from the moment the judge said "man and wife," and that she'd tried to settle it herself, but that it hadn't worked out quite the way she'd planned. Noah knew then that she must have tried something and failed. But he didn't warn Joel. Instead he'd let himself be sweet-talked and played and coaxed and convinced that *they* were the two who were meant to be together, forever. Add to that the illicit sex and the escalating value of the Turner Field and Grain Systems, and you had a heady hormonal cocktail guaranteed to tempt a weak-minded person to be very bad indeed. Libby came up with the plan; Noah provided the action. Joel never saw them coming.

Frank had mentioned that cash flow was tight at the feed mill, with all the buyouts and closings and upgrades . . . but Libby wasn't planning to be in it for the long haul. Even before Joel was dead, she had secretly been in contact with potential buyers and assessors, looking for just the right number that would set her up for the rest of her life—and Noah, too, if he played his cards right—without the hassle of day-to-day business management.

It was too bad for Libby that Joel had underplayed the seriousness of his phobia. Had she realized, her plan might have been played out differently. Her inattention cost her everything. By the time Dr. Dorffman's eventual confirmation of the purpose for Joel's therapy came in, it seemed almost an afterthought.

Libby denied everything. She was the victim here. Why couldn't they see that?

I felt sorriest for Frank. He'd lost one brother; could he somehow find it in his heart to forgive the younger his selfishness and stupidity?

And so the wheel of the year turned another notch as the days swelled to their longest at the summer solstice barely a week later. Litha, Liss called it. A fire festival. How fitting, that. Liss had invited me and Marcus and all of the N.I.G.H.T.S. to a celebration of the event as a part of a communal effort by Keepers of the Old Ways throughout the area. I was a little afraid that the Reverend Baxter Martin might catch wind of the plans, but apparently the festivities went off without a single fundamentalist hitch. I had the feeling, though, that we hadn't seen the last of him yet. As for me, I had gotten close enough to the fire at the feed mill to want to avoid that element entirely. Instead I spent the longest day with Mel, my own personalized version of the pregnant Goddess incarnate, and the two little faeries who danced at her feet, feeding my soul with family things. Healing it with love.

Once the more threatening spirit had been evacuated from her home, Mel seemed to kind of enjoy the remaining spirits. She asked the girls often what they were saying, what they were doing, and it would be a big topic of conversation whenever Mel had company over for months to come. Personally I think she liked having house ghosts almost as much as she liked having house guests.

The sun was setting when I made my way home. I stood quietly in the yard, watching its final descent in a resplendent glory of pinks and reds and golds. My own personal version of the Sun God joined me there without a word—Marcus, dressed casually in a pair of pale wash jeans and a simple cotton tunic in a woodsy shade of green that made his hair seem even darker where it curled down his back, his eyes even bluer, his teeth whiter. He slid into place behind me, looping his arms around my waist and touching his chin to the top of my head as we silently witnessed the last flare of red, the last glimmer of pink, the enveloping indigo blanket of dusk, while all around us the lightning bugs twinkled and sparked.

I didn't ask how he'd come to be there. I didn't ask

why. I simply accepted the gift from the Goddess for what it was.

Questions, you see, often brought answers.

I didn't know if I was ready for that.

I didn't know if I was ready for that at all.

FROM THE NATIONAL BESTSELLING AUTHOR
OF THE BEWITCHING MYSTERIES

Madelyn Alt

No Rest for the Wiccan

Maggie O'Neill reluctantly volunteers to care for her bedridden, oh-so-perfect sister, Mel, but strange spirits threaten to divert her attention. Then a friend of Mel's loses her husband to a dreadful fall, and the police call it an accidental death. Maggie's not so sure, and sets her second sights on finding a first-degree murderer.

M428T0309